TRADING UP

CATHRYN FOX

COPYRIGHT

Trading Up
Copyright 2022 by Cathryn Fox
Published by Cathryn Fox

This e-book is licensed for your personal enjoyment only. This e-book may not be re-sold or given away to other people. If you would like to share this book with another person, please purchase an additional copy for each recipient. If you're reading this book and did not purchase it, or it was not purchased for your use only, then please return to your favorite e-book retailer and purchase your own copy. Thank you for respecting the hard work of this author.

ISBN Ebook: 978-1-989374-47-4

ISBN Print: 978-1-989374-46-7

CASSIDY

"Are you going to marry a prince, Cassidy?"

I drop to my knees and adjust the diamond tiara on little Lacey's head. "I'm not so sure about that," I tell her, even though my mother has been grooming me to be a princess since the moment I was delivered and the doctor announced I was a girl.

A mixture of sadness and disappointment comes over Lacey's angelic face—I'm very familiar with the look—and since she's had enough letdowns in her five young years on this planet, I say, "Maybe someday I will, though." I guess there's no harm in letting her believe in prince charming and happily ever after. I prefer to live in reality, and why shouldn't she have a few more years before she becomes jaded like the rest of us?

A smile lights up her face and brightens her pretty blue eyes and precocious child that she is, she reaches for the tiara. "Well then, you're going to need this."

I capture her hands to stop her. "No, this looks much better on you than it does on me." I gently place her hands at her sides and admire the gorgeous blue gown I'd given her earlier, and the way the tiara brings out the shimmering jewels in the little dress.

I have gowns of all shapes, colors and sizes. Most are back at my family home in Southern California. On my last visit home, I grabbed a few to give Lacey and her friends here at the shelter. I have no need for them. In fact, I hate them. They remind me of all the pageants my mother forced me to enter. But I can't forget that if I'm going to catch the attention of Swedish prince Stefan Lundin, who transferred to Kingston college for his senior year, those debutante lessons and pageantry skills that were thrust upon me are going to come in handy. And why can't I forget? Oh, because mother dearest keeps reminding me.

Can you imagine it? Me, Cassidy Collins, catching the eye of a prince? What a joke. I grew up a tomboy, the bane of my mother's socialite existence. She spent years trying to beat that boyish behavior out of me, and while I can dress and act like a debutante when need be, deep inside I'm still a girl who prefers big juicy cheeseburgers over salads, jeans over dresses and ponytails over flat irons. Which means I don't stand a chance at getting a rose from the handsome Swedish prince who is here at Kingston College seeking a proper American bride, much like his brother Jonas had last year. Do they not have suitable women in Sweden? What the hell is up with that anyway? I really don't know, and of course, my mother told me not to question such good fortune and get straight to work on finding a way to catch his eye. Even if I do manage to get him to notice me, I'm sure he'll be bored in minutes. What on earth would I have to talk about? I'm sure we have nothing in common.

"Of course, she's going to marry a prince," my best friend Becca says as she comes into the room. I stand as the scent of rich dark chocolate reaches my nose. She sets a plate with two freshly baked cupcakes down on the coffee table in front of Lacey and me, and as I inhale the decadent scent, my mother's voice erupts inside my head. *You need to watch your weight, Cassidy.*

"Eat," Becca says as I stare longingly at the fresh-baked treat. Becca and I have been best friends since childhood, debutantes together, and she knows my struggles as much as I know hers. Two young girls, with chocolate all over their cute little faces, come racing into the room, their ponytails bouncing.

"I baked this one just for you," Bethany says, giving me a toothless grin as she picks up a cupcake and holds it out to me, hints of chocolate on her little cherub face. My heart misses a beat. Here I am lamenting about being on the pageantry circuit—about not being good enough for a prince —while these little girls have all been living in this women's shelter with their moms and siblings for months. Becca and I visit once a week, not just to pad our resumes, and not just because volunteer work is required for our Public Relations degree, but because we enjoy hanging out and helping out. These little girls always brighten our day.

I graciously accept the cupcake, peel the wrapper back and take a big bite. "Bethany, this is the best cupcake I've ever tasted."

She glows under my praise, and then her gaze goes to Lacey's tiara. Her eyes jump wide open, and sparkle like the vibrant gemstones. She holds her hands together, like she's working hard not to reach out and touch the jeweled crown fit for a princess. "That's so pretty."

Lacey takes it off and hands it to her. "Want to try it on?" My heart pinches as I watch her place the tiara on Bethany's head. "You look just like Cinderella," Lacey tells her and little Bethany spins.

"Bethany, I bet there's a dress in here you'd like. You too, Clara," I say to the other young girl who's a bit standoffish. She's new here and doesn't quite know who, and maybe even how, to trust, which breaks my heart. She takes a tentative step closer as I pull out numerous dresses from the bag I'd brought, and the girls begin to squeal in delight. Lacey's mother Patricia comes into the room, and I turn to her as the girls all appraise the dresses with glee.

"Mommy, Cassidy is going to marry a prince," Lacey blurts out and puts both hands to her heart and sways.

Patricia raises her brow. "Is that so?"

"No, not really," I say and a stupid unladylike snort shoots from my nose. Like I said, that tomboy still resides inside of me.

"Would this prince happen to be Stefan Lundin?" she questions with a gleam in her eyes.

"You've heard?"

She laughs, the overhead light glistening on her gorgeous dark skin. "Who hasn't? It's all anyone can talk about. He's all over the news and in the papers. He's quite the handsome young man, don't you think?"

"Don't get any ideas. He's taken," Becca says playfully and loops her arm through mine. "Isn't that right, Cassidy?"

"No, that is not right." My stomach knots. I know Becca means well, but the pressure to snag a prince is getting to me.

Mom has been calling non-stop, asking if Stefan has given out any roses yet—like the campus is his game show and love is the prize. What-the-fuck-ever.

"Well, he'll soon be taken." Becca lifts her chin an inch. "He can give out as many roses as he likes, but Cassidy is in it to win it and will no doubt end up his princess."

"You deserve your very own prince charming, Cassidy," Patricia says. "Just promise me you'll never forget one thing."

I frown, having no idea what she's getting at. "What?"

She taps me on the nose. "Never forget, you're the prize."

"So are you," I tell her, and her lips pinch tight. She's here at the shelter because of a bad marriage. She thought she'd found her prince, only for him to turn out to be an ogre, and not the cute kind from Disney. But one day I hope she finds love again—with the right guy.

"Mommy, don't I look pretty?" Lacey says as Bethany puts the tiara back on Lacey's head. Patricia turns to her daughter, and I check the time on my phone.

I catch Becca's eye. "We should get going."

Becca nods, and we say our goodbyes and head out into the warm day, and I glance up to take in the thickening clouds that threaten rain. It's mid-September, and it's still stinking hot in SoCal. I'm not complaining. I love the heat. If I ever married the Swedish prince, I have no idea how I'd survive the cold Stockholm winters. From what I hear they're long, snowy and dreadful.

Wait, I'm only in my junior year, if I was given the final rose, would I have to forgo my public relations degree and move, or would I stay and finish? My mother doesn't even expect me to get a degree. She went to college to get her MRS and wants the same for me. What century are we living in anyway?

"Ohmigod, there he is," Becca says and grips my hands. Our steps slow as Stefan comes toward us, his head down, scrolling through his phone. He briefly looks up, his glance moving through us like we don't even exist. Put a leaf on my head and he'd think I was just another tree on the campus grounds. I shake my head.

"He doesn't even know I'm alive." Honestly, I'm not even sure I care, or that I want to marry a prince—or marry at all. My mother tells me once I'm married to royalty, I'll be the happiest girl in the world. Do I really need a prince to be happy, though? Do I even need a guy?

What do you want, Cassidy?

"He is so hot," Becca says dreamily, and I'm about to tell her maybe she should try to get herself a rose, when she squeezes my hand and adds, "Go, walk straight into him. Make him notice you once and for all."

"I'm not doing that." My phone pings and I pull it from my pocket and read the message from my brother.

James: Hey is Becca available? Asking for a friend.

"Eww."

"What's going on?" Becca asks.

I stare at my phone. No way am I going to hook my brother —who happens to be a star defense player for the Falcons football team—up with my best friend. Not only does she have a boyfriend, the thoughts of her with my brother disgusts me. Don't get me wrong, I love James, and I'm totally proud of him but he's a total man whore. Even if she was available, I wouldn't hook any of his friends up with her either. They're all about the catch and release. With the exception of his best friend Braden Murphy. I sometimes wonder how the two guys are so close when they're so different.

I chuckle as I think about Braden's belief that he can't have sex during the football season because it will interfere with his performance. His superstitions make him all that much more interesting and appealing to girls. They like the challenge, I guess. Personally, I like Braden. I've known him forever, but I've never been attracted to him. I do, however, appreciate that he's not driven by sex, and that he has other goals and ambitions. I think he's actually one of the good guys. Not that my brother isn't. He's good to me, and the women who sleep with him know what they're getting themselves into.

I tuck my phone away. "What's going on is my brother asked if you were single."

Her face doesn't twist in disgust quite the way I expected. Heck, she's known James as long as I've known Braden. I wouldn't want to go out with Braden any more than she'd want to go out with James. Right? Man, the thought of the two together brings a lump to my gut. Besides, it's never going to happen. She has a boyfriend.

Becca sucks in a fast breath, and it pulls my attention back. "Oh no."

"What?" I ask, and my gaze jerks to hers. My heart thumps as Becca's eyes go saucer wide. I follow her gaze to Stefan, as Kate Hilton—my frenemy—steps onto the path, right in front of him.

"You have got to be kidding me," I murmur under my breath as my blood boils hot. I'm not sure what it is about Kate, but she brings out the absolute worst in me. Maybe I do know, and it's because she's always beaten me at everything. For as long as I can remember, my mother has been comparing me to her.

Why can't you be more like Kate?

Why can't you play with dolls instead of trains?

Why can't you smile like she does?

Why...why...why.

Ugh, I am so sick of hearing about how wonderful Kate Hilton is.

I hike my bag over my shoulder, ready to go slamming into Stefan. Heck, five seconds ago, I wasn't even sure I wanted his attention, but now thanks to Kate, I'm determined to get it. Becca grabs my arm to stop me.

"Wait."

"What?" I ask.

"Last year, remember how Stefan's brother Jonas stole Bianca from her boyfriend?"

"I remember." I actually thought it was horrible. Bianca's boyfriend, who played center on the Falcons, had been devastated when she dumped him for the Swedish prince.

Her brow furrows the way it always does when she's deep in thought. "I think there's something to be said about the chase."

"Meaning..."

"Maybe Stefan is like his brother. Maybe, in order to get him to notice you and take chase, you need to be already taken, or unavailable."

Kate flicks her hair over her shoulder and her laugh curls around me. God, I hate her so much. I'm sure she's the reason I didn't make the cheerleading team. There was one position left and she got it over me. But of course, she did. I should probably be thanking her for that, really. I could never admit that I was secretly happy about it. Mom was a cheerleader and was quite disappointed that I didn't make the cut. I'd rather focus on my degree.

"You might be missing one small detail. I am available," I say. Cripes, I hadn't had a boyfriend since my last year of high school—after my brother went off to college. I've been busy studying, and well...I'm sort of under the radar where guys are concerned. Throw in an overprotective older brother—and his protective best friend Braden, who would beat the crap out of any guy who did me wrong—and you have yourself one very hands-off girl.

"You know how all the girls want Braden simply because he stays celibate during football?" Becca asks.

"Yeah, they like the chase. It's all rather disturbing."

"Maybe, but it's all about the chase, right? If Stefan thought you were off limits, my guess is he'd want you all the more."

"I don't know about that."

"But you don't not know about it."

"Uh, what?"

She laughs. "Look, all you need to do is get yourself a boyfriend."

"Yes, that's easy to do because guys are falling at my feet." I look down at the ground. "Oh, there's one, oh, and there's another."

She nudges me with her hip. "Stop it. I'm not saying a real boyfriend. I'm saying get someone to pretend to be your boyfriend."

I stare at her like she might have just arrived from outer space. "You can't be serious. My life is not a rom com, Becca."

"No, it's not." We both stand there and watch Kate and Stefan turn and head toward the campus pub. "But if you want it to be a fairy tale, you'd better get yourself a guy and soon."

"Who?"

She puckers her lips and glances around, her gaze going to the football field as the players begin their drills. She points a finger. "How about him?"

My gaze settles on my brother's best friend as he tugs on his helmet. I snort. "Do you have a brain tumor or something?"

She laughs. "Think about it. He's totally focused on football and won't so much as look at a girl until the season is over." She pokes my stomach, and I almost giggle like the Pillsbury dough boy. "If you were on his arm, it would turn a lot of heads. Think about it. The guy who is off women turns his back on his superstitions because he's so totally in love. That, my friend, would raise a lot of brows and bring a lot of attention."

She's not wrong. My gaze goes to the star running back, as he fixes his helmet and prepares for a drill. We've been friends for a long time, and while he's always been overprotective of me, his loyalties are to my brother. "Forget it, he'll never do it. Besides my brother would never let him."

She cocks her head and her lips quirk. "You never know. With the right motivation, you can get anyone to do anything, Cassidy."

2

BRADEN

Seconds after I put my helmet on, a weird sensation raises the hairs on the back of my neck. I turn and spot Cassidy and her best friend Becca staring at us from the path that cuts around the football field. "Hey James. Why is your sister staring at us like that?"

James laughs. "Probably because I shot a text off to her a few minutes ago asking if Becca was single."

I turn to my friend, as he stretches his arms out. "You're interested in Becca?"

"No," he says with a non-committal shrug. But I know him well enough that he might be hedging the truth. Could James be into Becca? "It's a big brother's job to mess with his little sister," he says, like he's trying to backtrack. "You know that as well as I do."

I put my hand on James's shoulder. "Maybe so, but even if you did like Becca, she won't let you near her with a ten-foot pole."

For a brief second, I think I spot disappointment in his eyes. "Yeah, I know, but it's fun to mess with her."

Coach Meyers blows his whistle, and we head down the field toward him. I cast another fast glance Cassidy's way, and she's no longer looking at me. We walk past a few of the cheerleaders practicing for Friday night's game, and they start waving their pom poms and calling out to me.

"Christ," I murmur under my breath.

James throws his arm around me. "Dude, you're really missing out. You could have your pick of girls."

It's true, I could, but only because I'm a challenge. I'm just so over that and let's face it, I'm no prince charming. "I'll just have to live vicariously through you, I guess."

I steal another glance at the girls bouncing around on the sidelines. They're only calling out to me because I'm the only guy on the team who remains celibate for the season. It's a weird superstition I picked up in high school, and it's gotten me this far, so I'm not about to go breaking it now. My only goal is to make it into the NFL, and I'm not about to get sidetracked by some girl who only wants me simply because she can't have me. I'm not what you'd call classically handsome like my bro James. I'm no one's prince charming and without football or my superstitions, no one would even notice me. But that's perfectly fine. I have a career to focus on, and my education to fall back on.

For the next hour, we practice drills and once we're done, we all head back to the locker room for a shower. After washing, I towel dry and toss it over my shoulder and walk back to the change room. The guys are all laughing and carrying on and talking about our upcoming game with the San Diego Sharks.

I join in the conversation as I tug on my jeans and reach for my T-shirt.

Beside me, James finishes dressing, and grabs his phone from his locker. My stomach takes that moment to grumble. "Do you want to hit up The Growler for a burger?" I ask. Neither one of us are great cooks, and even though we share a house with a state-of-the-art kitchen, most meals are spent at the campus pub. Instead of answering me, he stands there staring at his phone like it might have cooties, or crabs, or...something worse.

"Ah, is everything okay?" Worry races through me as I tug on my shirt and step up to him. Truthfully, I love the guy, but he's been sleeping around a lot, and I'm worried cooties might be the least of his problems. Honestly, I'm not sure what's going on with him. It's not like James to keep things from me, but he's been screwing like the devil is driving him. He holds his phone out to me and I read the message from Cassidy.

"She has dinner ready for us?" I frown as I scratch my head. We're all friends, the three of us as tight as three siblings can be—not that she's my biological sister—but cooking isn't Cassidy's thing either, even though she's good at it. She's good at a lot of things, despite the fact that she considers herself a failure at most. Just because she never won a pageant growing up, and failed at cheerleading, does not make her a loser. I hate that she thinks she is. "Since when does Cassidy cook for us?"

"Never." He shoves his phone into his back pocket, a scowl on his face.

My stomach grumbles louder this time, the thoughts of a warm meal urging it on. "Maybe not, but I'm not going to say no to a homemade meal."

"Not even if it comes with a favor?"

"A favor?"

"Yeah, Cassidy obviously expects something in return. No way is she doing this out of the goodness of her heart, and since she hates to cook, it's obviously something we're not going to like."

"I'm pretty hungry, bro." James shakes his head at me and I consider what kind of favor I'd do to taste one of Cassidy's homemade meals. The consensus is: pretty much anything.

He reaches down, tosses his bag over his shoulder and heads toward the doors. "Come on. Let's go find out what our little sister is up to."

I snatch up my bag and follow him. We often call Cassidy our little sister because I've known her since she was just a kid, and she was like my sisters too—annoying. I chuckle at that. While it's only James and Cassidy, I'm the oldest with two younger sisters. I had no trouble taking Cass on as another sister to look out for.

We cut across campus, and as we walk past Wolf House, I spot Kate chatting with Stefan, the Swedish prince who recently transferred here. Kate was in Cassidy's grade growing up, and I don't know her all that well. What I do know, I like. She touches Stefan's arm and laughs when he says something.

Come on, Kate, you're better than that.

Sure, Stefan is attractive, and the entire campus is abuzz with his presence, every girl vying to be his princess, and although I don't know why—I've never really considered myself a great judge of character—there's just something about him that rubs me the wrong way. It's not the way he walks around like he's better than everyone else. I couldn't care less about his stature. Nor is it the way the privileged entitlement rolls off him in waves. All I know is I want Cassidy to stay as far away from him as possible. Seriously though, what kind of guy gives out roses and then decides who he'll take for a bride? I guess maybe that's what bothers me. That he thinks he can have his pick of women. That love is some kind of a prize. This is Kingston College, for Christ's sake. Not some reality game show.

James nudges me when he sees them. "Look."

"Yeah, I see them."

A half snort, half groan crawls out of James' throat. It's a Collins thing. I've heard his sister make that exact same sound. "That guy's a fucking douche."

"I know."

James' steps slow, and I can almost hear his heart crash against his chest. He swallows, hard, and curses under his breath. Unease clutches onto my balls with the death grip. I've only ever seen that look on James' face once before. It was when one of our teammates back in high school asked about taking out his sister. Murder. It's the only way to explain it.

"What?" I ask quietly, as every muscle in James' body tightens.

"I have a bad feeling."

"About Kate and Stefan?"

"No," he says picking up the pace. "About Cassidy and Stefan."

"Oh fuck." I double my steps to keep his pace. "You think that's what this dinner is all about?"

"You know my mom. I can just imagine she's all over Cassidy." James grips the handles on his bag harder, and the muscles in his jaw clench. Neither of us like the pressure his mother puts on Cassidy. Christ, when we were kids, and she used to play baseball and dodgeball and tumble in the dirt with us, his mother would go into hysterics, demanding she put on a dress and act like a lady.

I hated how it always deflated Cassidy, how her vivacious and contagious smile would run away from her face. It hurt my heart back then as much as it hurts it now. She's a good kid, down to earth with a kind heart—heck, she wouldn't even hurt a spider and she hates spiders—and in my world, that's all that matters. I pray to fuck her mother isn't pressuring her into impressing prince Stefan Lundin from Sweden. Like Kate, she's better than that and better than him.

We reach our place, and James rushes up the three stairs and bangs open the door. He's already questioning Cassidy by the time I reach the stoop. I don't know whether to hang back or not. This is a family matter. Then again, I consider Cassidy family too. I quietly close the door, drop my bag next to James' and walk down the hall to the kitchen.

My stomach grumbles loud as the scent of freshly baked bread reaches my nostrils. Cassidy made bread? My entire body stiffens. This is bad, so very bad. I lean against the door jamb when I reach the kitchen, and her gaze darts to mine. Her lids flicker nervously and she tears her gaze away, like she can't quite bring herself to look at me. What the hell?

"Cass," I say, and her chest rises and falls, her lids briefly closed like she's bracing herself for something. I push off the door and step into the room.

"Just give me a minute," she says, and James and I exchange a worried glance.

"Tell me this has nothing to do with Stefan," James says, but she doesn't need to answer for me to know it has everything to do with Stefan.

"Sit, have something to eat first. You guys look like you're starving." She pulls two chairs out, and we drop into them, keeping a laser focus on her. She bends and pulls a fresh baguette from the oven. After cutting it into slices, she sets it on the table. I reach for a piece, ravenous, and when James doesn't move, I pull my hand back despite the grumble in my stomach.

James eyes his sister. "You're not in some kind of trouble, are you?"

"No, no of course not. Now eat."

With that, James hesitantly grabs a slice and so do I. I take one bite of the sweet buttery soft bread and in that instant, I don't care what kind of favor Cassidy wants. I'd agree to anything...well, just about anything.

"School going okay?" James asks.

"Yes, in fact I have been thinking about some ways to fundraise for the football team. There were rumblings about the team wanting new uniforms, but it wasn't in the coffers this year."

"That's true."

A wide smile lights up her eyes. "If I could pull off a big fundraiser, with the help of you guys and your teammates, it would be good for you all, don't you think?"

James nods, a measure of relief moving across his face as I bite into another piece of bread. "I'm sure the guys would love to help out. I know Braden and I are in." He looks at me as I chew and I nod in agreement. James reaches for another slice of bread and his hand stops mid-air. "Wait, what's in it for you?"

"Extra credit."

"Oh, okay."

She goes to the stove, grabs a set of tongs and dishes up two generous plates of pasta and meatballs. Only my favorite meal on the face of this earth. I'm pretty low maintenance like that. James' favorite meal is steak and fries. Wait, why is she making *my* favorite meal and not his? Oh, because this meal isn't at all about fundraising and extra credit. She wants another favor and it has something to do with me.

Motherfucker.

I toss a big meatball into my mouth, and note the way Cassidy's gaze keeps flickering my way. Yet every time I lift my head to see her, she busies herself.

"Aren't you going to eat with us?" I ask.

Her hands go around her waist, and she hugs herself. "No, I'm not hungry. This is just for you guys."

"That's what this meal is about, then? You wanting to do the team a favor for extra credit?"

"Well yes, but..." She takes a big drink of water, draining nearly the whole glass. She's stalling. I get it. After she finishes drinking, she gingerly sets the glass down and wipes her mouth with the back of her hand. I grin. This is the Cassidy I know and love. If her mother was here, she'd be demanding that Cassidy dab the corners of her mouth with a napkin. I'm glad she doesn't feel the need to do it around James and me. It's not like she doesn't have manners. She does, she just doesn't need to pretend to be something she's not. She's loveable just the way she is.

"But what?" James asks, suspicion back in his eyes.

"Okay, so…" she begins, and checks to see how much we've eaten. She obviously wants our bellies full before she tells us what this is really all about. "You know Stefan…"

James drops his fork onto his plate and it lands with a clang. Cassidy jumps from the clatter, and holds her hands out, cutting James off before he can get a word out. "If you'll just hear me out."

James curses and his fingers fist at his sides. "I already don't like this, and—"

"James," I say, cutting him off. "Let's hear what she has to say. It can't hurt to listen and it's obviously important to her if she went through all this trouble."

Cassidy gives me a grateful smile. She takes a deep breath, and with her gaze still locked on mine, she blurts out, "I need you to pretend to be my boyfriend." My mouth drops open. So does James'. "It's just pretend, for a bit. You know how guys want what other guys have. I mean, Braden, you know how all the girls want to sleep with you during football because they can't. Because of your superstitions." I sit there, staring at her, trying to put the pieces together as she rambles on. "Remember last year…when Stefan's brother Jonas was here…and how he—"

"How he stole Bianca from Carlos. Is that what you're getting at, Cassidy?" James asks.

"Well, yeah."

"Carlos was devastated," James adds.

"When you put it that way, it sounds horrible. But my guess is Bianca and Carlos must have been having problems." There's hope in her eyes as she says that. "Otherwise, she wouldn't have dumped him, right?"

Is she trying to convince us or herself that anything about that was right?

"Cassidy, if you're doing this because of Mom—"

"I'm not. I really like him. He's handsome and sweet, and I think we'd make a great couple. Only problem is, I'm not on his radar, and—"

"Then he's an idiot," I blurt out and all eyes turn to me. "What? He is. You're smart and beautiful and if he doesn't see that, that's on him, not you."

"Yeah, okay sure," she says like she doesn't believe me. "I still think if he saw me with you, Braden, he might begin to notice me."

"Is that what you want in a guy?" I ask. How could she be attracted to a douche bag who'd only want her if he thought she was good enough for someone else, someone he could take her from? What kind of guy does that make him? Rage races through my veins and I work to tamp it down.

"Are you sure about this, Cass?" James asks. "He's who you want?"

"Yes," she answers, her gaze on me. "Braden, would you be able to help me out? Pretend to be my boyfriend for a little while, and once I have Stefan's attention, we can stage a breakup?" As I take in her big blue eyes full of hope and worry, and the way she's nervously coiling a long strand of dark hair around her finger my stomach clenches because damned if she didn't just ask the one thing I wouldn't do for a homecooked meal.

Fuck me six ways to Sunday.

3

___

CASSIDY

I take a deep breath and hold it as Braden stares at me like I just asked him to go skydiving without a parachute. James pushes back in his chair and the scraping noise seems to take Braden out of his trance.

"It will never work," Braden finally says.

"Why not?"

"Because I'm not into you and you're not into me."

"We can pretend though."

"Come on, Cassidy." He drops his fork onto his plate and rakes an agitated hand through is hair. "You're like a sister to me. Everyone knows that."

"Stefan doesn't know that. He doesn't know our history."

James clears his throat, and I glance at him. My heart sinks. From the way his mouth is twisted, it's clear he's going to side with Braden and I'll be back to square one. If Braden doesn't do it, who the heck could I ask? My mind races through the roster of the guys on the Falcons. Heck, I'm sure any other guy would expect more than a fundraiser in return, and I'm not giving my virginity to some hound who has a different girl in his bed every week. At least with Braden, I'm safe. He's not going to ask for more than I'm willing to give. It's not that I'm holding onto my virginity for any particular reason. Sure, Mom insists I have to wait until I marry—which makes me want to give it up all the more, truthfully. Her words race through my brain. *He won't buy the cow if he's getting the milk for free.* Wait, is my mother calling me a cow?

Maybe I'm old fashioned in a way though, and when I sleep with a guy for the first time, I want it to be about more than just sex. I want to like him, love him, even. But the guys on campus are juvenile at best, and I'm not about to give it up for the sake of giving it up.

"You know..." James begins.

Braden angles his head, his eyes narrowed. "What?"

"We really could use a good fundraiser for new uniforms."

"You can't be fucking serious, James."

He shrugs. "I mean, what can it hurt? You're not dating during the football season, and Cassidy wants the extra credit. A little tit for tat."

"There will be no tit or tat involved," Braden blurts out.

Okay, so he doesn't like me like that. Which is good. Perfect really.

James laughs. "Exactly. You're the only guy on the team I trust to do this." My brother turns to me, his smile falling.

"You really want him, Cassidy? This is what you really, truly want?"

"Yes," I say, and ignore the unease mushrooming in my stomach.

He reaches out to me, grabs my hand and gives it a little squeeze. "This isn't just pressure from home?"

"No," I say quickly. It's not a lie. Not really. Sure, Mom is pressuring me, but I want this too. I mean, it's not just the need to finally win over Kate, right?

James turns to Braden. "Do a girl a favor?"

"Jesus Christ." He shakes his head and blows out a hard breath. "I don't know the first thing about being a pretend boyfriend, Cassidy."

"I'll show you," I say.

"And you know about that how?" he shoots back. "This is something you do often?"

"Well, no, but we'll learn together," I say casually. "We've been friends forever, and we're comfortable with one another, so I don't know how hard it could be."

"I'm not kissing you or anything."

"I don't want that either," I say, my body stiffening. I've never thought about kissing Braden before, so I don't know why I'm suddenly all offended.

"If I do this—" A squeal jumps from my throat, and James angles his head towards Braden. "I didn't agree to it yet."

"Okay, sorry." I take a breath and hold it.

"All I was going to say is, *if* I do this, and it doesn't work out, I don't want you to be upset with me."

Before I can think twice about it, I throw my arms around Braden, and he just sits there, his arms at his sides. I let go and back up. "I would never blame you. Thank you so much, Braden."

He holds his hand up. "Not so fast."

"Okay, what?"

"How much time do we have to spend together?"

I crinkle my nose as I think about it. "Maybe just be seen around campus, and you coming and going from my dorm, and me coming and going from here."

"Since you're going to be here," he says, and twirls his fork through the pasta, "Do you think you could cook for me every night?"

"Us," James pipes in quickly, catching on to what his best friend is doing. "He means us, right, Braden?"

"Yeah, us." Braden lifts his chin an inch and stares up at me with those amber eyes. The color is hard to describe, but they always reminded me of the forest when the leaves turn golden during the fall. "Every night," he adds, playing hardball with me. It's laughable really, because he's a softie at heart and instead of looking mean and domineering, he looks sweet and adorable.

If cooking is a dealbreaker, then of course I'm going to do it. But I cross my arms and say, "I think that's blackmail."

He grins. "So that's a no?"

Oh, he's way too hopeful asking that and assuming it's enough to make me back out. "It's a yes."

He grumbles some more. "So we just need to be seen together, that's it?"

"Well, yes, and pretend we're into each other. No kissing but you might have to put your arm around me. It's not like you haven't done that before anyway," I begin, and he groans. "Also, there's the beach party tomorrow night. I'd love it if you could come."

He holds me with his stare and silence fills the room for a very long time. He finally breaks it and says, "The meals better be gourmet."

I can't help but laugh. "They will be, I promise."

He grumbles something under his breath. "Fine and just so you know, I spotted Kate Hilton with him earlier, and they looked tight, so we might have our work cut out for us."

My nerves jump, the competitiveness in me gripping my stomach and urging me to get this game started. I'm not surprised, really. She brings that out in me. Braden finishes his pasta and stands to take his plate to the sink.

"I'll take care of that," I say and take it from him.

He grunts his response. "Maybe this won't be so bad."

"I know I could get used to it," James says with a laugh.

"When I'm done here, do you think you could walk me back to my sorority?" I ask. "We might as well get the charade started."

"Fine," he grumbles, and disappears into the other room as I start the clean-up. Honestly, this went way better than I thought it would.

James comes up behind me and slides his dish into the soapy water. I glance at him and he looks like he wants to ask me a question.

"Something on your mind, big brother?"

"Ah, no. Just wanted to make sure you know what you're doing."

"I do," I say, injecting a measure of confidence into my voice that I don't really feel.

He grabs a dishtowel and starts drying. "Do you know anything about this Stefan guy, other than he's a prince looking for a princess?"

"I know as much as I need to know. He's a good guy, James. You don't need to go all alpha on him, and while I appreciate you looking out for me, I'm a big girl now and don't need your protection." He goes quiet and I glance at him. There's a strange look on his face, one that says he might actually realize that I am a grown woman who can take care of herself. "What?"

"Nothing...just...we're all family, you, me and Braden."

I stare at him for a long second, then burst out laughing. "Ohmigod, are you worried about me and Braden?"

"Well, no."

I splash water at him, and he rolls his dishtowel up and snaps me with it. I yelp and he chases after me, just like we used to do when we were kids, and I can't stop laughing. Braden comes into the kitchen and snatches the towel from James, he comes around the other side of the table and gives me a good snap on the ass.

This time I actually cry out, and drop into one of the chairs.

"Braden, that really hurt."

"Oh, shit. I'm sorry, Cass. I didn't mean to hurt you." I rub my backside and whimper. "Let me see."

"I am not showing you my ass."

He shakes his head. "I didn't mean..." The sweet, vulnerable look on his face wraps around my heart when he tucks a strand of hair behind my ear. "I'm so sorry, Cass. Do you want me to get you some ice? You can go up to my room, and I'll bring it to you."

"No, I'll be fine."

"I feel like shit."

I touch his face. "Don't. It's fine. You were only fooling around." I lift my head and note the way my brother has gone deadly still, watching the tender exchange between Braden and me with a horrified look on his face.

"Come on," Braden says, and takes my hand to pull me to my feet. "I'll walk you home, and tuck you in to make up for it."

I grin. Braden and James used to tuck me in when we were kids and I couldn't get to sleep. I never was a great sleeper. They took great pride in wrapping me so tight in the blankets I couldn't move, but I liked it. It always made me feel safe and secure. Today I use a weighted blanket which gives the same affect.

"It's been a long time since you've tucked me in, Braden."

His gaze moves over my face, and a smile tugs at the corners of his mouth. There's something about that tender grin of his that always wraps around my heart and squeezes tight. While he's not Hollywood handsome, he's a sweet guy. Someday, some girl is going to see past the conquest and see him for the amazing man he is. Honestly, I hate how they throw themselves at him, eager to be the girl to make him abandon his beliefs. He's so much more than a contest amongst the cheerleaders.

"Then I'm past due, don't you think?" he asks.

"Yup."

"Um...ah..." James says, his words shaky and broken. "You didn't finish the dishes."

I glance at him, take in the deep concern in his eyes and suspect that's not what he wanted to say at all. My God, if he's worried about anything happening between Braden and me, he's out of his mind. Braden and I are friends—family—nothing more.

"I'll take care of them when I get back," Braden informs James, and tosses him the dishtowel.

I head to the main hall, and pick up my backpack. Braden takes it from me and tosses it over his shoulder. We step out into the night, the low sun hidden behind heavy clouds. I breathe in the warm night air, and Braden's body brushes mine as we walk down the driveway.

I steal a glance at him, take in his features, and the scars on his face, from playing the game. "How are classes?" I ask.

He nods. "Good, actually."

"Are you ready for mid-terms?"

"Pretty much, how about you?"

I shrug. "I guess. Sometimes I wonder if I really know what I'm doing, though." I laugh, but it's strained and forced.

"You don't like Public Relations?"

"I do, I just...I don't know." Mom was the one who pushed me into it. She said this way, when I'm a wife of a prominent man, I'll know how to host the best parties. I actually do kind of like it, though, and maybe I could put it to better use, do something a little more meaningful with the degree.

"Are you really going to hold a fundraiser for the team?"

"Of course, I'm a girl of my word. You of all people know that, Braden." He told me a secret once, how he had a crush on Jessica Barnes back in high school. Jessica was James' girlfriend at the time. I could tell he was hurting about something, and when I asked—he was tutoring me in math at the time—he blurted it out. I never told a soul, not then and not now.

"Yeah, I know," he says, making a fist and nudging my chin.

The sound of keys rattling in the distance catch my attention. I glance up and beneath the streetlamp, I spot Stefan headed our way. The house he lives in, or rather, the mansion he lives in, is just a few blocks from the house Braden and my brother share.

"Ohmigod, it's him." I turn into Braden, my breath coming fast. "What do we do?"

He puts his hands on my shoulders. "Relax, he's just a guy."

"He's not just a guy, he's a prince," I say under my breath.

My entire body quivers and Braden rubs his hands up and down my arms, to calm me down. He presses his forehead to mine. "He's still just a guy, Cass."

"Yeah, you're right."

As Stefan gets closer, panic erupts inside me and I go up on my toes and do the one thing Braden said we couldn't do.

I kiss him.

BRADEN

Holy fucking shit. Cassidy is kissing me. Sweet Cassidy, my best friend's younger sister, who I've known my entire life is kissing me. As her warm soft lips press urgently against mine, I have one takeaway. Nothing about this feels like a kiss between family, between brother and sister. Nope, not at all. Wait, I have two takeaways and the second is, I don't hate it. Christ knows I want to—I should—but dammit, I don't.

A breeze washes over me as Stefan passes by us, and from the corner of my eye I note the way he's slowing, surprise registering on his face when he sees it's me. Everyone knows I keep to myself during football season, so it's no wonder he's shocked. I'm sure news of this will spread faster than campus cooties. I'm not sure how I feel about that, but I do know how I feel about her kissing me and I need to put a stop to it, now.

The second Stefan moves past us, I put my hands on her shoulders and push her away from me. "Cass," I say failing to keep the arousal from my voice. "He's gone."

She blinks up at me, and for a second I think I spot something in her eyes, something that looks awfully close to what I'm feeling, but it's quickly replaced with mortification.

She puts her hands over her face, and mumbles into her palms. "I'm so sorry. I don't know what came over me."

"It's okay." I take her hands from her face and press them to her sides. "You just panicked. Right?" Obviously, she panicked. Cass has never wanted to kiss me before and I've never wanted to kiss her and I need to know she only did that out of desperation. It can't be anything else. Ever.

"Yeah, I don't know what came over me." She blinks up at me, her eyes pleading. "Please don't tell James."

Christ. "I don't keep secrets from James, Cass."

"Well, you sort of do."

Is she bringing that up now? "Low blow, kiddo."

"I'm sorry. It's just, if he knew I kissed you, he'd put a stop to this right now."

"Unless of course he knew why, and that we both hated it. You did hate it, right?" What the fuck am I doing? Why am I fishing, and hoping she didn't hate it?

Her face twists like she'd just eaten a bag of worms. "It was kind of gross."

I laugh and it eases the tension between us. "Why don't you tell me what you really think?"

"Okay," she says and starts walking again. She gives me a little bump and begins, "Let's start with your tongue action."

"I didn't use any tongue."

Her soft chuckle curls around my dick and tugs.

What the fuck?

"That's the problem. You don't have any. When you kiss a girl, they like a little tongue action, and you could probably angle your head more. Your nose was in the way."

"Listen," I say and grab her in a headlock. She yelps but I don't let go. Instead I rub my knuckles over her mess of hair, working hard to remind myself she's like a sister to me. "I've never had any complaints in the kissing department, or any department, I'll have you know."

I let her go and she crinkles up her nose. "Great, now I'm thinking about you...*doing it?*"

Yeah, so am I, and the problem is, as that image invades my brain, it's sweet Cassidy I'm *doing it* with.

Fuck me sideways.

"I need brain bleach," she teases.

"It's not too late for me to back out of this, you know."

"Yeah, but you won't."

I shove my hands into my pockets and note the gleam in her eyes as we walk under a streetlamp. "You don't think?"

She gives me a wide grin, and puts her hands over her heart, looking very much like the young, innocent girl she is. "You love me and want me happy."

"It's true, I do." I'm just not sure Stefan is the right guy for her. Then again, what do I know about relationships? I've never been serious, and sex is for sex—in the off season. I get that's why the girls want me. I'm a challenge. Once they've had me, they move on.

She goes quiet for a moment, and then nudges me with her hip again. "Any critiques on my kissing?"

"It was bad, Cass," I lie, and she frowns, air leaving her lungs like I just poked them with a big fat needle. "Hey, I'm kidding."

"No, you're not. I'm just…" She blinks at me. "I'm not all that experienced."

"Good." Every protective instinct I possess grips me by the nuts. Honestly, the thought of her in bed with a guy bothers me—and in the last five minutes, it's not just because I've always thought of her as a sister.

What the hell did that kiss do to me?

"Maybe I should get some experience." She shrugs as she stares off into the distance. "What if Stefan gives me a rose, and kisses me and it's horrible?"

"Not going to happen. You're a good kisser. I was just kidding." She eyes me, like she doesn't believe me.

"You're just saying that."

"No, I'm not."

She whacks my stomach. "You are so."

I grab her hand, and not having any idea what's come over me, I pull her to me. Her body aligns with mine, and I slide one hand around her head, and tug on her hair, forcing her mouth to open for me. A growl I have zero control over crawls out of my throat as I dip my head and press my lips to hers. The kiss is soft at first, tentative, until some working brain cell registers her moan. I deepen the kiss and slide my tongue into her mouth to tangle with hers as I taste the depths of her sweetness and what I taste, I fucking love.

This is wrong, Braden.

Her hands slide around my back, and dip under my T-shirt. Fuck, that shouldn't feel so good. I grip her hair harder, fist it in my hand as I eat at her mouth like a man denied a treasure for too long. My dick thickens and I push against her. A little gasp catches in her throat as our tongues play and tease.

A dog barking in the distance trickles through my lust-fogged brain and snaps like a rubber band, pulling me back. I break the kiss and suck in a huge breath. She stands there immobile, staring up at me, her lashes blinking rapidly, her lips still parted, like she's waiting for more.

"What...what was that for?" She glances around, like she's checking to see if we have an audience and that was for show.

I try not to sound breathless when I say, "It was to show you that I know how to kiss, and prove to you that you do too." Okay, okay, fine, I wanted to kiss her. Was driven by a foreign force I don't understand, but I'm not about to tell her that and scare her off. Although scaring her off might be in my best interest. I don't want her with that douche bag Stefan, but she's a force to be reckoned with when she sets her mind to something, a tenacious girl who will find a way—ask someone else to fill my shoes—and that doesn't sit well with me at all.

"Well...just so you know, I was wrong about your tongue action."

I laugh, a strange new kind of intimacy blossoming between us. It seeps through my veins and fills my chest with unfamiliar cravings. My heart pounds a little faster as I rub the back of my knuckles over her flushed cheek and push her hair back. "And my nose."

"Not at all in the way."

"Just so you know, you're a great kisser, Cass. Believe me when I tell you that."

"That's because you've kissed a lot of girls."

"Something like that." I have, but probably not as many as she thinks. "Don't believe for a second that you're not great, okay?"

"O...okay."

"Now come on, let's get you to your dorm. It looks like rain any second now."

I put my arm around her and turn her until she's facing the right way, and we both fall quiet as we hurry our steps. But we're not quick enough. The skies open up and she yelps as we start running, the rain soaking us in seconds. We're both laughing, sexual tension still surrounding us as we reach her sorority and dash inside.

She grabs my hand and we hurry up the big set of stairs and down a hall to her apartment style place that she shares with Becca, each having their own bedroom. She opens the door and I ease her backpack off my shoulders and drop it onto the nearby table as she bends forward, presenting me with the sweet curve of her ass.

Dear mother of God and all that is holy.

I've looked at Cassidy a million and one times, and never once was it sexually until she kissed me and stirred something deep inside me, something that was better left dormant. Yeah, if James knew what happened on the walkway, he'd put a stop to this now, which means I need to tell him. Because I'm not sure I can do this, not after that kiss.

"I should go," I say. Christ, I sound like I'd just eaten sandpaper.

"No way. You owe me a tuck in, remember?"

She ties her hair back and flips it over her back as she stands, and my gaze instantly drops to take in her damp T-shirt and the mind-blowing way her hard nipples press against her damp T-shirt. Fuck, it's football season, which means I can't even tug one out. Why again did I think celibacy in all forms was a good idea during the season? Right, it helps me keep my focus and my head in the game. Right now, however, my head is anywhere but in the game.

"Just give me a second to dry off and get into my pajamas."

I run my hands through my wet hair as she waves me into her bedroom. I reluctantly follow her into her bedroom, and she gestures for me to sit on the bed as she grabs some clothes from her dresser.

"Be right back."

I catalogue her room, and grin. Everything about the space is so Cass. Unlike other girls' rooms I've been in, hers isn't filled with stuffed toys and trinkets from home. She has one picture on her dresser and I stand and walk over to it. It's from Halloween when we were kids. She was dressed as a hot dog, and James and I were the mustard and ketchup. I laugh remembering that night, and how Cass ate too much candy and had a stomach ache. I tucked her in that night, and gave her a kiss on the forehead.

"Something funny?"

I turn around and my smile falls when Cassidy walks into the room, dressed in a snug T-shirt and pajama shorts. Um, not funny. Not funny at all. Sexy, alluring...downright fucking hot. But definitely not funny. When the hell did Cassidy grow up?

"I...was just looking at this picture." She steps up to me, takes it from my hands to examine it. The warm minty scent of her toothpaste reaches my nose.

"I love this picture of us." She sets it on her dresser and stifles a yawn. "By the way, I checked my butt, and I have a big red welt."

I bite down on my cheek to stop myself from asking if I could see. "I really am sorry."

"No worries. A tuck in will make up for it."

I glance at her bed and nearly bite off my tongue. "Get in."

She practically skips across the room, her gorgeous tits jiggling as she does, and I give myself a hard, mental lecture to keep it together. This is Cassidy, a girl I used to think of as a little sister.

Used to?

Jesus mother fucking Christ!

She tugs the sheets down, crawls in and squirms around like the bedding is warm and cozy and it's all I can do not to climb in with her and see for myself. But it's not the bedding I want to squirm around on.

I step up to her and grab the blankets. "Stop squirming," I command in a soft tone as I press my hand to her stomach to hold her still. Her shirt lifts slightly, and when my hand brushes her soft skin, her lips part and a needy, breathy sound escapes her throat.

"Sorry."

Why the hell does that one word sound so sexy, so inviting? Maybe I'm imagining it, you know, because all the blood has left my brain and is currently filling my cock.

I slowly take my hand off her still body, as the heat of her flesh travels along my arm and settles in my balls. She straightens her arms and places her hands at her sides, and her tits jut out just a little more. I cover her body and bend forward, tucking the bedding tightly around her until she's practically mummified.

I fix the blankets around her shoulders and the scent of her hair, her skin, wraps around my cock and tugs. I swallow. Hard.

"Are you okay?" she asks, her voice low and husky. Christ, I hope she's not onto me.

"Fine," I grouch. "Are you good?"

"I'm good, are you good?"

"You just asked that and yes, I'm good," I lie. I stand back and look at her body, all tucked into her bedding. "G'night."

"Night." I turn to leave, desperate to get back outside. "Braden?"

"Yeah."

"Thank you."

I grumble under my breath and leave her room. I let myself out and walk home in the rain, hoping the fat droplets will cool my hot body, and reduce the swelling between my legs before I have to face James. The pathway is quiet, and because I'm taking my time, I'm completely drenched when I reach the front steps. I step inside, moving quietly in case James is studying or sleeping.

I head upstairs, and as I walk past his room, he calls out to me. I push open his bedroom door and his brow furrows as he takes in my damp clothes.

"Caught in the rain," I say for lack of anything else.

He nods and closes his laptop. He sits up straighter in his bed. "You and Cass..." he begins quietly, and I can almost hear his brain racing.

"What about us?"

"You're good with doing this?" He frowns. "I mean, I trust you, Braden. I just don't want...I guess what I'm trying to say is...I mean she's like a sister to you, right?"

Tell him, Braden. Tell him she kissed you and then you kissed her and you are no longer thinking she's like a little sister.

James' eyes narrow. "Is everything okay?"

"Yeah, uh, Cassidy..."

"What about her?"

"Well, um...I..."

He sits up a little straighter. "You what?"

"She uh...I uh..."

James' gaze narrows in on me. "What's going on?"

"She's all tucked in for the night."

The air is crisp tonight, if not a bit cool after last night's big rainstorm. Stripping off to my swimsuit and jumping in the lake doesn't sound all that appealing anymore, but that's not what's really stirring around inside my brain. No, I can't stop thinking about that kiss last night. My God, I've been kissed before, but I've never been kissed like that and when he tucked me in, I swear I almost asked him to join me, which is insane! I'm saving my virginity for a guy I like, a guy I love, and while I love Braden, I don't love him like that.

I steal a glance at my brother's best friend—my protector since childhood—as he walks beside me, his body strong, confident as he kicks out his muscular legs, his strides a little slower to keep pace with me, and for the first time in my life I'm so aware of him, his every move, his every breath. A strange wave of need careens through my blood and honestly, my body is a hot mess, every nerve alive, standing at attention, waiting for his body to simply brush mine, his lips to lay claim again.

But after that kiss, he was pretty nonchalant, so I'm not sure it smacked him over the head quite like it pummeled me, and it's best I keep that to myself, for fear of making a fool of myself. Plus, if I said anything, he might put a stop to the charade here and now, and I need to be on his arm if I'm going to shake things up on campus.

Braden glances my way, and grins as he throws his arm over my shoulder, the way he's done a million times before, but not once in those million times did it send me into sexual overdrive. "You good?" he asks.

"Yeah, just a bit nervous," I say to hide my body's reactions.

His gaze moves over my face, and I suddenly feel self-conscious. He's used to seeing me without makeup, and tonight, I have a face full and he probably thinks I look like a clown. But if I'm going to be 'dating' the star running back and make Stefan notice, I have to go all out. Basically, be everything I'm not.

"Just be you, Cass. If he can't see, or doesn't like the real you, well, fuck him." I grin at that and he adds, "Don't ever change. Not for anyone. I get that in your Public Relations classes you're learning to be an image shaper, that you're in the persuasion business where you influence opinions, but you never have to sell yourself."

As his words reverberate around inside my brain, and I'm a little surprised that he knows what public relations is all about, we head toward the big fire burning on the beach, and I relax a bit when I spot Becca with her boyfriend Jared, who is on the baseball team. He has his arm around her much the same way Braden has his around me. Jared's brows raise as we come close, and he recognizes Braden. Becca clearly hasn't let him in on the ruse and the fewer people who know, the better.

"Hey Jared," Braden says, and they do some kind of guy fist pump as I lean into hug Becca.

"Girl," she squeals and hands me a red cup. "I can't believe he agreed to this."

I take a big drink of the beer and wipe my mouth as Jared hands a cup to Braden. "Same," I say and don't tell her about last night's kiss with my brother's best friend. I probably will, later, but right now, as I scan the beach in search of Stefan, I'm not interested in an inquisition.

"He's here," Becca whispers, and I don't miss the tightness in her tone or the way she's shuffling closer to me.

"What?" I ask.

She fidgets with her necklace, running the stone back and forth over the chain. "He's been talking to Kate."

A loud squeal reaches our ears as a bunch of senior guys toss a handful of freshman girls into the water. It's tradition, Kingston's initiation, and I'm so glad I'm not a freshman anymore.

"Do you want to swim?" Becca asks.

As the guys talk, I bite my lips and hug myself. "I don't know. It's a bit chilly."

"Yeah, well, once Stefan gets a look at you in your swimsuit, it's going to change everything."

"Oh, please," I say and give a dismissive wave. Braden moves closer, his heat wrapping around me.

"Cass, the only one who doesn't know how hot you are is you. You are smoking, girlfriend. Am I right or am I right, Braden?"

His grip on his red cup tightens and he almost crushes it. "I... I don't know." He gives an easy shrug, and snorts much like my brother and I do. "I guess."

"Of course, she is, and she's going to make Stefan's eyeballs pop."

Braden's body brushes mine as he inches closer, and when his hand lands on the small of my back, my brain backfires. Is he touching me for show, or showing possession? I'm not sure. The only thing I do know is that I like the way his fingers are splaying, the warmth of his touch teasing all my girly spots— spots I didn't even know existed until that kiss last night. I have no idea what Braden did when he went home afterward, all I know is I touched myself, and it wasn't Stefan I was thinking about.

I turn to him and he gestures toward the lake. "If you want to swim, I'll go in with you."

No longer cold, in fact I'm downright hot, I nod. "Do you guys want to join us?" I ask Becca and Jared.

"Maybe later. You guys go ahead."

We walk toward the water, and the wind blows my hair from my face. I left it down tonight, heck, I even used a flat iron. Sure, I burnt a few strands, but that's the price one has to pay for beauty. At least that's what was drilled into us at the pageants.

At the water's edge, Braden peels off his T-shirt, and holy... when did he get so hard? His body is so cut, so well defined, my hands itch to touch him. I grip the hem of my coverup dress, my bikini on underneath, and lift it over my head.

"Dammit," I squeal. I tug but the stupid elastic waistband gets stuck on my face, my nose to be exact. I hop around like a contortionist on crack and struggle to get it off without taking my bikini top with it.

"Here, let me help." Braden's knuckles brush against my neck as he fixes the dress, and pulls it over my head. His grin is sexy, adorable as he stares at me.

"First time undressing?" he asks.

"Clearly it's not your first time undressing a girl." I cringe as those words leave my mouth. I sound like a jealous girlfriend, for God's sake. Not good. Not good at all.

"No, it's not," he admits, his voice casual, not at all bothered by my accusations, and why should he be? His sex life is his business not mine, and I've never been jealous before. His gaze drops, takes in my body, and a frown comes over his face. I cover my breasts.

"That's not much of a bathing suit."

"You don't like it?" Oh God, why does that bother me so much. I should only care if Stefan likes it.

"No, Cassidy. It's not that. I just...you're showing a lot of skin."

"My God, you sound like my brother." I drop my hands. "You two need to stop being so overprotective. I'm a grown woman in case you haven't noticed." I poke his chest. "I can wear whatever I want."

"I...noticed." His throat makes a sound as he swallows. Wait, does he like what he sees? His head lifts and he looks around. "Everyone is noticing."

"Is Stefan noticing?"

He turns back to me and steps closer, like he's trying to keep me from prying eyes. "Yeah."

Before I realize what's happening, someone scoops me up from behind, and I shriek as I'm carried out into the water and tossed into the freezing lake. Shocked and confused, I sink, and gasp for air as I struggle to find my footing. Oh my God, I'm going to die, and I haven't even had sex yet. A big hand reaches down, and pulls me upright.

"Braden," I spurt out, and choke on water. A hard shiver wracks my body, not just from the cold water, but from the trauma. "Braden, ohmigod."

His jaw clenches hard, and he curses under his breath as he gathers me into his arms like I weigh no more than a football. I put my arms around his neck and hold on.

"What the hell just happened?"

"Some asshole dunked you. If you didn't need me right now, I'd hunt him down and beat the crap out of him."

I press one hand to his chest, and revel in the way his strong heart beats against my palm. "No need. He must have mistaken me for a freshman. It's not a big deal."

"It is to me, and he needs to know you're with me now and no one, and I mean no one messes with my girl."

Holy shit.

The way he said my girl, and the possession in his words make me momentarily forget this is just for show. He's probably shouting those words just so Stefan, and anyone else within ear shot, gets the message, though. That still doesn't stop my stupid mind from wandering. What would it be like to be Braden's girl? He's strong, protective, kind and sensitive. Like I said before, any girl would be lucky to have him. But I'm not any girl. I'm his best friend's kid sister. I'm family and these inappropriate thoughts aren't conducive to my ploy to catch the attention of a prince.

I swipe at my face, my makeup running. I must look like hell. "Braden, I need to get out of here before Stefan sees me."

He frowns. "Isn't that why we're here?"

"My makeup, it's running."

He sets me down on a log, and kneels before me. He lightly brushes his finger under my eyes. "You look better without it anyway."

I stare at him, feeling a little deflated. Tonight, I tried really hard to put on makeup and look pretty. I guess I failed. "Please, can we go." I start coughing, and he goes still, his gaze moving over my face, assessing me.

"Can you breathe okay? I don't know much about mouth to mouth…"

Ohmigod, he's going to give me mouth to mouth?

"What the hell happened?" Becca asks, as she and Jared come running over to us, and killing my opportunity to kiss Braden again.

Wait, I don't want that. Or at least I shouldn't.

FML.

"I got dunked," I explain. "Someone thought I was a freshman."

"She wasn't expecting it, and took in water," Braden explains.

"Are you okay?" Becca drops down beside Braden and pushes my wet hair from my face. I shiver a bit, and she rubs my arms.

"I'm okay, I think."

"Is there anything I can do to help?" I stiffen at the sound of Stefan's voice, and rub the water from my eyes as I glance up, past Braden's broad shoulders and spot Stefan looking down at me.

I cough, choking on nothing but air. I quickly pull myself together and say, "I'm...no...ah, yes."

He angles his head and I don't miss the way his gaze is moving over my half naked body. "What can I do to help?"

Oh, give me a rose, marry me, make my mother the happiest woman in the world...

Braden stands to his full height, a few inches taller than Stefan and blocks Stefan's view of me. Wow, someone give him an Oscar for best overprotective boyfriend performance. But I'm grateful. I don't want Stefan seeing me like this. I'm sure he's used to perfectly put together women—like Kate.

"If she needs anything, I'll be the one to give it to her," Braden says between clenched teeth.

Stefan grins, holds his hands up, palms out and backs up an inch. "Just checking to see if I could help out." As Braden squares off against Stefan, Stefan angles his head and glances at me again. "It's Cassidy, right?"

"Right," I manage to say before a violent coughing fit overtakes me. My entire body jiggles, my breasts included. Attractive, I'm sure.

"See you around, Cassidy."

"K," I squeak out between each spasm.

Braden stands over me until Stefan walks away. Once he's gone, Braden drops back to his knees. "You're shivering. We need to get you home."

He searches the sand for my cover up dress and tugs on my hands until I'm standing on shaky legs. He fumbles a bit as he tries to dress me, and something tells me he's used to undressing a girl, not dressing her. It's strange how that thought, which never bothered me before, suddenly churns in my stomach. He finally gets the dress over my head and I start coughing again.

"Here let me." Becca helps me get my arms into my dress, and then hands me a beer to wet my throat and help with the cough. I take a sip but it doesn't help.

"She needs some tea and honey. Come on, let's get you back to our sorority."

"No," I say quickly and back up. "I'm not tearing you and Jared away from this party. I can make it home myself."

"You're not going anywhere yourself," Braden says, the command, his take-charge attitude teasing the needy spot between my legs. He puts his arm around me again and tugs me to his side. I sink into his warmth. "Can you walk or do you want me to carry you?"

"I can walk."

"Are you sure you don't want me to go back with you?" Becca asks.

"I've got her," Braden says and Becca arches a brow as she glances at me, her lips quirked at Braden's possessive behavior. I roll my eyes to let her know that Braden going all caveman is part of the charade, but I'm not sure she believes me.

She touches Braden's arm. "There's some vapor rub in the bathroom. You should probably rub some on her chest. It will help with the cough. Don't let her do it herself. She gets it everywhere and makes a big mess."

Ohmigod.

I glare at my former best friend as she smirks at me. I'm not sure what she's up to but I don't like it. Okay, maybe I do, but no, Braden is not rubbing anything on my chest. I'm using him to get Stefan's attention, and nothing more.

Braden puts his arm around me and walks me to his truck. We get in and he turns the heat on high, turning to check on me.

"I'm okay," I say to him, and try to fight off a cough. I'm totally unsuccessful.

"You need a hot shower," he says.

"Yeah. I'll do that once I get home."

He pulls into traffic, which is light, and a few minutes later, he parks at the sorority. I open my door, but he's right there, on my side and helping me out.

"I'm okay, Braden. You don't have to come in with me. Charade is over for the night. There's no one around to see you."

He shakes his head, and his eyes are dark, almost angry as they lock on mine. "You think that's why I'm walking you to your room?"

"What other reason could there be?"

A noise crawls out of his throat. "Here I thought you knew me better than that."

I do know him better than that, but he's never had to walk me back to my room on campus before. Sure, he's overprotective like a brother—although I'm not quite thinking of him as a brother anymore, and growing up he always hovered, but I'm safe, and feeling much better. I'm about to tell him that, but my throat is so sore from coughing, I fall silent. And maybe just maybe I like the idea of him taking me to my room. *Oh, God, Cassidy get yourself together*. He keeps his arm around me as he walks me to my room and once inside, he flicks the kettle on, and guides me down the short hall to my bedroom.

"I think I'm too tired for a shower. I'm just going to crawl into bed, okay?"

"I'm going to make you tea and honey, like Becca said."

I yawn and fall onto my mattress. "Okay."

"Get undressed and I'll be right back."

"What?"

He scrubs his face. "I mean, get into some pajamas or warm clothes. You can't get into bed all wet."

Oh God, if he only knew just how wet I was...

I slide off the bed and stand on wobbly legs. "Right." He disappears and I tug off my wet dress and bathing suit. I pull on a warm T-shirt and pajama pants, and crawl between my comfy sheets. My eyes are heavy, my throat sore, yet oddly enough, a warm contentment pulls me under, but I don't want to go to sleep just yet. Braden is going to be back with my tea. It's weird, I kind of like him being in my space, looking out for me. I hated the overprotectiveness when I was a kid, not to mention in high school when Braden and James scared all the guys away, but I like hearing him walk around in my small apartment.

"Hey," he says quietly, walking slowly as to avoid spilling the tea as he comes into my room, the light from the hall spilling over his body.

I sit up a bit straighter, as he takes a seat on the side of the bed. "Do you think you can drink?"

I rub my scratchy throat and I nod, and he hands me the cup. I take a sip, and moan. "This is so good. The perfect amount of honey."

"I've got skills," he teases with a sexy wink.

Oh, I have no doubt.

I take another sip and he stands and heads toward the door. I assume he's about to leave me sleep. "Braden?"

He turns back to me. "Yeah."

"Thanks for the tea, and for fishing me out of the water."

"No problem."

"G'night."

"I'm not going anywhere. Not until...hang on." He disappears and a minute later comes back into my room with the vapor rub. "Becca said I need to rub this on your chest."

Did he...wait no, he didn't just say what I thought he said, right?

As his warm gaze moves to the V in my T-shirt, his chest rises and falls a bit quicker. "Do you want to lift your shirt up, or tug it down."

Ohmigod, he did.

6

BRADEN

It's been twenty-four hours since I put my hands on Cassidy's hot flesh, and my palms are still tingling with the need to ravish her. And if we want to talk about my dick—and of course we all do—let's just say it's still half-mast. Christ, she was so soft, so supple, and when I breathed her in, filling my lungs with her delicious grapefruit scent...let's just say, I'm surprised I didn't combust into a million tiny pieces. The delectable scent of her skin is still imprinted on my brain, and completely throwing me off my game, and I'm not just talking football here. I'm sure her brother would beat the crap out of me if he knew I had my hands on his sister, but when it comes right down to it, I had no choice. It was a medical emergency, for fuck's sake.

Yeah, sure, Braden. You keep telling yourself that, if that's what you need to ease your conscience and help you sleep at night.

The goddamn truth is, I wanted to touch her and I damn well know it. I wanted my hands on her, my mouth on her, my dick inside her. I have no idea what's coming over me since she kissed me. It's like she awakened some deep-seated need inside me, something I kept buried, and behind locked doors —something I need to marshal into submission again and chain behind impenetrable bars. At least I didn't touch her inappropriately. I could never forgive myself if I did. This is not some random cheerleader looking to score with the celibate player, this is Cassidy Collins and I can't forget that. Ever.

Nevertheless, my brain keeps playing over the way she tugged her top down to expose her chest, keeping her lush breasts covered as I spread the vapor rub over her cool, glistening skin—which rapidly warmed beneath my fingers. It was all I could do not to dip my cock in the jar of vapor rub and tug one out. How many more weeks before the football season is over anyway? Christ, it could end tomorrow and it wouldn't be soon enough, and that's insane. I need to keep my head in the game, and off women if I want to make it to the NFL. I never found it hard until Cassidy, and can we please not talk about hard...

My pants grow tighter as Coach blows his whistle, and James hits my helmet with his. It's snaps me back to the present and we both run to the huddle. Our QB goes over the play. This time, I'm a decoy, pretending to receive the ball from our quarterback, and run left, to throw off the Sharks' defensive line. Mason, the team's other running back, will be handed the ball, and run down the middle.

We all line up and I scan the stadium in search of Cassidy. She always comes out to the games and usually sits in the same spot. I find her, and she gives me a little wave like she was waiting for me to search her out. I wave back, and grin like a damn fool, and that's when I catch the way James is watching me. I quickly wipe the smile from my face, and regroup to get my head in the game. I'm almost successful, until I spot

Stefan making his way to Cassidy and plopping down into the seat next to her.

Motherfucker...

I hate that fucking guy and every possessive bone in my body rages to life. My hands fist with the need to hurt something or someone. If I can't stand the sight of Stefan with Cassidy, why then am I pretending to be Cassidy's boyfriend so she can entice him by dangling her unavailability in front of him? Oh, because I'd do just about anything for her.

Seriously though, she doesn't need me. All she had to do was walk onto the beach in her bathing suit. There wasn't one guy at the party that hadn't noticed her—myself included. But, douche bag that Stefan is, he likes the chase and she wants to give it to him—thinks she needs to give it to him. Maybe she does, which makes him a double douche bag.

The play starts and I turn back to the QB. I'm sure I hear Cassidy calling out my name to cheer me on. I steal a fast glance her way as the fake-handoff takes place, but I fumble it so badly, it's easy to guess our play and when Mason gets the ball, the Sharks' defensive end is all over him

Shit.

"What the fuck, Braden?" our QB calls out, and I shake my head, angry with myself. This right here is why I keep to myself during football season. Women are a distraction I don't need.

"Won't happen again," I assure him, and work to put Cassidy out of my mind and pour every ounce of concentration on my game. Not an easy task with Stefan up there beside her. But fortunately, the game continues, and I don't fuck up any more plays and we end up winning by a few points. As our cheerleaders scream out names and the fans go wild, we walk off the field and I don't miss the way James' eyes are drilling into me.

"You good?" he asks when we get to the showers.

"Yeah. It's just…" I shake my head. "I really don't like Stefan. Does Cassidy really know what she's doing?"

James shrugs. "She's all grown up now, bro. I can't tell her what to do anymore."

"Yeah…" is all I say, and soap up.

"It's nice of you to help her out."

I mumble my response as I rinse off. If he knew what was going through my head, he might not be so happy about me helping her out.

"I put another hole in my jersey tonight, so I'm glad she's doing a fundraiser for us," he adds, a reminder that the team is getting something out of this too and while I don't want to let the team down, I'm questioning my judgement. James sticks his face under the water, rinses and turns off his shower. We grab our towels and dry off as we head back to our lockers.

"How does she plan to raise funds anyway?" I just hope it's not some stupid auction where girls bid on us and we take them out. Kill me fucking now.

"No clue. I'm sure whatever it is, it will be great. She's a great influencer."

I laugh. "No kidding. Look at what she talked me into."

James smirks. "Is it so bad?"

"Hell yeah, it's bad." Oh, he doesn't know the half of it.

He arches his brow. "Then why the hell did you agree?"

"The new equipment, and you seemed like you wanted me to."

"I just didn't want her asking any of these assholes," he glances around the shower as the guys soap up and razz one another. "When she puts her mind to something, there's really no stopping her."

"So what, I'm the lesser of two—or fifty—evils?"

"Better the devil you know."

I grin. "Love you too, buddy. I just think she could do a hell of a lot better than Stefan, and maybe she should be concentrating on school instead of marriage."

James looks aghast, like I just asked him to calculate the square root of eight million by hand, or I decided to forgo celibacy for the season—which I can't do, under any circumstances. Not even if Cassidy asked me. Not that she would but...Jesus, I'm losing my shit here.

"Don't let my mother hear you say that."

"Come on, James. You can't want her to give up her education to be some ridiculous princess in Sweden."

"Not my call, bud. Like I said, she's old enough to make her own decisions."

I frown at my best friend. Did he get an injury at practice or something, or suddenly develop a brain tumor? It's so not like him to be so easy-going where his sister is concerned. He loves her, and wants what's best for her. How can he possibly think this is it?

I tug on my jeans and long sleeved T-shirt and toss my football bag over my shoulder. We head outside and the cheerleaders jump on our backs, looking for a lift to the pub. I grab James' bag.

"You go ahead. I'll drop these off at home and meet you there."

"I could help you," Chloe says, and runs her finger up and down my chest.

"I got it."

She pouts. "Fine, but don't be long. We have some celebrating to do, you know."

I'm surprised she's not heard about me and Cassidy. Or maybe she has and she too likes a challenge. I hurry home, and when I'm about to put my key in the lock, I notice the door is slightly open. I push it, step inside and hear movements down the hall in the kitchen.

"Hello."

"It's me," Cassidy calls out. "I made lasagna earlier, and I'm putting it in the fridge for you guys. I'm sure you'll be starving when you get home tonight and if you're going to keep playing kickass games, you need real food, not greasy burgers from the Growler."

I step into the kitchen and I'm presented with an unobstructed view of her gorgeous backside, framed in tight jeans as she bends over and slides the lasagna into the fridge. She stands and turns my way, a big smile on her face. Dark eye shadow coats her eyes, and her cheeks are flush with makeup. She has a rosy, red color painted on her lips and damn if I don't want to pull her to me and smudge it. She looks beautiful, but she doesn't need all the crap to get a guy's attention.

"I made garlic fingers too. I know how much you love them."

"Thanks." I jerk my thumb over my shoulder and hope it's not as shaky as I feel. What is this girl doing to me? "Are you headed to the Growler?"

"Yup, I just wanted to drop this off first."

"That was nice of you."

"All a part of the bargain, remember."

"I remember. I'm headed to the Growler. If you're ready, I'll walk you."

"Yup, it's good for us to be seen together." She picks up her purse and crosses it over her body, the strap separating her breasts and I do my best not to look, not to remember how nice it felt to put my hands on her. We walk through the front door and I lock up.

"You're feeling better. No more coughing?"

"Yes, thanks to the warm tea and…um…vapor rub."

I steal a quick glance at her. It's dark out, and I can't tell for sure, but I'm pretty sure her cheeks just turned pink.

"Glad I could help." I shove my hands into my pockets and bite my cheek before I ask if she'd like a repeat treatment tonight.

"I…uh…saw Stefan talking to you in the stands."

A big smile lights up her face, and in that instant, my heart wobbles, partly because she looks so adorable, and partly because it shows that she really is into him.

What, did you think she might be into you because she kissed you? I remind myself that was all for show, and slow my pace to keep hers.

She puts her hands over her heart, something she does when she's excited. "He invited me to a party at his place tomorrow night."

Stefan hasn't been here long—no parties yet—but his brother used to throw epic parties last year. I guess he really is following in his brother's footsteps.

"Are you going?"

"We're going," she says and bumps me.

"I think you already have his attention, Cassidy. You don't need me."

She loops her arm through mine as we crossed the street. "We've got a long way to go yet, Braden. He hasn't made his choice yet."

"I'm just saying, he's noticed you. That's what you wanted, right?"

"Well yeah, but we can't give up too soon. I mean, if the chase is over..."

I bite my tongue to prevent me from saying what I really want to say. Hey, if she wants a guy who only wants her because he can't have her, that's her business. James pretty much told me she was grown up and her decisions were hers. I guess it doesn't matter what I think. But you know, that doesn't seem like James. He has been acting strange lately and whatever is going on with him, he's keeping to himself. I don't like it. I don't like any of it.

Music reaches our ears as we approach the Growler, and Cassidy's hold on my arm tightens. I pull my arm from hers and slide it around her back, pulling her close. She smiles up at me, and I almost forget how to breathe. God, she's gorgeous.

We step inside the Growler and the mood is high. The dance floor is full, and I scan the crowd for James. I spot him at the bar, and reach for Cassidy's hand, but can't find her. I turn, and spot her being dragged into the crowd by Becca. Disappointment settles in my gut, and knowing she's in good hands, I cut across the bar and take the seat beside James. He gestures for a beer, and the bartender slides one in front of me.

James swivels on his stool, and I do the same. I follow his gaze until it lands on Becca and Cassidy, who are dancing in the middle of the crowd. But I don't think it's his sister he's watching. I'm about to ask him what's going on when Kate comes up to us.

"Kate," James says. "What are you drinking?"

"I'll have a beer." James orders her a beer and she turns her attention to me. "Great game today."

I snort. "Thanks." I almost fucked it up and she knows it.

"I heard there's going to be a big fundraiser for the team. Cassidy is organizing it."

"Yeah," I say, even though I still don't know what she has planned. "What did she tell you about it?"

She frowns as her gaze seeks out Cassidy. "She didn't tell me anything." Something in the way she's frowning catches my attention. Are the two not friends? "Nothing really. I heard it through the grapevine."

"I didn't even realize she had anything planned already. We just talked about it the other night." She turns to James, and showcases perfect white teeth as she smiles. "You'll be part of the auction?"

"Fuck me," I blurt out and both James and Kate turn my way. "An auction?"

James grins. "It'll be fun."

I can only imagine how many of the cheerleaders will try to buy me, simply to see if they can make me break my convictions during the season. This is going to be hell.

Kate smiles at James again and leans into him. "Are you hoping anyone in particular bids on you?"

Whoa, does Kate like James?

My gaze goes back and forth between the two of them until someone nudges my leg. I turn and spot Stefan moving close.

"Hey Kate," he says in that ridiculous accent of his. "Great game tonight, guys." James holds his cup out and clinks it with Stefan's. I don't need to turn to know Cassidy is watching us. I can feel her eyes burning into me.

"Where's Cassidy?" Stefan asks me, and before I can answer, before I can tell him to shove his cup and his roses up his ass, Cassidy comes bounding over and plunks herself on my lap. Her arm goes around my neck, and I slide mine around her small waist. Before I can think better of it, I let my hand slide up until I'm cupping the back of her head, and I bring her lips to mine for a kiss so deep, and so passionate, there's no way anyone can question what she means to me—her brother included.

CASSIDY

I briefly lift my head up from my laptop and shrug. "For the millionth time, it was fake. The kiss was just to drive the point home that I was taken."

Becca arches her brow at me, as I work on posters for next week's auction. "Fake, my ass."

I turn back to my laptop as someone in the library hushes us. "If you don't believe me, there's nothing I can do about that."

She leans into me, her voice low. "Did you see the way James was looking at him? He didn't believe that kiss was fake any more than I did."

In an effort to redirect, I say, "What's going on with you and James anyway? After Braden kissed me and we went off to dance, you two seemed to be awfully chummy. Is there something going on I should know about?"

"James and I are friends."

"Just like Braden and I are friends."

"We were talking about you and Stefan, and the way he was noticing you."

"Good, that's the whole plan."

"All I can say is if that kiss was fake, Braden deserves an Oscar."

"Exactly. He's good at acting. Remember, he took drama back in high school. He was amazing in Macbeth."

"Yeah, I mean he was but—"

"But nothing." I spin my laptop so she can see the posters I'm making for next week's auction, which she promised to help with. Extra credit for both of us, and new outfits for the team. It's a win/win, even without Braden agreeing to help me with this ruse. "I already talked to the manager at the Growler and he said we could have it there."

"Those are awesome."

I stare at the pic of Braden mid-play, the ball under his arm as he goes for a touchdown.

She leans down for a better look. "Where did you get that picture of Braden?"

"My phone."

She eyes me. "Oh, you take pictures of Braden now, do you?"

"I did the other night because I needed a good picture for the posters."

"Uh huh."

I roll my eyes so hard at her I'm sure I've given the librarian a headache. "I'll print these off and we'll go distribute. I also have a small rally in the student union building in..." I stop to check my watch. "Less than an hour."

Becca tosses her backpack over her shoulder. "Let's get this party started."

I head to the front desk and use the library equipment to print my posters. The librarian gathers them for me, and pauses to take a look at Braden. He looks awfully impressive in the photo, if I do say so myself. I almost missed the shot, with Stefan talking to me.

We head to the cafeteria to hang the posters and put some on the board outside the student union.

"Do you think Jared will be jealous if I bid on one of the guys?"

"Most likely," I tell her as I put the last tack in and stand back to examine my handiwork. "How are you two doing anyway?"

"Good, why?"

Oh, just because my brother has been asking about you... which totally freaks me out. Just like he sort of freaked out when Braden kissed me. I guess it does have an ick factor.

"No reason. You don't have to hang around for my rally," I tell her.

"I've got nothing better to do."

I head inside the building, and spot Kate sitting there, flipping through her tablet. The hairs on the back of my neck stand up. Does she always have to look so perfect, in her short skirt, her makeup and hair on point? I turn away and my ponytail bounces over my shoulder.

I get set up with the microphone to speak to the small crowd, and that's when Stefan and Braden both come into the building together. As I see the two talking, I nearly bite off my tongue. What the hell could they be saying to one another?

They separate when Stefan sees Kate and he goes to sit by her. Her pretty face lights up and she instantly goes into flirtation mode. My God, I don't stand a chance against her.

"You know..." Becca begins, like she can read my mind, and she probably can, or at least read my body language.

"I know..." I answer, and expel a heavy sigh that reeks of failure and surrender.

"I'm just saying, if you go to the party, and Stefan wants to see if you two are compatible, you know, in the bedroom area..."

Blood drains to my toes. "Ohmigod." I thought about kissing, but not more. What would Stefan want with an inexperienced virgin? He's the kind of guy who'd want a woman who knew a thing or two about pleasing him, and about what pleases her. I know nothing about either. I turn to Becca, panic all over my face.

"Don't worry," she assures me quickly, putting her arms on mine. "I have a plan."

"Thank God."

She turns slowly, and I follow her gaze until I'm staring directly at Braden and he's staring back. My gaze leaves his face, and takes in the way he's casually leaning against a bookshelf, his feet crossed at the ankles, looking relaxed...hot...as he watches me with those dark eyes of his. Braden is delicious, even out of his jersey. Why am I only realizing this?

As I stare, Becca says, "Ask Braden to help you."

I continue to watch Braden as he pushes off the bookshelf and starts my way. His steps are long, and confident as I slowly turn to Becca, her words not registering in my mushy brain.

"What?" I say in a dreamlike state, her words coming at me like the adults in a Charlie Brown cartoon.

"Ask Braden to give you sex lessons."

This time her words hit like a wayward football to the head and snap me out of my stupor. "What the hell?"

She gives a casual shrug. "I'm sure he wouldn't mind."

"It's football season, Becca. He's celibate, and I would never do anything to interfere with his beliefs. I'm not that girl. You know that. Besides all that, I am not asking him for sex lessons. It's not like that between us."

She shrugs. "I know, but this is Braden. He'd do anything for you, and I'm sure he'd enjoy it. All you have to do is ask him."

"Ask me what?" Braden says his voice low and hoarse as he crowds me. My heart jumps into my throat as his warm scent, his presence, his dominance, overwhelms in the most mind-blowing ways.

"Nothing," I say quickly. "Nothing at all."

He angles his head slightly, taking in Stefan and Kate. I look at the two of them all snuggled close and the competitiveness in me leaps to the surface

"Is there something I should know?" Braden asks.

"No."

"If we're going to pull this off, Cass, I should know what you and Becca were just whispering about."

"We were talking about you giving her sex lessons," Becca blurts out and I nearly lose all ability to stand. My gaze jerks to hers, and while I expect to find her smirking, she's not. She just stands there, completely stoic—like she didn't just ask my brother's best friend to take me to bed and teach me all kinds of deliciously naughty things.

Deliciously naughty things?

Okay, well maybe she didn't say that, and I have no idea why I'm thinking it.

Oh really, Cassidy, you have no idea?

I shut that stupid inner voice down, and put my hand on Braden's chest. Completely embarrassed and hating that Becca would announce that and put him in a hard position, I counter with, "She's kidding, B."

As soon as I call him B, like I used to do when we were kids, something comes over him. His entire body stiffens, and I can almost hear the air leaving his lungs in a hiss.

What the hell?

Becca jumps in with, "I wasn't kidding."

Braden adjusts his backpack over his shoulder, and that's when I realize I still have my hand on his chest, and his heart is pounding beneath my palm. He's as upset as I am, clearly.

"I...uh..." he begins.

"No," I blurt out. "This wasn't my idea, it was hers, and it's ridiculous."

He stares at me long and hard, his eyes leaving mine and settling on my lips. For a second, I think he's going to kiss me. "Yeah, ridiculous," he murmurs, his voice an octave lower.

Just then the student council president comes out of her small office and puts the microphone on the podium. "Are you all set, Cassidy?"

"Yes," I squeak out. How the hell am I going to give an inspiring speech when my entire body is on hyperdrive? I'm going to sound like a chipmunk with two cheeks full of nuts.

I step up to the podium, and Stefan's eyes are on Braden as he walks to the back of the room and takes up position against the bookshelf. I grab the microphone, and start talking about the upcoming auction, and smiles go around the room. I'm happy everyone is excited by the idea.

James steps into the room and nudges Braden. They speak quietly, and Becca makes her way to the back of the room. She disappears with James for a few minutes, and my stomach tightens. There's definitely something going on between the two of them. It's not like Becca to cheat on Jared, but still… they seem to be talking a lot more than usual. Then again, maybe they're plotting ways to help me snag Stefan. They both seem on board with it.

I continue to give my speech and get the students excited, and I smile at Stefan as he grins up at me. *Take that, Kate.*

My gaze moves to Braden, standing there looking all hot and sexy.

Take that libido.

Good God. I finish up quickly, letting everyone know the auction is next Friday at the Growler and they should spread the word and show up ready to support the football team.

Everyone claps as I set the microphone down. My frenemy pushes to her feet and tentatively approaches me.

"Hey, Cassidy, great speech. I'll be sure to show up in support."

"That's great," I say, plastering on my best smile.

"So, you and Braden..."

"Yeah, me and Braden."

"He's a really nice guy. I've always liked him." She glances over her shoulder and jealousy rips through me. Honestly though, she can have Braden if she wants. It's Stefan I'm after and maybe Braden would be a good distraction for Kate. Or not. "Are you going to the party at Stefan's tonight?" she asks.

"I am."

She gives me a big smile. God, she always acts so sweet, like she's my friend, but then goes and competes with me for everything. "I look forward to seeing you there."

"I'm sure you do."

Her smile falls. "What?"

"Oh, I look forward to seeing you too."

She stands there like she wants to say more, and after an awkward five seconds, she says, "Okay, see you later."

She walks off and I gather up my bag. Stefan comes toward me and for a second I think he's going to shoulder it, but Braden gets to me first and snatches it up.

"Ready?" he asks.

"Yeah, sure."

Stefan backs up, and puts his hands in his pocket. "Great speech, Cassidy. I'm looking forward to the auction, and I'll see you tonight, right?"

"Thanks, and ah, yeah, right," I say for lack of anything else and Braden puts his arm around me to lead me outside.

I glance up at him. "You can't keep butting in like that, Braden. You have to give him a chance to talk to me."

"I'm doing what you asked, Cass."

It's true, he is, and I could never be mad at him anyway. "Yeah, okay, I know, but...I don't know. Stefan sure is noticing me, so maybe you pretending to be all possessive is actually working."

"Who's pretending?" he mumbles.

"What?"

"Nothing. Are you headed home?" I nod and we turn left on the path. "What's going on with you and Kate, anyway?"

I tense as her name slides off his tongue. "Nothing why?"

"Are you two friends?"

"Sure, we go way back." He eyes me like he doesn't believe me. "It's just that she always beat me in everything, you know. Every pageant, and she took the one last spot on the cheerleading team."

"And now you're determined to beat her and win over Stefan?"

"This isn't about Kate," I tell him, even though my voice lacks conviction.

"If you say so."

"What were you and Stefan talking about when you came into the student council building?"

"I ran into him, and he was asking if we were going to his party tonight."

"Are we?"

A strange noise crawls out of his throat. "I'm not letting you go alone."

I put one hand on my hip. "Hey, I'm a big girl. If I want to go alone, I'll go alone."

"Do you want to go alone, Cassidy?"

Oh, God, when he says my name like that, I can't help but think about sex lessons. Thanks for putting that into my brain, Becca!

"No." He shakes his head at me and chuckles. "But the point is, why don't you want me to go alone?"

"I don't know." He scrubs his face and frowns. "I just don't want you to, and I can't explain why."

"That's fine. We need to be seen together anyway."

He nods, and his hand brushes mine as we walk. It sends shivers skittering through me. "You did a great job on the posters and the speech. You really have a way of inspiring people."

I snort. I'm not great at receiving compliments, usually because I receive more criticism than anything, so I blow it off and say, "I don't think I'm really great at it. But I do enjoy it."

"I don't think you give yourself enough credit."

"Yeah, maybe, maybe not."

He goes quiet as he walks me back to my place. It's easy to tell he has something big on his mind, but I don't press. I have enough on my own, thinking about what I'll wear tonight, and what I'll do or say to Stefan if I find myself alone with him.

We reach my sorority house and he comes up the steps with me. I reach for my bag. "I got it," he says.

"You don't have to come up."

"I know." He walks inside and heads up the steps. I follow behind and try not to stare at his ass and the nice way his jeans hug his bottom.

He reaches the top and waits for me, and we walk side by side to my room. I push the door open and he drops my bag onto the table. I face him and his eyes are narrowed, as he scrubs his chin again.

I'm about to thank him for walking me, and tell him I'll see him at the party, but he says, "Cass."

"Yeah."

His head lifts and his eyes meet mine. "I'll do it if you want. I mean, if you think it will help."

"Do what? What will help...?" My pulse jumps. Ohmigod, is he saying what I think he's saying?

He swallows, and he reaches out and takes my hand. He gives it a squeeze, and I feel the pressure all the way to the needy spot between my legs when he says, "Give you sex lessons."

8

BRADEN

I take one look at Cassidy and nearly bite off my tongue as I consider what she's wearing under that mid-thigh dress that showcases her curves and too much breast. God, I really do sound like an overprotective brother. My thoughts however, are anything but brotherly, and I still can't believe that earlier today, I straight up offered to give her lessons. She shut me down quickly, saying she would never put me in that position during the season, and while I appreciate her thoughtfulness, all I can think about is the positions I'd like her to put me in—positions I'd like to put her in.

"You're in a dress?" *Way to state the obvious, dude.*

"Can't get anything by you, can I?" she teases as she grabs her phone and unceremoniously drops it into her purse.

"But we're going to a party and well...you don't wear dresses. Not usually."

She shrugs and from the way she's averting my gaze, I'm guessing I touched on a sore spot. "But there's nothing usual about tonight now, is there?"

"Right, you're trying to get Stefan's attention." I don't tell her it's gotten mine, but she's more than what she looks like, and that's always held my attention. She's sweet and kind and brilliant. I've always known that, but suddenly the idea of her with someone else woke me the fuck up in a hurry, and of course the kiss. "I think this will work," I mumble under my breath.

"Besides, I wear dresses." She smooths her hand down her stomach. "Believe me, I've worn plenty of dresses over the years."

"Yeah, the pageants, I remember. I also remember you hated them."

She crinkles up her nose. Is that embarrassment I see spreading across her face?

"I just thought he might like it."

I nod in understanding, but what Cassidy isn't saying is that Kate is always in a dress or skirt of some sort, and since she's her biggest competition and has been seen cozying up to Stefan, she needs to up her game and become the kind of girl he's drawn to.

"I'm still running a bit late," Becca says, pulling our attention as she darts from her bedroom to the bathroom in her robe. "I'll meet you there, okay?"

"Okay," Cass yells back as we step into the hall. She glances at my jeans and long-sleeved T-shirt. "You look nice."

"I look the same."

"I'm just saying you look nice."

"Thanks." Jesus, why am I suddenly in such a shitty mood? Oh, maybe because the woman beside me isn't the same girl I grew up with and I hate everything about it. We make our way outdoors, and because there will be alcohol tonight, we walk to Stefan's place instead of driving, not that it's far. Cassidy fidgets with her purse, and curls her hair around her finger.

"What's wrong?"

"Nothing, just...I don't know. I'm nervous, I guess."

"You don't have anything to be nervous about," I tell her, and throw one arm around her shoulder to pull her against me. I like the way her body fits against mine. "Remember, you're the prize, not him."

"Stop it," she says and whacks my stomach.

"You know I don't lie." Is omission the same as lying? If so, then I guess I am a liar. I haven't told her brother that I enjoy kissing his sister, or any of the insane thoughts running around inside my brain. I supposed that's because I'd like to keep my teeth inside my mouth and if they do get knocked out, I'd prefer that to happen on the field, not with his fist.

She goes quiet for a long time, and I say, "If we're in this together, you'd better tell me what's really on your mind."

She gives a curt nod, in agreement. "I love how protective you're being. I really do. But if Stefan starts talking to me, and you know it seems like things are going good, maybe you could just pretend you don't see."

I bite down on my jaw hard enough to break bone and my arm around her tightens possessively. "Yeah, sure," I say my words easy and light, a contradiction to everything I feel. I take a quick second to remind myself that I'm a token in a game, nothing more. "I guess that makes sense." Wait, if she spends time with him, she'll see that he's a complete douche bag. "You know what, spend all the time with him. It's a great idea."

She gives me the side eye like she's suspicious, but I concentrate on the path as we cut across campus until we hit the street. A few friends come over and walk with us. I turn to Mason, and he nudges me.

"What's going on with you and Cassidy, bro?" He runs his fingers through his hair, and I don't like the suggestive look in his eyes. He and a few guys on the team are known to party and share women. He better not have any ideas about Cassidy and me.

I roll one shoulder. "We're seeing each other."

His brows pull together, and really, why shouldn't that surprise him? With the way James is protective, and my celibate streak, it's a lot to digest.

He makes two fists and hits them together. "You two banging?"

Anger bursts inside me. "Don't talk about her like that."

He holds his hands up. "Sorry, just a question." He looks around me, taking in Cassidy in her dress as she chats with one of the cheerleaders. "I always thought she was off limits. If I'd known—"

"She is off limits to you and everyone else, so back off, or I'll break your face." I say it playfully, but there's a storm going on inside me.

He laughs. "Okay, dude. I get it. I'm just surprised is all. I figured she, like every other girl on campus, would be trying to get a rose from Stefan."

"I take it you don't like him either."

"I don't hate him. His brother threw great parties last year, but I don't like them fishing from my pool, if you know what I mean."

"Yeah, I know...so last night's game," I begin, switching topics.

We fall into conversation about last night's game as we head to Stefan's giant house that he shares with no one. Music spills out onto the street as we approach, and the knot in my stomach grows tighter. I have no idea why I have such a bad feeling about tonight. I've been to numerous parties, and I've been to this house before. Last year, Stefan's brother had many parties. I guess it's the first time I'm going disguised as Cassidy's boyfriend and while everything about that feels right, everything about it is wrong.

We head inside, and I keep close to Cassidy as she glances around. She waves to a few girls, and two red cups are thrust into our hands. I hold mine out to her, and she taps it. Here's to...snagging a prince, I guess.

Someone jumps on my back and my drink spills. Cassidy takes it from me, and my hands automatically go to whoever's legs are wrapped around me.

"Buy a girl a drink?" Chloe whispers into my ear.

I shrug to get her off me, and she slowly slides down my back, her warm body pressed hard against me. I take my drink back from Cassidy. "Here, have mine."

She grins, and swirls the beer. "You didn't put something in this, did you?"

I know she's kidding, but I'm still insulted. "Don't drink it then." I go to snatch it back, but she jerks it away.

"I'm kidding." She steps closer and squirms against me. "You don't have to roofie me, Braden." She puts her finger on my chest and slides it down. "I'm game for anything."

I stop her hand before she gets to my cock. "Chloe, I'm with Cassidy now."

Her eyes go venomous. "I thought that was just a rumor."

"Hi," Cassidy says, as she steps up beside me.

"Really?" Chloe asks. She takes a big drink of beer, her gaze going back and forth between the two of us. Something on her face softens. "I'm sorry, Cassidy. I thought it was a rumor. You two are actually cute together."

"Nope, not rumor, and thanks," Cassidy says, and puts her arm around me. She hugs me tight and I like it. A lot.

"Well, at least someone is getting laid tonight," Chloe says and blows out a slow, disgruntled breath.

"What?" Cassidy blurts out, stiffening beside me.

Chloe laughs and waves her hand at Cassidy. "Oh, I know it's not you. Unless you were able to break Braden's celibacy streak." She raises her brow, curiosity dancing in her eyes.

"I would never do that to him."

"Exactly, and while that sucks for you, good for you for standing idly by until the season is over." She leans in and whispers, "I hope you have a good vibrator, but it looks like little miss Kate won't need BOB tonight." She points her finger and we both turn to find Kate standing close to Stefan as he touches her hair, running the strands through his fingers.

"Go Kate, go," Chloe says and disappears into the crowd.

"What are we looking at?"

I turn to find James scanning the room, his arm thrown around Nikki, one of the team's cheerleaders.

"Stefan," I tell him, and he nods as he seeks him out.

"Well, let's get this party started," James says and throws his other arm around me, ready to guide me to the kitchen to get a drink.

I glance at Cassidy to check in and she gestures with a nod for me to go as Becca and Jared come in behind James.

"How's it going so far?" I hear Becca ask before I'm out of ear shot. In the kitchen, a bunch of guys are lifting each other up to do a keg stand. No thank you. I fill my beer, and take a sip, anxious to get back and check on Cassidy even though she wants time alone with Stefan.

I stand back and laugh, pretending to be into all this, but catch the way James is looking at me. Shit, does he know I like kissing his sister, that I offered up sex lessons? No, he couldn't. Cassidy would never tell him, but she would tell Becca. My gut tightens.

"You good, bro?" James asks.

I take a big swig of beer, and trying to pull off being casual, I wipe my mouth with the back of my hand. "Fine, why?"

"You seem upset."

"Nope, just tired. Long day. Shit ton of homework tomorrow."

He nods, and when Kate comes into the room, alone, James excuses himself to go talk to her. I guess he's checking out the competition for his sister. Speaking of his sister, with James distracted, I casually head into the other room and glance around, but Cassidy is nowhere to be found. Panic grips my nut sack, and I make my way out into the backyard as the party spills outside.

I stand on the back deck as a few people jump into the pool, fully clothed. Maybe I should jump in and cool myself down. I scan the backyard, and spot two people talking inside a gazebo. I can't make out their features, but I don't need to. It's Cassidy and she's alone with Stefan. I set my cup down, ready to go out there and drag her from him, but stop myself.

This is what she wants.

Fuck me twice.

It takes every ounce of strength to force my legs to take me back inside. My mood is as dark as the night sky as I walk through the big-ass house until I find James and Kate playing beer pong with Becca and Jared.

"I'm next," I say, wanting to do something, anything to get my mind off Cassidy and how Stefan might be drooling over her in that too-tight dress.

What if he touches her?

"Take my spot," Jared says. "I need to hit the head."

He takes off and I step up to Becca, who's grinning at me like she knows a secret I don't. I take the ball, toss it and it lands in a red cup. As James takes a drink, I glance at Becca.

"Why are you looking at me like that?"

Her voice is low when she says. "Because Cassidy told me you were going to take my advice."

Fuck. Honestly, I expected it, but why the hell is she bringing it up here and now, while James is within earshot?

"It's not happening," I tell her. "Let's drop it okay?"

"Okay, but if you really wanted to help her, if you really cared about her, you'd give it more thought." She puckers her lips, and her head bobs, indignant.

"I do care about her, but I don't fuck during football," I say through clenched teeth as James picks up his ball. "Can we not talk about this right now? Besides, I offered, she was the one who said no."

"She's too sweet to allow you to break your 'no fucking during the season rule'," she adds, doing air quotes around those words. "But there's other things you can do, you know. It's called foreplay."

James's ball lands in my cup and I fish it out and down the beer. Becca lines herself up with Kate, as James stands behind her, his hands on either side of the table. Is he into Kate? If so, he's barking up the wrong tree. Kate is trying to get herself a rose. Of course, she could be just trying to mess with Cassidy's head and throw her off her game. Although I'm not sure she's as horrible as Cassidy thinks.

"You do know what foreplay is, right?" Becca says, refusing to let it go.

"Becca…"

"I mean, maybe she needs to learn to give a blow job. Technically that's not fucking."

Jesus Fucking Christ. Is she trying to cause trouble between James and me?

"Stefan would probably like a wife who could give a good blow job."

I rake my hand through my hair, not wanting to think about Cassidy sucking any guy's cock as Kate tosses the ball and misses.

"No," James yells, and picks her up by the waist and spins her around. Kate squeals in delight as Becca focuses on her shot. She tosses the ball and it goes into a cup. Kate groans and grabs the cup.

"I bet Kate gives a killer BJ."

"Becca," I warn through gritted teeth.

"I'm just saying, and you know Cassidy really needs to know what she likes, too. Maybe you could experiment with her, help her learn her body." She holds her two fingers up to her lips and sticks her tongue out.

Kill me fucking now.

"You don't want her to have a pleasure-less sex life, do you?"

As I think about experimenting and touching Cassidy's body, my dick thickens. Goddamn traitor.

"Becca..." I warn.

She waves her hand at me. "Fine, fine, I'll drop it, but you could at least think about it."

Like I haven't been. Ever since Becca put the idea into my head, I haven't been able to get it out. Oh hell, who am I kidding? I've been thinking about it since Cassidy surprised me with that first kiss and stirred a deep-seated need inside me.

We play a few more rounds, and I check my phone about a dozen times. "Got somewhere to be bro?" James asks.

"Yeah," I say, even though I don't. Jared comes back, like thirty minutes later. I guess he must have gotten sidetracked along the way, and I relinquish my spot and go searching for Cassidy. I roam the house for what feels like forever and check the backyard again, but she's nowhere to be found.

Unease coils itself around my veins and tugs so tight, I'm worried my limbs are going to go numb. Like I said before, I don't think I'm a great judge of character, but I do try to go with my gut, and right now it's telling me I need to find Cassidy and I need to find her now.

I head back into the house and walk through the massive dining room. I go completely still when I spot Cassidy on the stairs, Stefan's arm around her as he leads her up—to the bedrooms.

Fuck.

I fist my hands, and when Adam, our wide receiver, bangs into me, I shove him out of the way.

"What the fuck, dude?" he says.

Shit, none of this is his fault. "Sorry," I say quickly and hand him my cup.

He nods, and accepts my apology as I stand there debating my next move. Do I stop this, or do I let it happen? She wants time with him right, but did she want to be in his bed? I'm pretty sure she didn't want to go that far with him, not tonight anyway. I stare at her as she walks—or rather stumbles. My heart jumps into my throat. Something isn't fucking right.

I walk—or rather run—up the stairs and just as she's taking the last step, I put my hands on her waist to stop her.

"Cassidy," I say.

"Whoa," she mumbles and wobbles. I turn her to face me, and her eyes aren't in focus as she looks at me.

"Cassidy," I say again quickly. "It's me."

She frowns, and puts her hand on my arm, like she's trying to keep herself upright. "B?"

"What's going on?" I ask, accusation dripping from my tone as I turn to Stefan, who is standing there like the world is as right as rain and he has every right to lead a drunk, or drugged, girl to his room to do God knows what. My fingers fist, and I'm two seconds from tossing him over the banister when he speaks.

"I was looking for you," he says.

"And you thought I was upstairs?" I ask, disbelief in my tone.

"I think Cassidy might have drank too much." He frowns and gives her a deeply concerned look, and I call bullshit. "I was looking for you everywhere. I couldn't find you, so I was taking her upstairs to lay her down."

"How fucking kind of you." I glare at him, my heart pounding so hard, I'm sure it's going to break a rib. My gaze moves over his lying face. I can't prove he's a deceitful pig, I just know he is.

"I've got her," I say and put my arm around her waist. She sags against me, and before I take her outside, back to my place to take care of her, I say, "I was in the games room. If you were looking for me, I was easy to find."

9

CASSIDY

irds chirping loudly outside my bedroom window pull me awake. I try to open my eyes, but every little movement hurts my brain and my body. What the heck is going on? I roll to my side and peel my tongue from the roof of my mouth as my stomach churns. A loud groan crawls out of my throat, and the sound rattles behind my swollen eyes.

"Hey," Braden says in a soft voice. "Easy."

I slowly open one eye and find him sitting at his desk chair, watching me. "B?" The room comes into focus, and that's when I realize I'm not in my bed. I make a move to sit up, but my stomach recoils. Braden jumps from his chair and sits on the bed beside me. He inches me up slowly.

"Drink this and take this." My mouth salivates at the big glass of water in his hand, two pills in the palm of his other. "This will help with the headache."

"Did you get the name of the running back who ran me over?"

He chuckles at my joke. "It wasn't a running back. How much did you drink last night?"

His head is angled, his brow furrowed as I struggle really hard to remember how many times my cup was refilled.

"I can't remember, but I don't think I drank that much."

"Did you leave your cup alone at all, or did anyone refill it for you?"

"Whoa, what's with the interrogation?" I pop the pills, take a big drink, and snuggle back down onto Braden's pillow.

"You were pretty messed up last night, so I'm just trying to piece things together."

I shut my dry eyes tightly. "It hurts to think."

"Okay," he says, his voice softer and lower. "You don't have to right now, but I want you to try to remember later."

"Why?"

"I think you were roofied."

My lids fly open. "No way."

"I don't have any proof, but you were pretty messed up and I've seen you drunk before, Cass, and this was different."

Panic bursts inside me. I turn and search for my phone. "I need to call Becca."

He puts his warm hand over mine. "I already talked to her. I messaged her and James and told them you had too much to drink and I was going to take you home."

"Okay, thank you." I frown and search my foggy memories. "I've been here all night?"

"Yeah."

I let my gaze roam over him. He's still dressed in last night's clothes, except now they're all rumpled. "Did you sleep?"

He shrugs like it's nothing. "Not much. I was worried about you."

"Where's my brother? Does he know I slept here?"

"It's okay," he says and fixes the blankets around me. "He didn't come home last night."

"Why didn't you put me in his bed?"

"I didn't know he wasn't going to come home, and I took you here because it's closer than your place."

I nod, and I think it all makes sense. I sink down further into the bedding, and the warm scent of Braden curls around me. I breathe him into my lungs and hold it for a second before I exhale.

"Braden..." I begin, working hard to pull back the veil clouding my brain as I think about being drugged and how badly things could have gone. "I don't know what to say..."

"You don't have to say anything."

I meet his gaze as my mind plays out numerous bad scenarios. "Thank you for being there and watching out for me. I owe you."

He shakes his head like that's ludicrous. "Stefan said he was taking you upstairs to lay down. Do you remember any of that?"

"Not a whole lot." He nods, but his eyes are murderous. My stomach cramps and I put my hand over it. "You don't think...do you?"

"I don't know what to think just yet. But I do think you should have something in your stomach. Do you think you can eat? Maybe some toast?"

My heart wobbles in my chest as this great big football player, a guy who runs through the defense team like they don't even exist, sits here taking care of me. Honest to God, he's rough and tough and would be the first to jump in to protect me or his friends, but underneath it all, he's a damn teddy bear, and I love it.

"I think maybe toast is a good idea." I sit up and glance to the left, and that's when I see myself in the long mirror on his wall. "Oh my God," I say and slap my hands over my face, to hide the makeup dripping down my cheeks. "I'm disgusting."

He takes my hands from my face. "You're fine, but you didn't need all the makeup in the first place."

"Yeah, well, didn't anyone ever tell you nice guys come in last?"

"What's that supposed to mean?"

"It just means if I want to play the game, I have to play by their rules." I never wanted to be in all those pageants, never played by their rules like Kate, and that's the reason she always beat me. Not this time. I'm determined to win.

"I like when you play by your own rules," he says, and stands. Using slow movements, I push the bedding down, and he drags it down my legs. My gaze follows the movement to see I'm still in my dress.

"Why am I in pajama pants, and how did I get in them?"

He glances around, almost sheepishly. "I didn't want you to get cold, and your dress didn't cover up much. I didn't want to...I wasn't going to..."

"Take my dress off?"

"Yeah." He grabs a T-shirt from his drawer and tosses it to me.

I stand on wobbly legs, go up on my toes and kiss his cheeks. "Always the gentleman."

"Not always."

"What?" I say, not sure if I heard him correctly.

"Toast?"

"I need to go wash my face first. I can't stand the sight of myself, so I'm sure it's killing you."

He steps ahead of me and opens his bedroom door. "There's a spare toothbrush in the bottom drawer."

"Thanks," I say even though I know. I'm sure I'll find a box of tampons and maybe some new panties if I searched really hard. My brother and his best friend are considerate like that, always making sure the girls who stay over have everything they need come morning. But I am not one of the cheerleaders he beds in the off season. Partly because I couldn't make the team, and partly because he's never liked me like that and I've never liked him like that before now either.

Before now?

Ugh, kill me now.

I tug my dress off, put the T-shirt on and step inside the bathroom. I groan as I stick my tongue out. Does Braden really think someone roofied me? Stefan filled my glass up, and I did set it down when we were at the gazebo. It could have been anyone, and really, I know better than to leave my cup unattended. It's a very sad reality, but nonetheless, it is a reality.

I turn the tap on, and cup the water and splash my face a few times until I'm feeling somewhat human again. I find the toothbrush and goop on the toothpaste. I've been in this bathroom before, of course, but in the past I never had the urge to snoop. I glance over my shoulder, expecting Braden to be standing there, even though I locked the door and he's probably already downstairs making me toast. Could he be any sweeter? But I already knew that about him. I honestly still can't even believe he offered me sex lessons. That's going above and beyond our deal and our friendship. There, of course, was a part of me that was intrigued, and while there are numerous girls wanting to break him during the season, it's not going to be me. I'd never do that to him.

I open the mirror to glance at the contents inside it, and I'm honestly not sure what to expect—maybe some ointment or something—but there's just some random crap like a comb, headache meds, and joint and muscle cream. I close it quietly and give myself one last glance in the mirror before heading to the door. It's a good thing I'm not trying to impress Braden. One look at me this morning would have had him running for the hills. He's seen me worse than this, though. There was a time I had a bad flu and could have won a contest for the best projectile vomiter. Poor Braden held my hair back and a few days later he ended up catching what I had.

I open the door, and come to a resounding halt. "Oh, what... what are you doing?" I glance up and down the hall, before my gaze settles back on Braden.

"Waiting for you." He pushes off the wall.

"I know how to get downstairs."

"I know, but you're a bit shaky and I didn't want you falling and cracking your head open, or anything."

"Such a good boyfriend."

His grin is cute. "I know, right."

"You probably just didn't want me to sue you."

He laughs as he walks to the stairs and I roll up the long pajama pant legs and follow behind. I grip the rail like it's a lifeline as I descend, and if I fall, I'll land on Braden and take him with me. Or not. He's pretty solid.

"Coffee?"

I glance at him like he just grew big elephant ears. "Do you really have to ask?"

He chuckles, pulls a chair out for me and I happily drop into it, as he puts on a pot. "Is your head feeling any better?"

"Actually, it is. I don't have time for a headache. I have so much to do to prepare for next week's fundraiser."

He takes two mugs from the cupboard and just the sound of them landing on the counter sets my head off again. I groan and put my hands over my temples.

"Does it really have to be an auction?"

"I think it will be fun."

"Yeah, because you're not the one who has to go on a date with someone who bought you."

"Actually, I'm putting together a spa date. I contacted a friend of Mom's who owns a spa here in town, and she's giving us a huge discount. The money we raise will cover it, and the uniforms. I'm excited."

His jaw is practically on the floor. "A spa date? Like I'm going to get a pedicure or something?"

I glance at his sockless feet. I'm not a feet lover by any means, but his toes are kind of cute. "Don't knock it until you try it." I wiggle my toes. "It's so nice."

His groan curls around me as he splashes milk into my cup and hands it to me. I take a glorious drink.

"Will you bid on me?" he asks.

Steam warms my face as I lift it to see a sad look on Braden's face. "Are you serious?"

"You know how it is during football season."

"I know but, everyone thinks you're with me now. I don't think any girl is going to try to get your pants down."

He grabs the loaf of bread and tosses four slices into the toaster.

"Do you have any other suggestions?" I ask.

He goes to the fridge and pulls out the butter. "No, but if you think this will work and bring in good money, I'll play along, and I'll even pretend to be happy about it."

"I'm sorry, B." He angles his head and looks at me over his shoulder. "I just assumed all the guys would enjoy being in the spotlight and that it would be fun. You don't have to do it. Maybe I could find other ways to involve you."

"It's fine, I'll do it. For you, I'll do it. I'll do just about anything."

Even give me sex lessons.

As I glance at him now, take in his strong body as he butters my toast, small sparks begin at my core and spread onward and outward. It's so strange. I've known Braden since I was a kid, thought of him as another annoying brother, but I'm not quite thinking of him that way anymore, and maybe I do want lessons, and maybe not just because I'm trying to marry a prince.

Oh boy.

"B?"

He sets my four slices of toast in front of me. "Yeah."

"I would never ask for sex lessons."

He picks up a piece of toast, takes a bite and holds it out for me. "I know, that's why I offered."

"But...football season." I take a small bite, and watch him carefully as I chew.

"Yeah, I know," is all he says, and glances down in thought and takes another bite of the toast, and while we've shared food before, there's something weirdly intimate about it today. "I don't fuck during the season, but..." his head lifts and his eyes are a shade darker when they meet mine. "There are...you know...other things."

10

BRADEN

The front door opens and closes quietly, and Cass and I stare at each other, the tension thick between us as footsteps come our way. I lower myself into the chair as James steps into the kitchen and goes completely still. He frowns when he takes one look at his sister.

"What's going on?"

Without taking her eyes off me, she waves a dismissive hand and says, "I drank too much and Braden took care of me. He was a perfect gentleman."

"It's not like you to drink too much," James says, his hair mussed from a wild night of hot sex—that I never missed until Cassidy.

James picks up her mug and takes a sip of coffee. "You look like shit, sis."

She takes her mug back and looking indignant, she puts her feet on her chair, wrapping one arm around them and says, "Why don't you tell me what you really think?"

"I just did. Why are you here?"

I debate on telling James the truth, but since I don't hide things from him—well, I never used to anyway—I push to my feet, and jerk my head, gesturing him to follow me into the living room.

Once we're alone, I explain. "I brought her back here because it was closer than her place. I think...I think she was roofied."

James jaw clenches with an audible snap. "Are you fucking kidding me?" He begins to pace, a wild animal ready to take down its prey. "Who did it? I'm going to kill him."

I tell him everything, and he turns like he's ready to bolt out the door. I put my hands on his shoulder. "We don't have proof it was Stefan."

"I don't need it."

As the more even tempered of the two of us, I squeeze his shoulder and say, "He's probably not even up yet."

"I'll get him up."

"I'll get to the bottom of things. You know I will. I care about her as much as you do. But right now, we can't just go around accusing Stefan or knocking his teeth out." Fuck, the last thing I want is for James to get kicked off the team. I'd go down before I let him go down, and football is my fucking life. "It could have been anyone, and maybe she really did drink too much, and Stefan was taking care of her."

He meets my gaze dead on. "Do you really think so?"

"I don't know what to think, but we can't be throwing punches until we know for sure and we may never know."

He exhales loudly, and puts his hand on my shoulder, giving it a squeeze. "When you talk to Stefan, I plan to be with you." I nod. Cass is his sister, and it's good to have back-up. "Thanks for taking care of her. You're the only guy I trust around her, you know."

Blood drains to my toes as guilt swirls through my veins. "Yeah. I know."

Just then my cell rings and I pull it from my back pocket. "We'll pay Stefan a visit later. Right now, you need to get some sleep," I tell him. "You look like shit."

He laughs. "Why don't you tell me what you really think?"

I shove him away, and he heads upstairs as I slide my finger across my phone. It's not like my mother to call me early on a Sunday morning. My heart picks up pace, hoping everything back home is okay as I step back into the kitchen to answer.

As Cassidy sips her coffee, most of her toast uneaten, I say, "Hey Mom, what's up?"

Cassidy sits up a bit straighter, her brows pulled together as she watches me intently.

I move around the kitchen, a slow pace as worry spreads through my body.

"Braden," Mom begins, her voice low and tired. "I'm sorry to call so early, but it's your grandmother..."

I sink into a chair, my brain racing as fast as the pulse in my neck. "Is she okay?"

"It was a stroke." Beeping sounds come through the phone. "We are with her in the hospital, waiting to hear more." Okay, she's obviously hooked up to machines, and none of this is good.

I jump from my chair, reach for my thermos mug and set it on the counter. "I'm on my way."

"No, no, you don't have to rush here, I know you're busy." More beeping sounds come through, a bit louder this time. "I can keep you updated over the phone."

"I'm on my way," I say again. My God, does she not think I'm going to come home if my grandmother's life is in danger? I come from a close-knit family, and I'm sure my sisters are a mess right now too. I glance at the clock. "I'll be there in three hours."

"Braden—"

"Mom."

She lets loose a long tired breath. It's senseless to argue with me when I set my mind to something and she knows that better than anyone. "Fine, drive carefully. I'll see you at the hospital."

I end the call and turn around, ready to dash upstairs and get changed. Cassidy is standing right there and I crash into her. "Whoa," she yelps.

I put my arms around her to keep her from falling. "Sorry. I didn't know you were standing there."

She nods. "It's okay, what's going on?"

"My grandmother had a stroke. I have to go."

I keep my arms around her and she puts her hands on my shoulders, giving me a little hug. "I'm so sorry, B. Give me a minute to run home and change."

With my brain racing, plotting out the fastest route to the hospital, I can't quite digest what she's saying. "What are you talking about?"

"I'm coming with you."

She's coming with me?

"No you're not. It's a three-hour drive and I don't even know if I'll be back tonight."

"I'm still coming."

I stare at her, my arms still around her back, because I just don't want to let go. "Cass, I have to go."

"I know, and I'm coming."

"You really want to come?"

"I'm not letting you go alone, Braden. Besides, I love your grandmother too."

"You said you had a million things to do today."

"I'll bring my laptop and work in the car. If we have to stay over, then we have to stay over. I can miss a class or two."

My heart pinches as she gazes at me with those big blue eyes, so full of worry. "You don't have to come."

"We can stand here and argue all day, or you could let me run home and get changed. The outcome is going to be the same anyway."

I shake my head at her stubbornness, which matches mine. "Fine, you can come. I'll drive you to your place to get a change of clothes. I just need to get changed first."

"Grab my phone when you're up there."

I let her go and step around her. I pause at the archway. "Do you think I should wake James, and let him know?"

"Let's just text him. He needs to sleep off last night, and while he'd want to go, might be pissed that we didn't wake him, me going with you will be enough to appease him."

"Okay." I nod and dash upstairs. James' door is closed and I listen for a second, but I'm guessing he's crashed hard. I take a fast shower, climb into a pair of jeans and a T-shirt and snatch Cassidy's phone off my nightstand. It lights up the second I do, and I turn my head to crack my tight neck—compliments of sleeping in my desk chair—when I see the message from Stefan, asking how she's feeling, and if she'd like to meet up for coffee later.

"Fucker."

Yeah, I get it. The message should make me happy because it's what Cassidy wants. I'm not convinced he wasn't behind her messed up state last night, and again, what kind of douche bag goes after another guy's girl? Cassidy is so blinded by his royalty and winning the competition, she can't see past her nose on this one. I stomp down the stairs, louder than normal, and Cassidy is waiting for me at the door.

"Maybe I should drive," she suggests after taking one look at my twisted-up face.

"I can drive. Here." I hand her phone over and she quickly reads the message. "I guess you're staying home now."

She tucks her phone away. "No of course not, B."

The knot in my stomach loosens, because it's true, I do want her coming with me. "Let's go then." I open the door and wave my hand. She exits and I follow her to my car. I back out and catch the way she's looking at me.

"You told James about what you really think happened last night, didn't you?"

"We don't keep secrets, and I thought he should know."

"We keep some secrets," she reminds me.

"I just thought he should know. If it were my sister, I'd want to know."

Her eyes go wide and she hugs herself as a shiver goes through her. I'm not sure if it's a sudden bout of fear, or she's chilly. "Wait, he's not going after Stefan, is he?"

"No, I talked him out of it." I turn on the heat. "I don't want him to jeopardize his spot on the team and if anyone is going after Stefan, it's me."

"Why you?"

"Because you're my girlfriend, and it's my job to take care of you."

"I can take care of myself," she says quietly.

I'm not about to throw what happened in her face last night, and how she wasn't able to take care of herself. Instead, I reach across the seat, snatch up her hand and give it a squeeze. "I know you can, Cass. Let me try that again. I don't have to take care of you, I want to take care of you."

She goes quiet for a long time, like she's having a hard time digesting my words. Her throat makes a sound as she swallows. "If you go after Stefan, it'll jeopardize your spot on the team, won't it?"

I grip the steering wheel tighter and turn down her street. "Don't worry about me."

"I..." She sinks back into her seat and stares straight ahead, and that's when it occurs to me. She might be more worried about Stefan than me. If I find out he did roofie her, she's going to have a hell of a lot to worry about.

I reach her sorority, and she opens her door. "Did you want to come in and wait? I'll only be a second."

"You go ahead."

She nods and darts up the steps, and I turn my car around and leave the parking lot the second she gets inside. Since I forgot my thermos, I make a quick trip to the drive thru and grab us both something to eat and drink for the long drive. It takes longer than I'd like, and my phone starts ringing. I see that it's from Cassidy as I pull up in front of her building and find her standing there staring at her phone.

Her eyes go wide when I stop in front of her. "I thought you left without me," she says as she opens the door and slides in, tossing her backpack into the back seat.

"I was getting us coffee and breakfast. I didn't think the toast was enough for you, and it's always better to have something greasy after a night out." She graciously takes the big cup of coffee from the tray.

"Good thinking."

"Are you feeling better, headache gone?"

Her smile is so sweet and adorable, my heart twists in my chest. "Yeah, thanks, B. You're so sweet."

Sweet.

Yeah, that's what I am to her and all I'll ever be to her, and I hate how much that pisses me off. Honestly, we can't have a future. She's after a prince, and her brother is my best friend

—a guy who trusts me with her. He'd veto a relationship so fast it would leave me spinning, and I don't want to do anything to jeopardize our friendship, which means I can never, ever, give her lessons. I was a goddamn idiot to even suggest it.

Thanks for putting that in my head, Becca.

I guess I can blame her—it's easier that way—but I was thinking about Cassidy ever since she kissed me, so this is on me, not Cassidy's best friend.

Beside me, Cass unwraps the egg sandwich, and hands it to me. "Thanks," I say and bite into it.

She bites into her own and moans. "This is exactly what I need for a hangover. You're the best."

I laugh at her as she moans and devours her sandwich, and once she's done, she sits back and sips her coffee. I drink mine, and we fall into conversation about the upcoming auction. She talks animatedly about it, and her ideas totally impress me. When she has a passion for something, she goes all out. Cass and I have engaged in many conversations over the years, but since college, we've mostly been busy doing our own thing. It's nice spending time with her, talking, and getting to know this grown-up version of the girl whose energy and enthusiasm was stifled into a frilly dress. The sun climbs higher in the sky and it's nearing noon when we reach the hospital. My stomach tightens as I circle the lot and search for a parking spot.

Cass goes quiet beside me, her worry as deep as mine, but she's one of the strongest girls I know. I pull into a spot, kill the ignition and reach for my phone to let Mom know I'm here.

"Ready?" I ask Cassidy.

She nods, and climbs from the car. I circle it to meet her, and do my best to hide the fear mushrooming inside of me. I love my family hard, and while I know my grandmother is aging, it doesn't make this any easier. She's a strong woman, robust, the matriarch of our family, and has been there rooting me on my whole life.

"Braden, I know this is hard, but I want you to know...." She loops her arm through mine and blinks up at me. "You had my back last night, and I've got yours today, B."

I nod my thanks. Only problem is, ever since that kiss sparked something in me, I don't just want her back, I want all of her and that won't—can't—ever happen.

11

CASSIDY

I keep a tight hold on Braden as we step inside the hospital and I crinkle my nose. God, I hate the smell of antiseptic and cleansers, and well... I hate being in a hospital, period. Who doesn't though, right?

My phone pings as he walks up to the counter to find out how to get to his grandmother's room, and I check my phone and read the message from my brother. I shake my phone at Braden. "That was James, asking how things were going. I'll let him know we just got here."

Braden is quiet and contemplative as he nods and we walk to the elevator. I shoot James off a text that I'll keep him updated and tuck my phone away. The elevator pings as the doors open and we stand back and wait until a middle-aged woman in a wheelchair exits, her husband—at least, I assume it's her husband—at her side.

We step on and other people join us. The air is so thick with sadness, you could dip into it with an ice-cream scoop. The doors open on the fourth floor and we step out. Braden takes a deep breath and glances around to figure out which direction we're supposed to go. Voices sound down the long corridor and I turn and spot his two younger sisters walking our way. They notice us at the same time.

"Braden," Lauren says and comes rushing to him. His other sister Jessica, who is one year younger than Lauren, is tight on her heels and they both throw their arms around their big brother.

After a good long hug that chokes me up a little and squeezes my ribcage, he breaks from the circle of their arms, and the worry on his face guts me as he frowns and quietly asks, "How's Nan?"

"She's awake, and Mom told her you were coming," Lauren says, her dark lashes falling over caramel eyes identical to Braden's. "She's excited to see you." Her smile fades. "She's having a bit of a hard time talking right now, though, but she's awake and that's a good sign. No numbness in her extremities. It was a mild stroke." Lauren turns to me and smiles. "Cassidy, what are you doing here?"

"I kept Braden company for the drive."

Her smile is warm and genuine, much like her brother's. Braden really does come from a nice, close-knit family and sometimes I'm envious. Luckily, I have James and we're pretty tight, and I mostly like him—when he's not scaring boyfriends away, but I guess we're past that, if he's cool with Braden helping me catch a prince.

"That was so nice of you," she says softly. "It's a long drive to take alone when you're worried."

"I'm glad to help."

Jessica touches my arm. "We were just headed to the cafeteria. Do you want to join us?"

I glance at Braden to see what he wants, and he nods. I guess he wants to see his grandmother alone and that's understandable. He's a sweet guy, and a great brother and friend, but he doesn't like to show his emotions in public. I nod, and Braden turns. His back is stiff as he walks down the hall, and I'm reluctant to let him go.

"Come on," Lauren says when the elevators ping back open. We step on. "Tell me, how is Kingston?" she asks. "I'm hoping to go there next year, but I only ever hear Braden's opinion of it, and that's all football talk and cheerleaders, and sometimes accounting, which gives me a rash."

I laugh. "It gives me a rash too. Math and numbers are not my thing."

"I want to be a cheerleader," Jessica says and throws her hands up, mimicking some routine she probably learned in high school.

"Yeah, me too," Lauren agrees.

"I have no doubt you'll both make the team." Truthfully they have it all. Confidence, poise, beauty, and, unlike me, they're both girly-girl beauty queens.

"You didn't want to be one?" Lauren asks me.

Truthfully no, not really. I never wanted to be one. It was forced on me, but they have enough on their plates with their grandmother and don't need to hear my first world problems. Honestly I come from privilege, and have no right to complain. "I tried out and didn't make it," I simply state with a shoulder roll, like it's nothing. It was nothing to me, but it was huge to my mother. It's baffling how she wants me to walk in her exact footsteps. Why can't I just be who I want to be. She says it's because I don't know who I am or what I want, and she's probably not wrong about that. But shouldn't I carve out my own path?

Her mouth drops open, indignation on my behalf. "That's ridiculous."

"Kate got the last spot. You guys know Kate Hilton, don't you?"

A smile lights up Jessica's face. "I just love her."

"Me too," Lauren pipes in. The elevator opens on the cafeteria floor and we step off. "What I really want to talk about though is the prince, Stefan." Lauren squeals. "Is he as dreamy as he looks in the papers?"

"He's dreamy," I tell her, as my thoughts go to their brother, who isn't a classically handsome Prince Charming. Looks aren't everything...they're not anything.

Lauren has a far-away dreamy look on her face when she says, "I hope when I get there, he has a brother or a cousin looking for a princess."

I push the cafeteria door open and chairs scrape the tiled floor as people hustle about and hurry to and from their tables. The scent of burnt coffee reaches my nose, shadowing the tang of sadness, and I make my way to the java station. Perhaps Braden will want another cup after his visit.

"Do you think you'll get a flower from Stefan?" Lauren asks, her eyes full of wonderment and hope as she follows me.

"It's possible. I went to a party at his house last night." They both squeal and grab hands to jump up and down. I leave out the part about getting roofied. I'm still not even sure it happened. I'm not sure about much that happened last night, other than Braden taking care of me.

"What do you want to take at college?" I ask Lauren as I fill two paper cups with the dark blend. That's what she should be concentrating on.

"I'm thinking about public relations, like you."

"Really?" I ask, thrilled to hear that. "If you have any questions, I'd be happy to answer them. In fact, I'm having an event next week. We're auctioning off football players to raise money for the team."

"No way, that sounds amazing. I can't imagine Braden would like that, though."

"You're right, he doesn't, but he's a good sport, so he said he'd play along. While I'd like you to see that in action, it's being held at the pub, so you can't get in. Maybe you could bus to campus Saturday, and if you stay, you can watch the game Saturday night and share my room."

She throws her arms around me. "That would be awesome, and I could meet prince Stefan."

It's strange, my first reaction is to scream no, that she should stay as far away from him as possible. Could he have been the one who roofied me? The more I think about it, the more ludicrous it sounds. He can have any girl he wanted. He doesn't need to use drugs to do it.

"Sure you could. I could introduce you."

"Introduce her to who?"

I turn at the sound of Braden's voice. His hair is mussed from raking his hands through it, and there are dark circles around his eyes. Why wouldn't there be? He stayed up all night watching over me.

"Stefan," Lauren blurts out. "Cassidy invited me to the campus next weekend."

"You did?" he asks.

"She's interested in public relations, and I thought she could come for a visit, and overnight if she wants, and I could show her around."

"I don't know if that's a great idea," he murmurs and Lauren's shoulders sag. He pulls her in for a hug, clearly hating to disappoint her. "Let me think about it, okay kiddo?"

"Okay."

He lets her go, and I hand him a coffee. "I thought you could use another. It's cafeteria coffee, but it's still coffee."

"Thanks." He peels the tab back and takes a drink, and winces. "Yum."

I laugh, and dig my wallet from my purse to pay. His sisters wander off to get some pastries, and he stays close to my side as I pay for our drinks.

"How is she?" I ask.

"She's sleeping now, and they're still assessing her. It could have been worse. Mom noticed the signs and called an ambulance right away."

"Thank God."

"Do you want to go up and say hi to Mom and Dad? I'm sure they'd love to see you."

"For sure."

His sisters meet us at the elevator and after we step on, I stand back and smile as big brother grills them on school and boys. It's kind of funny—I've been the recipient of the talk numerous times myself—but it's also kind of sweet and adorkable watching him do it to his sisters.

The doors open and he falls silent as we walk down the hall and enter his grandmother's room. His mom jumps up when she sees me and gives me a hug. "Cassidy," she says quietly. "It's so nice to see you. Thanks for coming."

"Of course. I'm so sorry to hear about your mom."

I hug her back, and breathe in her warm vanilla scent. His dad gives me a hug when she's finished, and I turn to his grandmother, who is sleeping quietly. Braden stands close, his warmth reaching out to me.

"Braden, you look so tired," his mom says. "Why don't you head back to the house and get some sleep? We'll call if she wakes up, and there is nothing more we can do. At least we know she's going to be okay and with a little therapy, she should be back to normal again."

"No, I'm not tired, I—"

"It's not a bad idea," I tell him, and reach for his dangling fingers. "You can sleep and I can get some schoolwork done."

He stifles a yawn. "I guess maybe an hour." He turns to his sisters. "Are you guys staying or do you want a lift back?"

"We both have cheer practice," Lauren says.

"Okay, I'll be back in a bit. Do you want me to bring you something to eat?"

"No, we'll get something here," his mom says, and I put my arm through Braden's, and after we say goodbye, he practically zombie walks down the hall.

"I'm driving," I say and he tosses me the keys.

He pushes back in the passenger seat, his big body worn out, and he closes his eyes and I take us both back to his childhood home. The streets are quiet this Sunday afternoon, and I make it back to his place quickly. I pull into the driveway, and I really hope Mom doesn't get wind of my return home. I am not interested in an interrogation about the prince.

Braden's eyes open when I kill the ignition. "Let's get you to bed," I say, and he nods.

I grab my backpack and he takes the keys from me and opens his front door and I stand there for a second. It's been a long time since I've been in Braden's house. We go straight upstairs to his room, which looks exactly like I remember it. Football trophies line a shelf, and I run my finger over them. He kicks off his shoes and drops down onto his bed, and I go to his desk, and dig into my bag for my laptop.

"Cass..."

"Yeah?"

"Thanks."

"Anytime."

"No, really...thanks. She's my grandmother. I...I was scared."

My throat closes over as I try to swallow, and pain shoots to the roof of my mouth. "She's going to be okay, B," I say softly, as the worry in his voice wraps around my heart and squeezes tight. I've seen a lot of sides of Braden, but never this one. He's afraid of losing someone he cares deeply about—

someone he's known and loved forever—and that isn't easy on anyone.

"You really think so?"

"Yeah, I do."

He sits quietly for a moment. "I think Lauren really likes the idea of coming to the campus. She really looks up to you." He chuckles. "The older sister she always wanted."

"She'd never trade in her older brother." I cock my head and take in his tired face. "You're not sure, though?"

He gives a humorless laugh. "I'm a guy, and I know how guys look at fresh bait."

"You never did though, B. You were never like the rest."

One shoulder rolls. "I'm not a saint."

I smile. "I know that, but you're a good guy. Don't worry about Lauren. I'll keep an eye on her. I promise." He nods. "Why don't you get some rest?" I push to my feet as sunlight slants across his bed. I pull down the room darkening shade and close his curtains over it. As my eyes adjust to the darkness, I take a few careful steps, about to go back to his desk, when a hand reaches out and grasps my waist. The next thing I know, I'm standing between Braden's open legs, his big warm palms sliding around my body.

12

BRADEN

What am I doing?

Yeah, what the fuck are you doing, Braden?

This is Cassidy. My best friend's little sister and I shouldn't be putting my hands on her body. Not only that, she's using me to catch the attention of another guy. I am so not her type. She likes the handsome Prince Charming—even though the one she's after is a jerk—and I'm anything but.

"B?" she says, her voice low and husky.

"Yeah?" Christ, I need to pull myself together. Maybe it's the fear of losing my grandmother—Cassidy—that's driving my actions. Or maybe I just really need to touch her, feel her arms around me right now.

"This isn't a good idea."

"I know," I say and I'm about to pull my hands back, take myself outside and kick my own ass when she presses against me, her breasts against my mouth. Sweet mother of God and all that is holy.

"Cass..." I breathe her in, as her nipple pokes against my lips through her shirt, beckoning for attention. "This is such a bad idea," I reiterate, even though everything about it feels good and right.

She rakes her hands through my hair, lifting my face to hers. As my eyes adjust to the dark, I take in the silhouette of her face, and body, and I don't need to see her to sense the need inside.

She's doing this for another man, Braden.

As that reminder hits like a power defenseman determined to keep me from scoring, I'm about to break the moment, but she dips her head and presses her lips to mine, and as my blood drains to my cock, all thought goes with it.

Why again is this a bad idea?

I taste her mouth as she kisses me, her lips parting hungrily to accept my tongue. My hands tighten around her body and slide down to cup her perfect ass. Her little moan of approval reaches my ears, and she writhes against me. Fuck, she is hot and needy.

"I won't...I can't..." she murmurs into my mouth and it sobers me in seconds flat.

"Right, of course." I let my hands fall to my side and instead of backing up like I expect her to, she climbs onto my lap, her knees on the bed beside me.

"Cass?"

"We can't go all the way," she says, her mouth saying one thing but her gyrating body telling a different story altogether, and even though my brain is so rattled I can't tell up from down, I will never forget no means no.

I grip her hips to stop her movements before I burst into dust. "No, we can't."

"B…"

Christ, the want and need in her voice is killing me. "Yeah?"

"I told you I wasn't all that experienced, but the truth is, I'm a virgin."

"I know you are, Cass. I've always known. I guess you're saving yourself for the right guy, huh?"

"Yeah, something like that."

"Nothing wrong with that," I tell her and totally mean it. "Your body, your choice." If she slept around, I'd probably hate it, but again, there's nothing wrong with it.

"And…your football. I won't do anything to break your celibacy streak and mess up your game…"

My heart thuds against my ribcage, each beat pounding in my ears and drumming home the fact that she's so fucking sweet and considerate, so different from the other girls I know.

"But if you're up to it…" She wiggles against my body, and my hard cock presses against her hot pussy. Yeah, she knows I'm 'up' for it. "I wouldn't mind a few lessons."

Smack. To. The. Face.

With that fierce, palm to the cheek wakeup call—a reminder of what's really going on here—fire races through my veins and I swear steam is about to come out my nose. I hate the thought of giving her lessons for another guy, especially if that guy is Stefan. But this is Cassidy and well…I'd do just about anything for her. Consequences be damned.

I slide my hand to the back of her neck and bring her mouth to mine for a deep, thorough kiss, needing almost desperately to taste the depths of her, and I do plan on tasting her body everywhere. She kisses me back, and I love the almost hesitant way her tongue plays with mine, like she's still not sure she's a great kisser.

I fall back on my bed, taking her with me, and slide my hands down her back, shifting her until she's pressing hard against my throbbing cock. She rocks against me, rubbing that hot pussy all over me and if I don't get her naked and get my mouth on her, I might go insane.

She sits up and grips her T-shirt, ready to peel it over her head when one working brain cell hammers on my head. "Cass," I say, touching her hands, and reveling in the softness of her skin. I want this. I want this so fucking bad, but I need to know... "Are you sure? Are you sure Stefan is worth this?"

She hesitates for a brief second, her eyes moving over my face. "I..."

"I need you to want this for you too, okay? I have to know I'm doing this for you, too."

She nods. "You are. I want this. I want you to do this for me, and I..."

"What?"

As I lay here gazing up at her, the words I really want to hear —I want *you*—don't come.

Because she doesn't want you, asshole.

"I want this," she says, but I sense that she wanted to say something else.

I let it go, for the time being. "Okay."

I let her hands go and she peels her shirt off, exposing a pretty white bra, and it's sexier than anything I've ever seen. The words, "You're beautiful," slip from my lips, and she draws her bottom lip between her teeth, a line forming in her forehead as her brows bunch together. "Don't believe me?"

"I just...I keep thinking this should be awkward, B, but it's..."

"...Not. I know."

"I'm just so...comfortable with you. This is so easy between us." Her voice is low and a bit broken, but full of warmth and honesty that wraps around my heart and holds tight. "I thought it would be harder."

I laugh, and lift my hips. "It is hard, babe." She laughs and whacks me, and the movement jiggles her gorgeous tits. I reach out and cup her breasts, shaping her soft flesh through her bra. "Just two friends helping each other out, huh? Nothing awkward about that."

"You are my friend."

"You're my friend too, Cass." I slide my thumb between her bra straps and shoulders, and run my fingers over her flesh. "Do you want to take this off?"

"Do you want me to?"

"More than anything."

I love the grin that she puts on her face as she reaches behind her back and unhooks it. The second her bra slips from her lush body, I nearly shoot off in my pants. "Gorgeous," I manage to push out past a tongue gone thick. "So fucking gorgeous, Cass." I caress the sides of her breasts, and run my palm along the soft swell of the undersides. Her eyes slip shut and a soft breathy moan escapes her lips.

"No one has ever touched you like this?" She shakes her head and her long curls swish over her shoulders.

"It feels so good, B."

My dick jumps, and I realize the gift she's put in my hands. I don't take it lightly, and honestly, I'm honored that she picked me to be her first. At least I know she's in good hands, because I will always do right by her.

I sit up, and slide my tongue over her nipple, and a soft gasp catches in her throat. "This is about what you like tonight, Cass." I have to think that way. I have to make this about her, not Stefan, otherwise I'll lose my fucking mind. "This is all about discovering your wants and needs."

"I like that idea. But it has to be about you too. I want to make you feel good."

So fucking sweet. Cass never puts herself first. She's genuine, and all about fairness and consideration. Those traits are what I've always liked best about her.

"For the record, touching you...kissing you is rocking my world."

"Are you saying you don't want me to suck your cock?"

Her words take me by surprise and shock the hell out of me. Probably because I'm not used to hearing her talk dirty. We've known each other forever, but it's been outside the bedroom. I kind of like bedroom Cassidy, and her dirty mouth. "I didn't say that."

Her laugh curls around me. "Didn't think so."

"I am a guy, you know."

She wiggles on my cock. "Don't have to convince me of that."

I laugh and wow, I have never had this kind of fun in the bedroom before. I'm not sure I ever had a conversation with a girl, and I kind of like it.

"So I'm going to do things to you, lots of things, and you're going to straight up tell me what you like and don't like."

"I'm pretty sure I'm going to like it all."

I grin, loving her confidence in me as I put my hands on her thighs and slide upward, toward her warmth. She moans and wiggles some more and I bite my jaw to keep myself in check before I shoot off like a teenage boy. Why does she bring that out in me?

I grip her hips and move her off my body, setting her beside me. I shimmy off the bed and stand over her, and she looks up at me with eyes full of desire. I know exactly how she feels.

"Lay back," I say and she immediately obliges.

I gaze at her as she spreads on my bed, offering herself up to me so nicely. "Cass..." I murmur as I bend over and press my arms on either side of her as I take one of her perfect breasts into my mouth.

"B," she whimpers as I lightly lick her pert, pink nub and draw in into my mouth for a deeper, more thorough taste. She wiggles, and I love how hot I'm making her.

"Like that, huh?"

Her hands go around my head and she holds me to her, showing me just how much she likes my mouth on her tits. But there is so much more we need to do, so many other areas of her body I need to discover and pleasure.

I inch off her breast and she frowns, but it turns to a moan as my fingers go to the button on her jeans. Her chest rises as she fills her lungs with air and holds her breath.

"Breathe, Cass," I whisper as I unhook the button and slide open her zipper. The hiss curls around us and my dick jumps, eager to be inside her, but that can't happen. Neither of us want that. Okay, that's not entirely true. She's saving herself, and while I want it, I can't fuck during football season. When did I come up with that crazy belief anyway?

I grip her jeans and she lifts her hips, making it easier for me to pull them off her silky legs. I drag them down, pull them over her feet and toss them away. Forget about thinking—hell, forget about breathing. Fuck, I lose all voluntary bodily functions the second I set eyes on her little white panties. Holy Christ, she's in little white panties that only a woman like her could make sexy.

I touch the elastic, and she whimpers, and I run my finger along her inner thighs.

"So very pretty," I say. I glance up at her, trying to keep my shit together. I'm the one giving lessons here and I'm about to blow it.

Are you saying you don't want me to suck your cock?

Holy shit, I can't wait for *her* to blow it.

"Can I take these off you, Cass. Can I see your pussy?"

"Ohmigod."

I grin at her reaction. She likes when I talk dirty too. With that knowledge, I continue with, "I bet you have the sweetest pussy, and I can't wait to put my tongue on you." As her eyes go wide, I swipe my tongue over my bottom lip and moan.

Her legs spread, the sweetest invitation I've ever seen. I slide my hand between her open legs, and nearly drop to my knees when my fingers connect with wetness.

"Does the idea of me my mouth on you turn you on, Cass?"

"Uh huh."

I grin, and unhook the button on my pants as my cock throbs. Her gaze drops, her eyes wide and eager as I release my zipper and tug my cock out to free it.

"Braden..." she murmurs.

I take my cock into my hand and rub it. Pre-cum pools on the slit and I'm about to dip into it, when she takes me by surprise, sits up quickly and runs her soft, pink tongue over me. I grip her hair, hard, and try to tug her off, but she won't allow me.

"Cass, you can't." Dark lashes fall over lust-imbued eyes as she glances at me in confusion. "I mean, you can, but right now this is all about you."

She bites her lips playfully. "I think your cock begs to differ."

I laugh out loud at that, and it eases some of the tension inside me. I love this playful side of her. "Okay, you're right. He wants you...badly." She smiles. She likes that she can make me hard. Fuck, I like it too, and I wish I didn't.

"Lay back, I want to take these panties off and get a good look at you." She nods and falls back, not at all shy about that, and I fucking love how easy we are with each other. My chest swells, a new fullness inside me.

"Do you want me to give you a hand taking my panties off," she asks and slides her hands into the elastic at the back. "You know, seeing how your hand is already so busy."

"Fuck yeah."

Her soft chuckle curls around me, and I continue to rub my cock. "Good, because I really like watching you do that."

I pull from base to crown. "This?" I ask, my cock growing thicker as she writhes on the bed and slides her panties to her ankles. They hover there for a minute as she lays back and once again, taking me by surprise, she picks her panties up with her feet, the band dangling around her toes and holds them out to me.

I should take them and put them in my pocket like a souvenir, a reminder of this day with her, because I'm not entirely sure there will be another.

13

CASSIDY

I don't know what's come over me. I've never talked dirty or handed my panties over to anyone, but Braden brings out this side of me, and I'm completely at ease with him. I arch a brow but say nothing as he tucks my panties into his back pocket. Maybe he's worried I'll lose them in our mess of clothes. But I'm not worried about my underwear. How could I be when this big powerful guy is standing before me, his face twisted with want as he gazes at my naked body and works his hand over his cock.

I bend my knees and inch them open slightly and his resulting growl not only turns me on, it makes me feel a little wild, a little brazen. Tonight, he's not taking my virginity, he made that clear. If he was, maybe I'd be a little more nervous, more afraid of the pain that might follow. Today, from the heated look in his eyes, all he's going to do is give me pleasure and I can't wait.

I slide my hands from my knees to my thighs, and I'm pretty sure he's stopped breathing. I keep the smile from my face as I let my legs fall open, completely exposing myself to him. He curses under his breath and my throat dries as pre-come spills from his slit. I can't believe that I—tomboy Cassidy who has known this guy forever—is able to turn him on like this. It's damn empowering.

"Are you going to stand there, or are you going to put your mouth on me?"

He shakes his head, his chest flaring as he takes a hard breath. "I never knew you were a tease, Cass."

"I guess today we're going to find out a lot of things we never knew. For starters, I'd love to taste more of your cock."

His muscles ripple and I grin, loving the way my words hit home. "You will, but I need my mouth on you first." He drops to his knees, and I yelp a little as he grabs my knees and pulls my legs until they're dangling over the bed. He taps me, and I instinctively know he wants me to wrap them around him, and I do as he requests. He's breathing so hard, his hot breath washes over my sex, and my clit quivers in response. Warm lips press against my thighs, and he presses hot, open-mouthed kisses to my trembling flesh before he sinks his teeth into my flesh, biting gently. The sensations zing through me and I whimper.

"Braden," I plead, desperate for his mouth on my aching pussy.

"Do you touch yourself, Cass? When you're alone in bed, do you rub your clit, or put your fingers inside yourself?"

"Yes," I admit, not at all embarrassed or uncomfortable telling him that. It might be different if I was with another guy, but I don't mind telling Braden these things. I go up on my elbows and find him looking at me.

"You've had an orgasm?"

I twist my lips, and shake my head. "I don't think so. I mean..." I look past his shoulders. "It felt good, and I would get really wet, but I'm not sure."

"Babe, you would know if you orgasmed, so I'm going to say you haven't."

"You're probably right."

He parts my lips, and his breath washes over me as he says, "I'm going to make you come, Cass. I'm going to make you feel really good."

I do love a guy with confidence, and judging by the way he's spreading me and lightly stroking my clit, I have no doubt he can back it up. I grip the bedding and tug on it as he teases my throbbing nub, and without shame, I lift my hips, begging for more. His soft chuckle curls around me, and that's fine. He can pretend all he wants that he's completely in control. I saw his cock, and tasted his pre-cum. He wants and needs this as much as I do.

He moves his finger, slides it downward and as much as I'm disappointed—I want him to continue to caress my clit—I also want to feel those thick fingers inside me. My disappointment is short-lived, however, because he replaces his hands with his mouth, and OMG and HALLE-FREAKING-LUJAH.

How is that so good?

"B," I moan and take my breasts into my hands to rub and pinch my nipples. I only ever touch my nipples or my pussy; never have both been treated to pleasure at the same time and let me tell you, touching myself pales in comparison. Cripes, if I knew it was going to feel this good, I might have jumped on the bandwagon earlier. But no, it's strange. I wasn't about to have sex with anyone for the sake of sex, and Braden isn't just anyone, he's Braden, and there isn't another guy on the planet quite like him.

"Feel good, Cass?" he asks, his voice hoarse and breathless. I go up on my elbows again, and while he doesn't need to ask—heck, my moaning alone is probably letting the neighbors know how much I like it—there's something in his face, some sort of need or vulnerability that suggests he needs to hear me say it.

"It feels incredible, B."

"How about this?" he asks, as he slides his thick finger inside me, stretching and filling me, and reaching spots that have never been touched. My eyes roll back into my head, and I let loose a loud moan that my brother might be able to hear back at Kingston. But I am not interested in thinking about my brother at the moment. Nope, I'm only interested in his best friend, and the magic he's performing between my legs.

He dips his head, and touches some enchanted place deep inside me, and as I begin to pant, he smiles. "Like that?"

"Yeah, I like that," I practically screech.

"How about this?" He takes my clit into his mouth and works that beautiful thick finger inside me, taking me to some faraway place. As I approach the highest mountain, the peak of some fairy tale castle, he inches another finger in and I suck in a fast breath and hold it.

He moves his fingers in and out of me and shifts positions, rubbing the butt of his hand against my clit. How is he so skilled? But oh no, that's not all he's got up his sleeve. His cock presses against my outer thigh as he reacquaints my nipple with his hot, wet mouth.

"Oh my God," I cry out as he sucks hard and finger fucks me. I move, writhe, cry out like a crazed woman who is about to explode into a million tiny pieces. My spasms begin in my core, and he lifts his head, his dark eyes on mine. He's not smiling, he's just lying there watching, learning my body as he brings me over the edge.

"B..."

"That's it," he says softly, gently, his encouraging voice trickling through my veins and taking me to a place I've never been before. My body completely lets go, and strong spasms grip my core, and my sex starts pulsing around his probing fingers. I try to talk, try to say his name, try to breathe, but I can't do any of those things. All I can do is lie still and take pleasure in every hard pulse between my legs. My God, this is what an orgasm is like?

"Breathe, Cass."

I suck in air and he breathes with me, his hand still between my legs as he brings me back down to Earth. He presses his forehead to mine, his hard breaths hot on my face. "Take your time," he whispers, and my heart pinches at the sweet way he's taking care of me. His fingers leave my channel, and he lightly strokes me, giving me all the time in the world to get my bearings.

I slide my hand around his head and bring his lips to mine. Never have I experienced such easy intimacy with any man. "Thank you," I say between kisses.

He chuckles lightly, but it sounds needy and strained, a reminder that this isn't just about me tonight, and I don't want it to be. "Trust me, Cass. The pleasure was all mine."

I wiggle my brows at him as my body continues to tingle in the most glorious way. My God, I hope there are more of these lessons in the future. A girl could get addicted to this kind of pleasure, and I like learning about my body—and his. "I'm pretty sure it wasn't, but it's going to be."

"Yeah?"

"I want to suck your cock," I say bluntly, honestly.

He groans, and his cock jumps against my leg. Clearly, he wants that too. I crinkle my nose and wait for an answer as he brushes the back of his fingers over my hot cheeks, so achingly tender, you'd think he was stroking my heart. "You don't have to do that if you don't want to, Cass."

"I want to learn."

He stiffens against me, every muscle in his body taut. "Right, yeah...sure."

He's about to inch back, and I hold him to me. "I want to pleasure you, B. The way you pleasured me. I just...maybe it's not just about learning. I want to do it."

He holds my gaze so long, his body so still, I begin to wonder if I've done or said something wrong. Or maybe I said something right.

His demeanor changes, all stiffness gone from his body— well, that's not entirely true, his cock is rock hard—and he shifts back into sex mode, "You want to suck my cock, Cass?"

"I do." I push on his chest, until he's flat on the bed beside me, exactly how I want him. I roll, and he groans as I go up on my hands and knees and crawl until I'm positioned between his legs. "Your pants." In a movement so fast it leaves my head spinning and my lips twitching, he peels off his pants and tosses them to the floor. "That's better."

I examine his big, thick cock and take it into my hands for a better look and feel.

"Fuck me sideways," he grumbles and I grin.

"I'm not really sure how to do that, but I would like to take you into my mouth." I lightly run my fingers along the long length of him and press down on his bulging veins. The whole time, I'm listening to his little grunts and moans, trying to gauge what he likes and doesn't like. I rub his crown, squeeze him a little and I'm pretty sure no matter what I do, he's going to like it.

"So a blow job," I say and lean forward. My hair falls over him and he grabs it to hold it to the side, either so he can watch, or so I don't end up choking on it. "Is there anything particular you like?"

"Put your mouth on me, Cass." His voice is low, strained, and so damn tortured it does the strangest things to me. It's weird, but I like that he wants me this badly. I don't think anyone has ever wanted me like he wants me right now, but again, I must remember that guys like and want sex, and this might not have anything to do with me at all. Heck, most of the guys on the team are with a different girl every weekend, and none of them are special to them. This isn't about me being special, though, so I push those strange emotions aside and stick my tongue out to lick him like a lollipop.

"Jesus," he curses as his hips jump, his cock pushing between my lips and forcing them open. I put my hands on his thighs and lean into him. His thick cock stretches my lips, and I relax my throat as he slides in deeper. I taste his tangy precum, and go a little deeper, until I nearly choke. "Cass..." He tugs on my hair, and I love that he's worried about me, but to hell with that. I want to play and experiment, and I want to know if I can take him without gagging, and how to take him deeper. Simply put, I want to learn as I pleasure.

I moan around his cock and he curses some more, and those little sounds let me know I'm on to something powerful here. He tucks my hair behind my ear and I glance up as he gives in to me. He's a powerful man completely at my mercy and there's just something sexy and empowering about that.

I swirl my tongue around his crown and that's when I remember he has balls. I steal another glance up at him, and let his crown sit on my bottom lip when I ask, "Do guys like their balls touched?" Hey, I know how sensitive they are from the time I accidently smacked Braden in the nuts when we were younger.

"I don't know about other guys, but yeah, I like to be touched."

I nod, and slide my hand down to cradle his balls. He hisses out a breath as I very gently massage them in my palm.

"Yeah, Cass, just like that. Put me back in your mouth and keep doing that."

I do as he says, and his moans grow louder. I take him to the back of my throat again, and this time I don't gag.

"You are so good at that," he murmurs.

I'm not, but I am a quick learner and he does seem to like it. I've heard girls can take guys down their throat, but I think that will have to be another lesson. I just hope Braden is up for more, but I'll worry about that later because right now he's *up* for this in a big way.

As I massage his balls, I put my other hand on his cock, near the base and as I move my mouth up and down him, my hand follows the motion. Okay, now this he really likes. He moves and writhes and I think he's talking in a foreign language that I'm not familiar with as he grips my hair again and wraps it around his hand. His pleasure reverberates through my body and I shift so I can rub my clit on his leg.

"That is so hot," he whispers as he moves his thigh back and forth to stimulate me. As I ride him freely, without inhibition, I work his cock in my mouth, becoming much more comfortable with it. I rub and suck and use my hands on him and his entire body stiffens as I manipulate his cock.

"Cass...you have to stop...I'm close."

His breathing and words are rapid and broken and I shrug his hand off me as he tries to pull me off him, but no, I want to taste him. I want to experience him coming in my mouth. I don't know if I'll like it or hate it, but I'm damn determined to find out.

I suck harder and lightly run my tongue over his crown. That seems to be what messes him up the most. My hands and mouth work together and he swells even more, his veins swelling with blood and my heart beats in anticipation. I take him deep again and he groans as he lets go, and that first spurt fills my mouth with his cum. I swallow and he keeps on coming until I can't swallow fast enough. Some spills onto my chin and down his cock. Neither of us care, though. We're both enjoying it, so lost in the moment, nothing else really matters.

"Cass...Cass," he repeats with each hard pulse, and I wonder if he's ever going to stop. That thought almost makes me chuckle. His cock finally settles, and I let it rest against the notch on my top lip as I lift my head and find him watching me intently.

I grin, and he grins back, another little secret we're sharing, and I like that we have secrets between us. I don't want to tell anyone else. I want this to be our private experience, not for anyone else but us.

"That was amazing," he says, and my chest puffs with pride.

"You weren't so bad yourself."

He laughs and grabs a tissue from the nightstand. "Come here." I climb up his body and he wipes his cum off my chin, and I lay there and lift my face to him, liking the way he takes care of me. "Messy girl," he teases.

He tosses the tissue away and I flop down on top of him, feeling a little giddy inside. He puts his hands around my back, and presses a kiss so steeped in tenderness to my lips that my heart jumps in surprise.

I blink once, then twice as I take in the warmth and satisfaction in his eyes. "What...what was that for?"

He smiles at me and he shifts back into teasing mode as he rolls a shoulder. "What? A boyfriend needs a reason to kiss his girlfriend?" he asks playfully.

"No, I guess not." I bend and press my lips to his. His tongue slides into my mouth and he deepens the kiss until I'm feeling it deep between my legs. His moan curls around me, and I nearly lose myself in him again, when a noise downstairs snaps me back to reality. I try to break the kiss but he holds me to him a moment longer, like he can't quite bring himself to let me go. I get it, I love this new intimacy between us too.

Another bang from downstairs echoes through the house, and he loosens his hold on me. I inch up, and as I take in his dark eyes, and the way they move over my face, I nearly forget how to breathe. I quickly remind myself he's helping me snag a prince, and right now, in this moment, I'm glad it's football season and he's not 'fucking' because there's a warning bell going off in my head, telling me that if I went all the way with Braden, he might just destroy me...in more ways than one.

14

BRADEN

As Mom and Dad walk around downstairs, I slide from the bed, pull on my pants, and pull Cass to her feet. We both dress and take turns ducking into the washroom to clean up before we meet my folks downstairs. I'm just not sure we'll be able to pull off casual, not when we have sex written all over us. I step from the bathroom and find her in the hall waiting for me, her cheeks still pink, her turned-up lips kiss-bruised. Jesus, I love it that I was the guy who put that look on our face.

"Hey, so what do we tell Mom and Dad? Do we let them in on the ruse, or let them think we're a couple?"

"I don't want to mislead them," she says. "Or let them know I'm using you to catch Stefan's attention."

My gut clenches at the word 'using' and without even realizing it I take a small step back. She realizes it though. Her hand touches mine, and she gives it a squeeze. "What we did in there was more about us, B," she says, soothing my battered ego and thoughts. I take in the concern in her eyes as they rush over my face. I have no doubt that what I did in there was about us and while we both enjoyed it, is it possible that she gave herself over to me because I was under emotional duress? Was this her way of soothing me? I've read about people falling for one another after they've been through a traumatic event. I'm sure this is different, though, and hey, Cassidy isn't falling for me, so there's that to remember.

"Okay," I say. "How about this? If it comes up and I doubt it will, why don't we just say we're friends and leave it at that."

"Good plan, and Braden, if they're home, that must be a good sign for your grandmother."

My heart jumps with hope. "Let's go see." We dash downstairs and find my folks in the kitchen making coffee. Mom turns, takes one look at us and goes quiet for all of one second, then she breaks out with, "Grandma is doing so much better." She cups my cheeks. "I think seeing you helped."

I grin. "I don't know about that." I give my mom a hug. "I'm glad she's going to be okay. What happens now?"

Mom explains the recovery process as Cassidy helps Dad with the coffee. She's easy around my house. She's been hanging around my family for a long time, and our parents are friends, so there is no awkwardness, other than Mom noticing that something might have transpired between the two of us upstairs. She didn't look all that surprised, actually. Maybe she looked a little pleased and maybe I'm just imagining it.

They bring the coffee to the table, and set it down. We all sit and Mom turns to Cassidy. "Lauren says you invited her to Kingston for a tour."

"I'd love to show her around."

She leans in, looking conspiratorial. "I think she's trying to get a glimpse of that prince from Sweden."

Cass laughs lightly. "Who isn't? But I'd love to show her around the public relations department. Show her what we do."

Mom touches Cassidy's hand. "You are so sweet to do that. She really looks up to you."

"The older sister she always wanted," I tease, and take a big sip of coffee as they all laugh, but I think Cass really likes the idea of being my sister's role model.

We spend the next hour sipping coffee and we have a sandwich, and as late afternoon approaches, I stretch and glance at Cassidy. "We should get back. You still need to study."

She nods in agreement, and helps pick up the dishes and place them into the dishwasher. I love how at home she is here, and there's no pressure from my mother regarding her single status or how she should dress better. She's in jeans and a T-shirt and couldn't look more beautiful.

"I'm driving back," she says to me. I'm about to protest, but she has the 'don't you dare' look on her pretty face, so I concede. The truth is, I'm exhausted, and I might not be all that safe behind the wheel. If I drove and anything ever happened to Cass, I'd never forgive myself.

I hand my keys over. "Thank you very much."

"I'll run up and get your bag." As she chats with Mom and Dad, I hurry upstairs and the second I look at my bed, my dick swells. I'm still a little shocked that we fooled around in my childhood home, but I'm even more shocked at how unbelievably mind-blowing it was. I quickly fix my bed and work to push down a measure of guilt. This is James' sister. I guess if he ever found out, I could spin it, remind him that he said I was the only guy he trusted with her, so if she wanted a partner to teach her, it had to be me, right?

And of course, after I tell him that load of shit, I'd better make plans to go straight to the Emergency Room.

Fuck me sideways.

I find Cass at the door waiting for me, and my stupid heart does a little flip when she checks in with me. "All set?"

I throw her bag over my shoulder and stifle a yawn as I hug Mom and Dad goodbye and ask them to keep me posted. Outside, I head straight for the passenger seat and tilt it back to rest. I don't want to go to sleep. I'm not about to nod off and let her drive alone. She was good enough to keep me company and I want to do the same for her.

She reaches across and squeezes my arm. "Great news about your grandmother."

I smile, a new kind of contentment over me. "Yeah..."

She backs from the driveway and we both fall silent, lost in our own thoughts as we drive, and about a half an hour into our trip, she eases off the highway and takes an exit. I sit up a bit straighter.

"Pit stop?" I ask.

"Something like that." She gives me a sly grin. "What do you do for fun during football season?"

"I play football."

She laughs. "That's what I thought." I wait for her to enlighten me and she doesn't.

"What do you do for fun?"

I catch her frown before she turns her focus back to the road.

"You know, I don't know what I do for fun. I'm not even sure I have fun. I enjoy putting together benefits and things like that, but it's still school and work." I steal a glance and find her watching me. "We should do more fun things."

"Yeah, you're probably right."

I glance around and try to figure out where she's taking me. She flicks on her signal and the second the tumblers fall into place, she grins and says, "We don't bird watch anymore."

I laugh at that. "No, we don't."

"Remember how much we liked it?"

I nod as I think about it. I was the one who really liked it, and Cass and James would humor me. As we grew older, and then college, it wasn't a hobby I continued to pursue or talk about. I can't even imagine what the guys on the team would say about me being a bird watcher.

As if reading my mind, she winks and says, "Don't worry, it's still our little secret."

"You think you know everything about me, don't you?"

"I don't think I do, I actually do," she responds with a grin.

She does know a lot but she doesn't know everything, mainly all the crazy things I'm starting to feel for her and it's best she never does.

"Well, maybe I know everything about you too," I add with a tilt of my head.

"I'm not arguing the point," she says. Her hand touches mine, and in the softest voice she adds, "Now we know much more about each other." My chest squeezes. We've always been close but I can't deny there's a new kind of intimacy between us. I just pray to fuck her brother doesn't notice it and if I was smart, I'd get my head on right and realize that I'm just being used. What can I do, though? I've always liked Cass, and would give her the world if I could. I know who Cass really is, deep inside. I know the pressures on her, the expectations, the way her mother tried to turn her into something she wasn't.

Hell, she volunteers at a shelter, not because it furthers her agenda or education. She does it because she wants to, and hasn't even told her mother about it for fear she'd want her to stop. So far, she's stayed strong despite all the pressures, and remained a sweet girl who would do anything for anyone—although I do worry that she might be caving now and Stefan isn't the guy she really wants, although that could be my own bias against him. Nevertheless, she just dropped everything to go home with me. How could I say no when she asked me?

"Why are we here, Cass?" She has to study and get things ready for next week's auction. "We don't have time for this."

"We're here because you love it, and for you, I make the time."

My fucking heart pinches so hard, it stops the blood flow to my brain, and I become a little lightheaded. She narrows her eyes, and she must read me wrong when she says, "If you really don't want to, we—"

"No, I want to." I suck in air and stare straight ahead. "This is just really nice." I slowly turn to her. "It's nice that you remembered."

A smile lights up her pretty face. "Of course I remembered. This was a big part of who you are, and you've been working and studying, helping me." She goes quiet for a second and squeezes my hand. "And the scare with your grandmother. I just thought the world could cut you some slack for a couple hours."

She pulls into the parking spot of the sanctuary and I sit there and smile like an idiot. "I can't believe you thought of this," I say quietly.

"Come on."

We both jump from the car, and she nudges me as we head inside the not-for-profit sanctuary. She reaches into her purse to make a donation.

"You took me here, so this is on me." I grab my wallet, make a generous donation, and my shoulders relax a little as the sound of chirping birds reach our ears. "Can we—"

She laughs and grabs my hands. "Parrots first, I know." Her finger pokes against my chest. "You're still that little boy in here, aren't you?"

"Maybe in here," I say and wink as her touch stirs things inside me and reminds me of the way I put my mouth on her, and she put her mouth on me.

Her grin is soft and sexy as pink crawls up her neck. "Let's just say I like the little boy and the big boy."

I laugh and throw my arm around her shoulder and enjoy being with her as we walk to see the parrots. "Oh, look, pelicans," she squeals, and points to the pretty white bird soaring over the lake. She points to the trees, her enthusiasm rubbing off on me, and I sort of do feel like that little kid again. "A little yellow warbler."

She's smiling from ear to ear, and it's nice to see the young girl in her again too. She loves this as much as I do, and I like that we have that in common. A little girl licking an ice cream cone passes by us.

"I'm going to need one of those," she announces.

"A trip to the sanctuary wouldn't be complete without ice cream, Cass," I say, like of course I know we're getting a couple of big cones.

She grins and we take a left in the path, knowing exactly where the parrots are. We could find our way around this place with our eyes closed. "Are you going to hold one?" she asks.

"Did you just meet me?"

She laughs, and before I realize it, she jumps onto my back for a piggyback ride, like she used to do when we were little. Although I have to say it hits me a little differently now, because yeah, after having her legs wrapped around me in bed...well, let's just say, as the heat of her sex seeps under my skin, it's making walking very difficult.

Down, boner.

I hurry to the parrots, and she slides off my back. We head straight for the trainer who's holding Pete on his gloved arm. Pete has always been our favorite parrot. We stand back as everyone takes their turn, Pete jumping onto their outstretched arms and greeting them. Children and adults laugh around us, and Cass leans in close when we get to the front of the line. The trainer glances at us and his eyes narrow as he angles his head.

"Do I know you?" he asks.

Cass gazes up at me with genuine pride in her eyes and I like that she's proud of the guy I became, "This is Braden Murphy, star running back for Kingston." I'm about to introduce her, and list off her accolades when the trainer shakes his head.

"No, that's not it," he says, and Cass and I chuckle. "You guys used to come here a lot, years ago, right?"

His glance goes from me to Cass, back to me again. "I can't believe you remember us," I say.

He speaks to Pete as Pete fluffs up his feathers. "Pete, do you remember Braden?"

For a second, I can't believe he knows my name but then I remember Cass just introduced me. Pete jumps onto my arm and says, "Hello, buddy."

"Hello to you too, Pete." I smile at the gorgeous multi-colored bird, as he takes small hops along my arm. He slightly flaps his wings.

"I think he remembers you," the trainer says as he pulls off his thick work gloves and adjusts his ball cap. "Want a picture?"

"Sure." I put my arm around Cass and bring her in close, and the trainer snaps a pic with his Polaroid. I hand him back and Pete says, "Bye-bye."

"See you, Pete."

"Don't be strangers."

Cass and I laugh. "We won't." I take the Polaroid and drop ten bucks into the donation box.

"Let's see," Cass says and takes it from me as we step out of line. She laughs hard.

"What?"

"Look at you. You're smiling like a kid on Christmas morning."

I pull her in to me. "I'm having fun, and you're smiling too, just so you know."

Taking me by surprise, she goes up on her toes and kisses my cheek. "I'm having fun. I'm so glad we came here."

If we weren't surrounded by people, I'd drag her into the trees and have my way with her. I tamp down my arousal and look for a distraction. "Time for ice cream?"

"Did you just meet me?" she says, and it totally makes me laugh.

She wraps her arm around mine, and we head to the on-site restaurant, and a change comes over her as she checks out the menu. I take in her frown, the way she begins to close in on herself and anger floods my veins.

"You're having an ice cream Cass."

She takes a breath, all the years of her mother badgering her about her weight—which is perfectly fine—is no doubt racing around her brain and making her second guess her choices. I fucking hate that.

"It's tradition," I point out. I lean in, and put my mouth close to her ear. "And after what we just did, we need to keep our strength up."

A small smile touches her mouth. "You might be right."

"I am right, and if we want to do that again, we're going to need to carb up."

15

CASSIDY

As I lick my cone on the way back to our car, I steal a glance at Braden's profile. Are we going to have sex again? My body tingles all over at the thought, and I have to say, I'm not opposed to the idea. I kind of like it. A lot. Fooling around with him is fun, and as far as I'm concerned, there's not a damn thing wrong with it, as long as we don't go all the way and I blow it for him. Well, I already blew it for him. But you get the gist.

Braden looks at me and asks, "Why are you staring at me?"

I laugh as he turns and meets my gaze, his brows raised in question. "I was just thinking."

He arches one brow and tries to pull off smoldering. It's not his specialty, and that's okay. He doesn't need any tricks to get me to like him. Not that he's trying. He's just Braden being Braden. "About how hot I am?" he asks.

He's teasing, I know it. Braden isn't an egotistical jock, and does not walk around thinking he's God's gift to women.

Why the cheerleaders go after the guys who do is beyond my comprehension. I prefer substance over self-absorbed.

"Maybe."

He rolls his eyes. "You don't have to lie."

"Why would I lie?"

"I'm no prince charming," he says and takes a big lick of his strawberry cone. I used to think strawberry was so weird, but this is Braden. He marches to the beat of his own drum and I like that.

"Dude, do you have any idea how hot you are?" I ask, not at all lying.

"I wasn't fishing for compliments, Cass." We reach his car and he opens the passenger side door and gestures for me to climb in.

"I thought I was driving."

"I've gotten my second wind." He waves his hand. "Get in."

"Wow, look at you being all bossy and telling me what to do."

Catching me by surprise, he pushes up against me, pinning me between the car and his body. "Don't pretend you don't like it, Cass."

A fierce shiver wracks my body and he grins as my reaction gives me away. "Yeah, well, I wasn't denying it, I was just pointing it out." I press my ice-cream free hand to his hard chest, and splay my fingers, wishing he was naked again so I could take pleasure in the play of his muscles beneath my fingertips. Does he react like that with every girl or only with me? I quickly berate myself at that thought. He's not a man-whore, but he's had his share of women, and honestly, I'm not special. The only reason Stefan is noticing me is because of Braden. I'm not sure I'll ever be special to any man.

His eyes darken as I touch him, giving me the feeling that sex again might be sooner rather than later. "If you keep touching me like that, I might demand you get in the back seat so you can slide that hand lower."

I pull my hand away, knowing now is neither the time or place, and his resulting groan swirls around inside me, setting my heart a little off kilter. I slide into the seat and he stands still a moment longer, his jaw clenched, his body stiff. After he takes a second to pull himself together, he circles the car, and I admire his confident gait as he walks. I also admire the way his jeans hug his thighs. The man has nice thighs. I never noticed them before, but after seeing him naked, I'm noticing a lot of things about Braden's body.

I feign innocence and go back to licking my dripping ice cream when he slides in beside me, but I'm not at all oblivious to the looks he's casting my way, or the groans catching in his throat.

"Why are you staring at me?"

"Because you're licking that ice cream the way I want you to lick my cock."

I choke, shocked at his blunt, dirty words. "Braden," I shout, and wipe my mouth with the back of my hand as he takes a huge bite of his ice cream like he needs it to cool him down.

"What?" he says around the mouthful. "I'm just being honest."

He's definitely an honest guy, but I never expected this kind of honesty. As I consider his words, and consider how much I'd like to take his cock into my mouth again, my phone pings

—my brother's special tone—and it snaps me back to the present, and a measure of guilt churns in my stomach. There's no way he's going to tell James about us, even though there is nothing wrong with what we're doing, but James has made it perfectly clear to all his friends that I'm hands off.

"James," I say and fish my phone from my bag. I read his text. "He wants to know how your grandmother is, and how you're doing."

"Tell him everything is good and we're on our way home." His demeanor goes from playful to serious in seconds and he quickly finishes his cone, starts the car and drives out of the parking lot.

I text back and take in the tightness in Braden's shoulders. I reach out and touch him and he flinches.

"Whoa." I pull my hand back so fast I nearly smack myself in the face. "Are you okay?"

He exhales as his grip tightens on the steering wheel. "It's just…"

I nod in understanding. "James."

He casts me a fast glance. "Yeah."

"I'm sorry, B. I never should have put you in this situation." I fold my hands across my tightening stomach.

"Cass," he says so quietly, and tenderly, the heat in his eyes scorching my skin. "I love all the positions you put me in." He's trying to ease my worries, when his stress levels are at an all-time high. God, I love that about him. "I don't want to lie to him, you know."

"I'm an adult, Braden, so are you." I'm not really sure I can say anything to make this better, but damned if I'm not going to try. "What we do is our business and no one else's."

"I know, but still."

"Why don't we just tell him then?"

He shakes his head fast. "He's my best friend. My brother. I can't risk ruining our friendship."

"I never should have asked you to do this. I would never ask you to choose me over my brother. I'm not worth it."

"What? No, I mean yes you are. I mean, it's not that..."

As he stumbles over his response, I say, "How about this? We keep this a secret. No one ever has to know. After we stage a breakup, what we've done will just be a memory." I honestly have no idea why that leaves me feeling a little cold and disturbed inside. It's not like Braden and I have, or even want, a future together. No, after our ruse, we go our own way, and continue being friends—without the benefits.

He stares straight ahead and nods. I do the same and a few minutes later we're on the freeway, and I give in to the yawn pulling at me. Cripes, I slept last night, yet Braden is the one driving. My thoughts turn to last night. Honestly, I'm not much of a drinker, and I'm still not sure someone drugged me. All I know is I'm grateful Braden was there to take care of me. When we get back home, I plan to take care of him.

I snuggle back into my seat, and engage in small talk to keep him awake and occupied during the drive. Braden talks about football, and his accounting degree, and I like how he has a plan B. I guess my back-up plan is public relations. It's strange though, a part of me thinks of that as my A plan, and marriage as my B plan—even though it's my mother's A plan. I wish my place in society wasn't so important to her.

Night has fallen over Kingston as Braden pulls up to my sorority. He parks and kills the ignition, ready to walk me inside like I knew he would. Chances are Becca is at Jared's place. They always plan special dinners on Sundays.

Braden is tired as he circles the car to meet me, and I gaze up at him beneath the streetlight and take in the dark smudges beneath his even darker eyes. He takes my bag and tosses it over my shoulder.

"Sorry you didn't get much homework done."

"I can catch up. No worries."

A car horn honks in the distance as we fall silent as we head up the stairs, enter the big house and down the hall. I open the door to my shared apartment and find it dark inside. Not bothering to switch on the light, I shut the door behind Braden before he can escape.

His eyes move over me in the dark room, and I tug on his shirt as I turn. "Would you mind tucking me in?"

He follows along, his footsteps heavy on my floor. I reach my bedroom, and stretch out. "It's been a long day. I was thinking I'd have a hot shower before bed. I hate to ask you to wait."

"I'll wait."

The sound of his teeth grinding echoes in my quiet room. "It's been a long day for you too," I say and tug on his T-shirt again. "Since you're here waiting, and you likely need a shower too, maybe you could join me?"

I expected a protest of sorts. An excuse that he has to leave. After all, while there is nothing at all wrong in what we're doing, we both know this will look like betrayal in my brother's eyes. He's wrong, of course, and I've held Braden's secrets before, and I'll hold this one too.

His hand grips the back of my hair, and tugs until my mouth is open and my eyes are on his. "You want to shower with me, Cass?"

I do love his bluntness. "Yes," I admit.

"Then...?"

"Then I want you to put me in my bed."

"Alone?"

"No."

"Good, because once I have you naked, I'm going to need to do things to you."

"One condition." His head angles and I add, "I get to do things to you too."

He tears off his T-shirt, makes quick work of his pants, and dressed only in his boxers, he leads me to the bathroom. I wince after he flicks on the light.

"Too bright," I groan in protest.

"I want to see you."

I slowly open one eye. "I want to see you too." Shamelessly, I let my gaze race over his hard body, and study his every move as he turns on the shower and adjusts the spray. He comes back to me, and without words, only moans of approval, he slides his hand under my shirt and inches it upward to cup my breasts through my bra. I arch into the warmth of his palms, letting his heat curl through my body.

"B," I murmur, and place my hands on his hard pecs as steam fills the room. Deft fingers unhook my bra and before I can even get my lust-rattled thoughts straight, he has me naked and under the spray. He steps to the back as my body gobbles up the warm water. The scent of grapefruit reaches my nostrils, and I brace myself as he fills his hands with my soap and begins to clean my tired body.

"Now I know why you always smell so good," he murmurs.

It takes a moment for his words to register. "You think I smell good?"

"Always."

Big palms move over my stomach and sides, washing me all over. I stand there like a rag-doll and let him do whatever he wants. The rough pads of his thumbs brush my nipples as he cups my breasts and massages, all under the guise of cleaning me. My hips cant forward and I ever so slowly part my legs to give him access to other, more needy spots.

He fills his palms with soap again, and his lips are inches from mine, his gaze locked on my eyes as his hand slides between my legs. I begin moaning, long before he even touches me, and it brings a grin to his face.

"Need something, Cass?"

I can barely speak, barely breathe, as he caresses my swollen clit. "I need you to wash me," I manage to get out on a hard breath.

"Is that what you need?"

"Uh huh," I groan, and put my hands on his shoulders. He lightly brushes my clit, and I rock into him, demanding more, and finally—finally—he slides a thick finger inside me. God, I love that.

"I give you an orgasm and look what happens," he teases.

"Yes, all this is your fault. I used to walk around content, and now I walk around needy and achy." He uses his palm on my clit as his other hand goes to my parted lips, and his groan is a telltale sign that he likes what he does to me.

"I've been semi-hard all fucking day thinking about this sweet mouth wrapped around my cock again." He pushes his finger into my mouth, and his growl grows louder as I suck on him. His finger stills inside me and the tip of his throbbing cock throbs against my leg. I move with his finger, and brush up against his thick cock, making him a little crazier, judging by the grunting sounds he's making.

I close my eyes as pleasure spreads through my body, arousing me from the top of my head to the tips of my toes. Is this better than the last time? I'm not sure and I don't want to think at the moment. All I want to do is concentrate on the points of pleasure between my legs.

"B, that feels so good."

His slick fingers change tempo, each thrust a little faster, deeper, as he works my clit, and closes his lips over mine for a smoking hot kiss. His breath comes quicker as my body tightens, my sex muscles gripping his fingers hard.

"Jesus, Cass. It's a good thing we're not fucking. I might destroy you."

"I had that same thought this morning." I grip his shoulders and hang on, and a moan I have no control over crawls out of my throat.

"That's it, come all over my fingers," Braden says. "Show me how much you like me inside you."

I whimper and buck against his hand.

"I want to taste you so fucking bad," he groans. I push against his chest, and practically score his skin with my hard nipples. "Jesus Cass, you're killing me."

Hearing what I do to him pushes me over the edge and my body lets go. A flood of liquid heat spills from my body, and burns hotter than the spray falling over us.

"Yes," he groans and lightens his touch on my clit. I come and come and come some more, until I can barely stand on my own. He snakes his hand around my body to hold me, and I gasp, struggling to fill my lungs.

"B," I murmur, and press my lips to his chest. I breathe in his skin and sag against him as he gently removes his fingers, and brings it to his mouth. I glance up as he licks my hot release from his fingertip, and a quiver goes through me.

"Next time, you come in my mouth."

"Okay," I squeak out. I wrap my hand around his cock. "Trade places with me."

"I don't want you to get cold."

"I won't." I shift so he has to stand in the spray and he lifts his head as it falls over his body and I run my hand up and down his rock-hard cock. "But I want you to get hot."

"I'm hot, Cass," he moans. "I'm fucking hot."

"Yeah you are." I take pleasure in the way his handsome face twists as I stroke him, the way he rocks into me, the way he loves how I touch him. I love it too.

I drop to my knees and he shifts so the water cascading down his body doesn't drown me. Good call. As the spray hits his back, I take him into my mouth, and drink in his tang. I never thought I'd like the taste of a man like this, but with Braden I do. I put my hands on his outer thighs and he rocks his body and fucks my mouth.

He pushes my wet hair from my face, and I close my eyes as he enjoys the show. We both move together, and I love this so much, I don't want it to end, but he begins to thicken, and curse under his breath and it thrills and shocks me that I can bring him to climax so fast. We had sex this afternoon. Then again, he's a virile guy who's been off sex for a while, so this shouldn't be a surprise.

"Cass," he mumbles and I take him to the back of my throat, a silent warning not to try to pull me off him again. He listens and lightly strokes my hair as he spills into me, and I do my best to drink him all in. Once he's depleted, I slowly inch back and he winces as I slide my lips off his crown.

"Sensitive?" I ask.

"Yeah." He reaches down and pulls me to my feet, turning to put me in the shower. The warmth feels glorious against my skin and Braden puts his arms around me, and we both stand like that, enjoying the intimacy and the heat until the spray begins to cool.

"Let's get you to bed," he murmurs into my ear, and as much as I hate to break the hold I have on him, I don't want us freezing to death. We step from the shower and he hands me a towel before grabbing one for himself. I can't seem to tear my eyes from his body as he dries. I like the way he moves, the way his muscles ripple as he knots the towel around his waist and focuses on me.

I tighten the towel around me, and he takes my hand and leads me to my room. It's weird how much I like him taking care of me. When we were young, I mostly hated how he watched out for me. I was determined to prove I was all grown up and could take care of myself. I've certainly proved that this week.

We reach my room and he scoops me up. I yelp as he carries me to my bed, and we're both so exhausted and sated, I expect him to dress quickly and head back home to get some sleep. He surprises me by sliding in next to me, fixing the blankets around us and pulling me to him. As the little spoon to his big spoon, I snuggle in and fight sleep. I want to enjoy the comfort of his arms a little longer.

"Go to sleep, Cass."

I chuckle. "I'm trying."

"No, you're not."

"Why do you want me to sleep? You're not going to do depraved things to me when I nod off are you?" I turn in his arms, until I'm facing him.

"No, I'm going to do them to you when you wake up, and you're going to need your energy so shut your eyes and your mouth and go to sleep."

A thrill goes through me. Okay, it's true. I'm addicted to orgasms. "So bossy." I quickly roll over and snuggle back until I'm pressed against him. A soft, contented noise crawls out of my throat, and I close my eyes, let sleep pull at me. "I love this," I murmur as my breathing slows and the world goes quiet in my brain. "I love you." As soon as the words leave my mouth, my lids fly open. "I mean..."

"I know what you mean. We're friends, we go way back. I love you too, Cass. Hell, I wouldn't be helping you get another guy if I didn't care about you."

He loves me.

Like a friend.

Of course, he does!

I love him the same way and there will never be more between us. He's helping me get another guy, and I can't forget that—mainly because he keeps reminding me.

16

BRADEN

I wake to find Cassidy sleeping soundly beside me, and I rub my eyes to check the time. Shit, it's later than I wanted, but early enough that James won't be up yet. I move quietly, not wanting to wake her. That's not entirely true. I do want to wake her and put my mouth all over her again. Last night we both drifted off and when I woke in the middle of the night, I crawled over her, and brought her out of her slumber with my tongue between her legs. As much as I'd like to do that now, I need to bail.

I slide from the bed and stumble around in the dark in search of my clothes. I dress quickly, and do my best to get out of her room without waking her. I'm not sneaking off, I just want to be back before James starts searching for me. I shoot Cass a quick text to let her know what's going on and I'm about to head down the hall when a door opens. I go perfectly still. Like that's going to stop Becca from seeing me.

"Oh, hey," she says, as she wipes her eyes. She glances around. "Were you..." She points to Cassidy's door. Confusion morphs to a grin. "Oh, yeah you were."

"It was a late night and I tucked her in."

She holds her hands up, palms out. "Not my business, but I do want to say thanks for helping her out like this. I mean, I'm sure Stefan is an experienced guy, and he's going to want his bride to know how to please him."

Fuck me twice.

I fist my hands without realizing it, and bite down on my jaw. Becca angles her head, and it's dark in the hall, but if I had to guess, I'd say she was smirking. "Something wrong?" she asks.

"No, something funny?"

"Not at all."

"Listen, what do you know about Stefan?"

She shrugs. "Pretty much what everyone else does."

"The party at his house, he told me he was taking Cass upstairs to rest. She really seemed drugged."

"You think Stefan was behind it?"

"I'm not saying that."

"But you're not *not* saying that either."

"Just keep your eye out, okay, and if you hear anything, let me know."

She gives me a salute. "Consider it done." She softens a bit. "I'm glad you were there for her. I know crazy shit can happen at parties, but I'd be really surprised if someone messed with Cassidy. They'd have you and James to contend with. Everyone knows better."

"You think she might have grabbed someone else's drink by mistake?"

"Anything can happen, and don't forget she's a lightweight when it comes to alcohol."

I scrub my face. "True. I better get going."

She moves to the side to give me room to pass her in the hall and as I do, she lightly touches my arm. "Braden, I'm sorry to hear about your grandmother."

"Thanks."

"I'm glad Cass was there for you."

I nod, and head to the door. When hasn't Cass or James been there for me? I can't even recall a time. That brings a smile to my face as I leave the dorm room and head outside. Long streaks of yellow claw at the parking lot as I jump into my car and head home. The second I enter the silence of our place, my demons come out to play. Fuck, what I'm doing with my best friend's sister isn't smart, and I'm not just talking about sleeping with her. What does she see in that douche bag Stefan anyway? I head upstairs, weary from a couple of sleepless nights and fall into my bed.

The sound of the toilet flushing pulls me awake, and I roll over. I guess a couple hours sleep is better than nothing. I push to my feet, and rake my hands through my hair and a big stupid smile lights up my face when my phone goes off and I see the message is from Cass, telling me that her bed was cold when she woke up.

Me: Sorry, I had to go but didn't want to wake you.

Cass: Did you have to do the walk of shame?

Me: LOL, no one was up, but I did run into Becca.

Cass: So she knows you slept with me?

Me: Technically we didn't sleep together.

Cass: Let me rephrase. Does she know you gave me a couple of mind-blowing orgasms?

Me: It didn't come up in conversation, but I'm sure she's going to interrogate you later.

Cass: What do you want me to say?

Me: Wasn't me sleeping with you all her idea?

Cass: Yeah, you're right. I'll swear her to secrecy.

Me: See you later?

Cass: Of course you will, boyfriend.

I grin like the idiot I am as she calls me boyfriend, and I quickly text back.

Me: Counting down the minutes.

I lift my head, sensing movement at the door, and the smile falls from my face when I spot James standing there scratching his balls. I hope he doesn't have crabs again.

"You okay, bro?" I ask.

"Yeah, you?"

"I'm good."

"I guess your grandmother must be doing okay, huh?"

"What?"

He nods at my phone. "You were smiling. I'm assuming your grandmother is good."

I toss my phone away, like it's a little white lie I don't want him to see. "Yeah, she's great."

"You should have woken me. I would have gone with you."

I give a casual shrug. "You were tired. Cass came and kept me company."

He stares at me so long, I'm sure he can see inside me, read all the dirty things I did with Cassidy. I expect him to call me on it, or at least pounce and beat the shit out of me. Instead he says, "Breakfast and then Stefan. Or do you want to do it in the other order?"

I stand and tug on my jeans. "Prince Charming probably isn't even out of bed yet. Let's grab something to eat at the diner."

I tug on a clean T-shirt and finger comb my hair. Yeah, I look like shit, but who really cares. I make a quick trip to the bathroom and a few minutes later, we're cutting across campus and headed to our favorite diner. I pull open the door, and James steps ahead of me. I walk in, and bump into his back. Why did he abruptly stop?

"What the hell?"

He glances at me over his shoulder. "Stefan and his friends are here." I look around his shoulder and find Prince Charming leisurely sipping coffee and laughing with the guys from the rowing club. Stefan doesn't look like a rower. I bet he bought his way onto the team because it looked good on his transcript.

James walks right up to their table, and I catch Rhonda, the server's eye. She looks horrified, but I'm not going to let a fight break out, at least not inside. I hold my hand up to ease her worries and follow James. As we present a united front, Stefan casually glances at us.

"Well, if it isn't the two best footballers on campus. What did we do to deserve this pleasure?" He glances at his friend in the seat across from him. "Get up and let these guys sit."

"We won't be staying," James says and presses his palm into the guy's shoulder to keep him seated.

Stefan stretches. "What's this about then?"

I fold my arms, and take a threatening step closer. "It's about my girl."

He puts his fork down and although he's trying to play it cool, I don't miss the slight waver in his hand. "Is she okay? She was pretty drunk the other night."

"Drunk or drugged?" James asks.

"If you're accusing me of something here—"

I study his body language as he speaks. "We're asking what happened."

"Look," he begins. "She's your girl, and it's not my fault she'd rather spend the night talking to me. If you're jealous."

I am jealous, dammit.

"This is about her safety," I say, working to keep my temper in check.

Before Stefan can answer, James says, "If you or anyone of your guys was behind this—"

"I can guarantee I didn't drug her." He puts a hand on his chest. "I'm a nice guy. I come from a good family and I respect women." He casts James a fast glance as if to insinuate he doesn't. "I like her, which is why I was taking care of her, until you showed up." He stares at me. "If someone roofied her, I'll get to the bottom of it, and believe me, when

I find out who's responsible, they'll pay for it. You have my word on that."

James grips the edge of the table. "You better not be fucking lying to us."

Stefan pulls out his phone. "I'll get to the bottom of this. If you say she was drugged and wasn't drunk, I believe you. I'm just glad nothing happened to her."

"If you find anything out, let me know first," I say.

"Of course," Stefan says and holds my gaze unflinchingly. I whack James' arm, unable to look at his face for another second. What does Cass see in him? Sure, he's got the looks, the money, the stature, but life is more than that, right?

"Let's go."

We move to the other side of the diner and Rhonda nods at me. I nod back and we slide into a booth. James grabs the menu. "Do you think he's telling the truth?"

"He better be, or he's a dead man."

"Yeah."

"He doesn't strike me as a stupid guy. Drugging Cassidy at a party in his house while her brother, and..." I poke my chest. "Her boyfriend and half the football team is there would be a pretty fucking stupid move." As I rationalize it out, it makes sense, but I still don't like the guy and my judgement could be clouded because it's Cass we're talking about here.

Rhonda comes and I flip over my mug.

"Everything okay, boys?" She pours the coffee and the bands on her wrist jangle together.

"Yeah, we're good," James grumbles. A group of girls come into the diner and Stefan waves them over. Giggling, they all start playing with their hair as they slide in beside him and I tear my gaze away and take a sip of the strong coffee. I'm glad we have practice this afternoon. I have a shit ton of energy to burn off.

We put in our orders and every now and then I check my phone to see if Cass messaged. The disappointment I feel when my search comes up empty is utterly ridiculous. Kate walks in and glances around. Her gaze lands on Stefan, and if sensing her presence, James sits up a bit straighter. Christ, one minute I think he's hot for Becca and the next he seems interested in Kate, although his flavor can switch faster than the wind. He waves her over, and she slides in next to him. A goofy smile that I'd never seen on his face before splits his lips from ear to ear.

"Good morning," Kate says. "Thanks for waving me over. I hate to eat alone." She frowns and looks at me. "How is Cassidy?"

"Why?" I ask, every nerve in my body going on high alert.

"I heard you had to take her from the party."

I relax. "Yeah, she drank too much. Wait, how did you hear?"

She gives James a small, secretive smile. "Oh, through the grapevine." James slides his coffee her way and she takes a sip. I wave Rhonda back over, and she fills a mug for Kate.

"So, are you guys excited about the auction?"

"No," I say.

Kate laughs. "Why not?"

"I hate that shit. A day at the spa, what the fuck ever." Christ, I'm grumpier than I should be considering all the sex Cass and I had, and I definitely shouldn't be taking it out on Kate.

"I get that Cassidy can't bid on you because she's master of ceremonies." She takes a sip of her coffee and stares at it for a second. "I have an idea. Why don't I bid on you, so you don't have to go on a date you don't want to go on? We can just pretend we did."

"You'd do that?"

She shrugs. "Sure, why not. Anything to help out the team, and Cassidy." She frowns, and I sense loneliness in her. I think she really wants to be Cassidy's friend.

"He's not going to go cheap, Kate."

Kate laughs. "I know. I'm a cheerleader. I know about all the bets on Braden."

"I'm with Cass now."

She laughs. "Clearly you know nothing about women."

"Meaning?"

She leans forward. "Now they want you even more. Cheerleaders don't like sharing their guys with non-cheerleaders and they're all envious that Stefan seems interested in her."

"What a bunch of bullshit."

She shrugs. "Hey, I don't make up the rules."

James nudges her. "What about you? Are you into ballers?"

Her smile is coy and demure, as she brings her coffee mug to her lips and says, "Maybe."

"I thought you were into Stefan," I say.

"We share a couple of classes."

At that non-answer, our pancakes arrive, followed by a fruit muffin for Kate. Kate and James chat and James forces her to take a bite of his pancake, which is dripping with syrup. She gobbles it up and he feeds her more. I take a big sip of coffee and glance outside. My heart jumps as Cass and Becca walk by the window. I'm ready to jump up and run out to meet her when Stefan beats me to it.

What is that little fucker doing?

17

CASSIDY

My stupid stomach, as well as other body parts, flutter as I walk past Braden and give him a finger wave. I love the way he smiles when he sees me. I'm about to head inside, just to say hello, but stop abruptly when Stefan comes out and practically knocks me over.

"Oh, hi," I say, and start coiling my hair around my finger, taking a cue from all the cheerleaders I've watched flirt. I'm not great at it, and hope I'm not coming off like a nitwit.

"Cassidy, Becca," he responds, flashing those perfect white teeth of his.

Becca touches my arm. "Shoot, look at the time. I have to run."

She has nowhere to run to, she's just giving me alone time with Stefan, and I'm not sure if I'm happy about that or not.

Standing before me in his polo and khakis looking very put together, Stefan's blue eyes narrow in on me. "How are you feeling?"

"I'm good, how are you?"

He steps closer. "If someone drugged you at my party, Cass, they're going to pay for it." From the corner of my eye, I spot Braden getting up from the booth. "I hope you don't think it was me. I'm not that guy."

"I didn't think it was you. Honestly, I'm not even sure I was drugged. I drank on a very empty stomach. Not my smartest move."

He moves even closer, and the scent of his cologne reaches my nostrils. "Don't be so hard on yourself. We all make mistakes." I drop my hand and let my hair go, and he lightly brushes the strands from my face. "I'm just glad you're okay, and hey, about your fundraiser for the football team..."

"What about it?"

"I'd like to make a big donation. To make up for what happened to you at my place. Everyone under my roof is under my care, and if I failed you, I'd like to make it up."

"That's sweet, Stefan, but I can't just take your money, and you weren't responsible for me. I'm all grown up and responsible for myself."

"Yeah, well, I still feel responsible. It's a good thing you didn't wander off when I made a quick trip to the bathroom. If I wasn't there, who knows what would have happened to you."

I can't help but think Braden would have come looking eventually, even though I told him I wanted alone time.

"So please, let me transfer the money to you." He grabs his phone to do the transfer. "The auction won't even be necessary."

I snort, and his eyes lift from the phone. Jesus, why am I snorting. I quickly call about my debutante lessons and say, "Braden will certainly like that?"

He runs his finger over his screen. "What?

"Oh, nothing." I give a dismissive wave. "He didn't love the idea of being auctioned off and spending a day at the spa."

"Sounds perfectly lovely to me."

"Me too," I say. I might not be a girly-girl, but a spa day does sound divine. Stefan is a prince, and I'm not a princess, but maybe we do have some things in common.

"What's your Venmo?"

"That's sweet—"

"What's sweet?" Braden steps in beside me, and puts his hand on the small of my back. I look up at him, take in the dark intensity in his eyes.

"Stefan just offered up a big donation for my auction."

Surprise replaces the irritation on his face. "Really?"

"You won't even have to have the auction if you don't want to." Stefan glances at Braden. "Now you're off the hook."

Braden frowns. "What do you mean?"

"Cassidy told me you didn't want to be a part of the auction."

"You told him that?" He glowers at me, like I broke his trust.

"It just came up," I say quickly. Was that supposed to be a secret?

He dips his head. "I told you I'd do it, Cass."

"Yeah, I know but—"

He shakes his head. "The auction will look good on your transcript. I mean, you have to go through with it. You've already gotten the ball rolling, and you actually seemed excited about doing it."

"You didn't, though and this will get you out of it."

Hurt registers in his eyes. Why do I feel like I've betrayed him somehow? "I also said I would. For you." His body is tense, as he gazes at me with a mixture of vulnerability and confusion in his eyes. "This is good for you, Cass. Good for class credit and good experience."

"Yeah, I know." Another thought hits. "Wait, is this about me cooking for you?"

As soon as the words leave my mouth, I realize what I said.

"What's this about cooking?" Stefan asks.

"Nothing," I say quickly. "Just...I told Braden I'd cook for him if he played along...with the auction."

With the ruse.

Stefan's eyes narrow in on me. Shoot, can he tell I'm fibbing? "I wish I was a footballer now. I bet you're a great cook."

Braden shifts his body, so he's practically standing between Stefan and me. "You're not, and she is, so no, you can't take part in the auction, and she won't be cooking for you."

Wow, Braden is a little over the top possessive. Is that what he'd be like if he had a real girlfriend? Would he go all alpha to protect her?

"If she decides to have it," Stefan counters, a challenge in his eyes as he narrows in on Braden.

"I'm going to have it," I blurt out, hoping to break the tension between the two. "Thank you for the generous donation, Stefan, but I'm going to have to decline. Braden is right. This is good for credit and experience, and all the guys are looking forward to it."

"Not all of them," he says and cocks his head as he continues to stare at Braden. Is the guy crazy? Pushing Braden's buttons isn't wise.

"I said I'd do it," Braden responds through clenched teeth. I put my hand on his arm, and he relaxes a bit.

"Maybe I could help out in other ways, then," Stefan suggests. "I could help with posters, or set up, or just be your right-hand man to run errands. Whatever you need."

"Oh, okay, that would work," I say.

"Yeah, that's a good idea," Braden says, and I turn to him so fast, my eyeballs practically roll in my head.

"What?" he asks.

"Nothing."

"It's settled then. Stefan can be your right-hand man. Help you out when you need it."

"Okay," I say, clueing in. I did tell him the other night that he needed to give me time with Stefan and that's exactly what he's doing.

Kate and my brother step from the diner and walk up to us. She smiles up at Stefan and he smiles back. Competitiveness flares inside me.

"Tonight I'll be writing up stories for each of the guys. Maybe you could help me with that."

"Oh, you're helping out with the auction?" Kate asks.

Stefan nods, and she continues with, "You're such a good writer, Stefan." She glances at me. "We're in English together and I read over his last paper for him." She puts her hand on Stefan's arm. "He'll do a great job with the write-ups, Cassidy."

Stefan's phone pings and he checks it. "Looks like my guys have a lead on who might have messed with Cassidy's drink."

My heart lurches. So I was roofied? Ohmigod, how horrifying!

"Who?" Braden and my brother ask at the same time.

"I'll get to the bottom of it," Stefan says. "It was my house, my party."

"Yeah, but it was my girl," Braden blurts out, tugging me against him in a possessive manner that I once would have hated.

"And my sister," James says.

Remaining calm as the two other guys fist their hands, Stefan holds his palms up and says, "It was my house, my party, which means Cassidy was my responsibility. I'll get to the bottom of things, and report back to you guys."

As the three stare at each other, I say, "Tonight, seven, student union?"

Stefan turns to me. "You could come by my place if you like. It might be quieter. I live alone, so no one will be around to disturb us."

Both Braden and James open their mouths, like they're ready to protest me being alone with Stefan. I jump in first. "Student union building is better. I'll need to use the printers and resources."

"Sure, seven it is. See you then." He gives everyone a nod and walks off.

"I need to get to class," Kate says.

James checks his phone. "Me too. Come on, I'll walk you."

"Are you headed to class?" Braden asks. I nod, and he nudges me. "Come on?"

We head down the sidewalk, toward campus and he's silent. "Are you upset that I told Stefan you didn't want to take part in the auction?" I ask, breaking the quiet.

"No, it just surprised me at first."

I nod. "You did good, acting all possessive like that."

"Yeah."

Okay, so he doesn't want to talk about it.

We reach my building, and he captures my arm before I head inside. "I have practice tonight," he says softly. His head dips, his mouth close to mine. "Will I see you after...Stefan?"

My lips part automatically as he leans close. "I'd like that," I murmur, and wait for the kiss that never comes.

He backs up and I blink my eyes back into focus. *What the hell, Cass?* I quickly pull myself together and remember what's real and what isn't. "I...uh...I'll have dinner waiting for you guys. I finish classes at two, and I'll head over and cook something and put it in the fridge, okay?"

"Okay," he says and turns. I stare at him, enjoying the way he moves as he jogs to his own class. Once he's out of sight, I head inside and work to get my head on straight. I've known Braden my whole life, spent plenty of time with him, so why now do the thoughts of hanging out with him tonight, after Stefan, excite me? I think all the sex has been messing with my brain.

I put everything out of my mind as I take my seat and for the next couple of hours, I concentrate on my schoolwork. When classes are over, I head to Braden and my brother's place, and let myself in with the key they gave me ages ago.

The place is quiet and I welcome it as my brain races from my earlier encounter with Stefan. I can't believe he offered to donate money, and took my safety so seriously. That's kind of nice really. It's also kind of nice how Braden jumped in and encouraged me to run the auction, despite how much he despised the idea of being auctioned off and honestly, I can't blame him.

In the kitchen, I pull out a package of chicken and decide on a hearty soup. With the cooler nights, and a hard practice, I'm sure they'll appreciate it, and it's easy for them to heat up. I grab my phone and put on some tunes as I cut the vegetables and get the soup going. Soon I'm singing along, and swaying my hips to the music.

I'm so lost in the music, I had no idea the front door had opened, or that someone was standing behind me, watching.

"Hey."

I jump and spin at the sound of Braden's voice. I catch the want in his eyes, the small smile on his face.

"How long were you standing there?" I ask, completely breathless, and not just because he scared me. I take him in, his long hard body, his crossed arms and feet as he leans against the doorjamb looking like sex. My body warms all over.

"Long enough." He pushes off the doorframe and takes a step toward me.

"Long enough for what?"

"To hear you sing. To watch you dance. To want you again."

My pulse jumps as my nipples tighten with bliss. "You want me again?"

He steps up to me, pulls me against his big, warm body, and glances over my shoulder. "You might want to turn the burner off."

"Why?" I ask, but that question turns to a moan, as he gazes at me, his hungry eyes letting me know he's going to do dirty, delicious things to me, and he doesn't want to burn the house down.

I reach behind me and turn the burner off. "What...why are you here?"

"You said you got off at two, didn't you?"

"Yes."

He unhooks the button on my jeans, and pulls my zipper down. "I didn't want you getting off alone."

I stare at him, a little confused. The second he slides his big hand into my panties and strokes my clit, I get the joke. "You're...you're going to get me off."

He chuckles. "That's the idea, Cass."

The rough pad of his thumb lightly brushes my sex, and my legs give a little. "You have class." What the hell am I saying? Do I want him to stop and rush off to class? That would be a hell, no.

"I can be late every now and then." His mouth finds mine and he kisses me deeply, thoroughly. He breaks it and we're both breathless. "You want to learn things, Cass, and I'm ready to teach you all about the joy of a quickie."

"Quickie, yeah," I say, my brain spinning so fast it's hard for me to think straight. "We're in the kitchen."

"Yeah, I know."

"Someone could come."

"Someone is going to come." He inches his finger into me and a low groan crawls out of my throat. God, that feels so good.

"B..."

"Door is locked, your brother is in class. It's just you and me, Cass. You can keep talking and worrying, or you can let me put my fingers in you and give you an orgasm."

I open my mouth, and he arches a brow, his finger toying with my pussy as he waits for an answer. I put my finger to my lips and pretend I'm sealing them, and he chuckles. It reverberates through my body and stimulates my clit.

He slowly sinks to his knees, and tugs my pants down, just until they're around my knees. I try to spread, but can't. Although I must say, keeping them tight together comes with its own pleasure. He presses his nose to my stomach and breathes me in.

"Grapefruit," he murmurs. "Fuck, I missed the smell of you."

I hold onto his head as he parts my sex with his tongue and brushes the soft blade over my trembling clit.

"Ohmigod, Braden." I stumble a little, and he stands and turns me around, pressing me against the kitchen counter. He puts his fingers on the back of my neck and urges me to bend. I do as he wants, and his groan curls around me. I picture myself from his view, pants at my knees, bent over for him, offering up my hot, wet sex.

I like it. A lot.

"This," he murmurs, and runs his hand down my spine. "This is perfect."

He cups my ass cheeks and squeezes, and I writhe, aching for more. "Are you hurting, Cass?"

"Yes," I cry out.

"Do you need my fingers inside you?"

I'm about to scream out that I want his cock, want to feel his hard cock thicken inside me. That I want him to bend me, break me, take me to places unknown, but catch myself before I say or do something that we'll both regret. He's on hiatus, and I'm saving myself for love. Why does all of that sound so ridiculous right now?

He inches a finger into me, and holy hell, with my legs jammed tight, squeezing my clit, the sensations are out of this world. He moves his finger in and out, and a keening cry catches in my throat. I grow so wet with each glorious pump, it begins to drip down my leg.

"Fuck yeah," he says and bends over my back, pressing kisses to my neck as he finger fucks me in the kitchen. It's all so surreal, like I'm in some sort of pleasure trance. I'll take it.

"You've been missing me, haven't you?"

"Yes," I cry out.

"I'll have to surprise you like this more often. I can't have my girl going around all needy."

My girl. Why does that sound so nice?

"No, no you can't."

He chuckles and his lips burn my flesh as he changes the pace, sliding another finger in and touching my body just the way it needs. Is there anything this man doesn't know about me? I scratch at the countertop as pleasure centers between my legs, and he growls, clearly aware that I'm seconds from coming all over his fingers. He likes it. He likes doing this to me. Dammit, I like it too.

"That's it, Cass. Come all over my fingers, then I want you to go lay in my bed until you recover. That way tonight, when I crawl between the sheets, I'll smell you...have you with me."

"B..." I cry out as my orgasm grips me, and I stop breathing as a wave of pleasure drowns the colors of the kitchen out. My body spasms and tightens and clenches around his probing fingers.

He stays inside me until I ride out the last clench, and I take a big, deep gasping breath. Have I ever come so hard before, and again, I'm sure every orgasm is better than the last.

Warm fingers slip from my sex, and land on my hips. He straightens, and pulls me up with him, holding my back to his chest. The room spins before my eyes.

"How do you feel?"

"Amazing."

"Can you walk?"

"I think so."

"Good." He tugs my pants up, but doesn't button them up again. "Take yourself upstairs. Get naked and crawl into my bed."

"Okay," I say, and he backs away, leaving cold where there was once heat.

His hot breath sears my skin as he presses his mouth to my ear. "See you tonight."

By the time I turn around, he's out of the kitchen and the sound of the lock on the front door sliding open echoes in my brain. I stand there for a good long time, listening. When he doesn't come back, I shake my head.

What the hell was that all about?

18

BRADEN

What the hell was I thinking, kissing her and fingering her in the kitchen? *Oh, just that you wanted her to be thinking about you tonight, when she was with Stefan.*

Christ, I knew her brother was in class, but seriously, that was stupid and reckless. Everything we're doing is risky, yet I can't seem to help myself. She's become an addiction I don't want to quit. I head down the street toward campus and outside of Wolf House, I spot Stefan and a bunch of his goons. They seem to be surrounding someone. I hurry my steps and when I reach them, I put my hand on Stefan's shoulder to get his attention.

He turns to me. "Just in time."

"Time for what?" He snaps his fingers and his goons move back. All except one, who is standing over some guy I don't know, as he bleeds on the ground. "What the fuck is going on?"

"This is Jonny Foster, the guy responsible for drugging Cassidy. I told you I'd get to the bottom of things." Anger flares through me, and I look at the goon standing over Jonny. He has blood on his knuckles, while Stefan's remain pristine clean. "Do you want to take a turn with him. Get a few good kicks in?"

I push the guy beating Jonny out of the way, and stand over him. "What the fuck did you do?"

He wipes his face, and wipes the blood on his hands against his pants. I'm not sure if I recognize him, but there were a lot of people at the party. Jonny steals a fast glance at Stefan and my stomach tightens as warning bells go off in my brain. Something isn't right here.

"I roofied her," he admits. "She's hot as fuck, and I wanted a piece."

Before I can even think straight, I kick him in the ribs, and he groans and clutches his side.

"Yeah, give it to him," Stefan says. I can only see red as Jonny moans.

"Stand up," I say.

Jonny doesn't move so Stefan's goons pull him to his feet. My gaze goes over his face, and once again, I can't help but think something is off. Blood pours from his nose, and he's hunched over like breathing is difficult. While I'd like to give him a thorough beating, I think these guys already did a number on him.

"You go near her, touch one hair on her head, or even look at her wrong, you'll have to deal with me, and what happened here," I say and circle my finger in the air. "This will feel like a goddamn party compared to what I'll do to you."

"Yeah, okay," he says, and I take deep gulping breaths to calm myself down. One of Stefan's goons pushes him and he stumbles off. I watch him until he disappears, no doubt on his way to the clinic. I turn to Stefan, who's standing there like a cocky asshole.

"How did you find him?"

He slowly rolls one shoulder. "I have resources." I stare at him, as smugness radiates off him in waves. "A thank you would be nice."

"You're the one who invited the asshole to your party." I push past him and he says something under his breath. I pause for a second and pull myself together, even though I want to turn back around and wipe the smirk off his face with my fist. This is the guy Cass wants to be with, so I can't very well knock him out because I don't like his face.

I consider texting Cass to ask her if she knows Jonny, but decide to wait. I'll talk to her later, in person. Right now, she's safe in my bedroom warming my bed, and I like the idea of it so much, it's hard to focus on anything else.

I make it to class late, and slide into a seat at the back. A few heads turn my way as I settle in. I focus as best as I can but I'm once again thinking about that strange exchange between Jonny and Stefan. Maybe I'm reading too much into it. By the time class is over, I head to the gym for a workout. I don't normally work out before practice, but I need to do something to clear my head. I change in the locker room, and hit up the free weights and do some bench presses.

"Hey Mason," I call out as he sits on one of the benches and checks his phone. "Spot me."

He comes over, and stands behind the bench, his fingers under the heavy bar as I lift it. "What are you doing in here anyway? We have practice tonight."

I set the bar on the rack and sit up. "Just felt like a workout." He grins, and I glare at him. "What?"

"Still not getting any? Need to work off a little steam?"

"None of your fucking business." I'm in such a shit mood, I swear if he says one thing about Cass, I'll knock his teeth out.

He holds his hands up and laughs. "Hey, I'm just saying, regular sex makes me a better player. You should try it."

My mind goes back to fingering Cass, and it takes all my effort to keep my dick down. I'm fucking lying to everyone now.

"You do you. I'll do me."

"I don't need to do me. I've got a handful of cheerleaders for that."

I add more weights to the bar and lay back down. "Have some fucking respect, dude."

He snickers. "Yeah, man, you need to get laid."

He's not wrong, but I can't with Cass. It's not me who she really wants, and I'm not about to take her virginity if she's saving it for Prince Douchebag.

I tune Mason out as I do my next reps, and my arms are exhausted by the time I finish. I set the bar back, and sit up. Mason tosses me his towel and I wipe my face. Before I can think better of it, I ask, "Do you know a guy by the name of Jonny Foster?"

He squeezes his water bottle and squirts water into his mouth. "Don't think so. Why? Should I know him."

I shrug, even though unease is once again tugging at me. "No. Just wondering. I need to hit the showers. See you at practice."

I hit the showers, and it's late afternoon by the time I head back home to get ready for tonight's practice. The front door is locked, which means Cass is gone. I open it and call out to James, but he's not back yet. I dart upstairs, and grin when I find my bed sheets mussed. I drop down onto them, and breathe in Cassidy's sweet scent. My dick thickens and I think about taking it into my hands. I stop myself, hoping Cass will do that for me tonight—after she's been with Stefan.

Fuck, do I really want her getting worked up from some other guy and then using me to ease the ache he created inside her.

"Hey."

I lift my head and find James at my door. Shit, I was so lost in thought, I hadn't heard him come in.

"Hey," I say and push to a sitting position.

His eyes narrow. "What's up?"

Oh, just that I could very well be falling for your sister?

"Jonny Foster, do you know him?"

He narrows his eyes in thought. "I think there was a Jonny Foster in my English class, freshman year. Yeah wait, I remember now. The guy with the red hair, they call him Red, obviously. He's a real douche from what I remember. He was friends with that asshole Cameron who tried to rape that girl, Ella, a while back. Why?"

"He's the guy who roofied Cass."

Every muscle in his body stiffens. "Come on, we're going to find him and I'm going to fucking kill him."

"Stefan and his goons kicked the shit out of him already. Pretty sure they broke his nose. I just...I don't know. Something was strange about it all."

"Like what?"

"I don't know. I can't put my finger on it." I press my feet to the floor and brace my elbows on my knees. "He admitted it, right to my face, then I kicked him in the ribs."

"Good."

"I mean if he admitted it, and he's a douche like you said, it must have been him."

"Have you talked to Cass, asked her if she knew him?"

"No, not yet. I haven't seen her..." Fuck, here I go lying again. "...since walking her to class."

"She was here earlier." He gestures with a nod to the stairs. "Made some food and left it in the fridge."

Then put her scent all over my bed.

"Okay," I say for lack of anything else. My stomach squeezes tight as I lie to my best friend. I fucking hate myself right now.

"Send her a text. Let her know we were wrong about Stefan."

Were we, though?

"I'm on it." He pulls his phone from his pocket, and jerks his head toward the hall. "Come on, let's get ready for practice."

I push to my feet and grab my bag. I hike it over my shoulders and head downstairs as James goes to his room to collect his things. I open the fridge, and there's a little sticky note stuck to the pot. I rip it off and my heart lurches as I read it.

A hearty soup to help keep your carbs up.

I crinkle the note in my palms and I'm about to shove it into my pocket when James steps into the kitchen, and asks, "What do you think she meant by that?"

Sweet fuck, he really doesn't want to know.

I shrug, and toss the note onto the counter. "She's your sister, you tell me."

He angles his head, and stares at me and I try not to flinch. "She's your sister too."

Yeah, no.

I nod, because Cass is anything but a sister to me. "Actually, I'm her boyfriend," I say.

"Seems like this whole pretend thing is working on Stefan."

"You think?"

"He offered to help her out with the fundraiser, didn't he? He's obviously interested." He turns and heads toward the door. I follow him down the hall, anger flaring through my blood.

"That's kind of fucking messed up, don't you think?"

"A guy wanting what another guy has? That's human nature, Braden. Just like all the cheerleaders want you during football season."

"That's fucked up too," I grumble. Jesus, I just want someone to want me for who I am. I'm beginning to believe that girl doesn't exist. We head to the field and make our way inside for a team meeting. We all take a seat and Coach talks to us and goes over some plays, and we watch a video of the team we'll be playing on the weekend. Once that's done, we all get changed and head to the field.

The lights over the field come on and I try to keep my focus on the game, and not on Cassidy and Stefan, and how they might be cozying up in the student union building. I stretch out, and put all my focus into my plays as we run drills. Once we're done, the coach whistles and we all line up for a scrimmage. I funnel all my rage about Jonny and all my want for Cassidy into my game, and when the ball lands in my hands, I run my fucking ass off to get a touchdown. But no matter how hard I run, I can't run away from the things I feel for Cass.

My teammates go wild as I slam the ball into the ground and throw my arms up in the air. Coach waves his finger for me to get back into formation for another play. Our quarterback, Jaxon, calls the play, and tosses me the ball. I quickly scan the field and do a clean pass to Mason, who manages to carry it four yards.

I'm not sure what's going on, but I'm really on my game tonight. We continue to play and I continue to kick ass, and I'm drenched and exhausted but exhilarated all at the same time. Coach blows his whistle for us to bring it all in and I tug my helmet off and head toward the locker room. I pass by Coach Meyers.

"Braden, you're really on," he says. "Bring that to the field on Saturday night."

I nod. "Will do."

"Jesus Christ, Braden, what the fuck has gotten into you?" Jaxon asks as he throws his arm around me. "You were lightening tonight, and your throws were dead on."

Mason catches up to us. "I think the question is, what has he *not* gotten into." Mason wags his brow. "If you know what I mean."

"Yeah, we all know what you mean, Mason." I roll my eyes.

"If no pussy makes you play like a machine, maybe we should all try it." Jaxon glances at James. "What do you think, James?"

As James looks at me, something dark and suspicious in his eyes, I'm pretty sure I don't want to know what he thinks.

19

CASSIDY

I smooth my hand over my dress, and set my phone down as Stefan pulls the doors open and steps into the student union building. I glance at him over my laptop, take in his perfectly put together appearance, and put on my best debutante smile. I'm glad Stefan got to the bottom of whoever drugged me. It's nice to know that he was trying to take care of me that night.

"Hey," I say, in a musical voice that I don't recognize. He smiles at me, his gait confident as he strides across the room, his backpack slung over one shoulder.

"Hey gorgeous." He glances around, as if to see who else is in the building, but we're currently alone. It was noisy at the party and hard for us to talk, so tonight is my chance to show him who I really am. Well, not really. I'm going to showcase my debutante side, the side that would make a good princess.

The side you hate, Cass.

"Were you here long?" he asks.

"Not long," I fib. Yeah, I was here on time, unlike him. But I put my time to use and started writing out bios for the guys. I'm so glad they're all onboard for the auction. Well, all except Braden. He hates the idea. But he's doing it for me, and that's so sweet of him.

"Sorry for making you wait." He slides his fingers through his longish hair and pushes it back off his forehead. Unlike Braden, who has a few scars on his face from football and his bout of acne when he was fourteen, Stefan's face is as smooth as a baby's bottom. "I got a little tied up."

"Not a problem." I turn my laptop toward him so he can see what I'm working on. "I got a lot done, actually."

He glances at the computer screen and checks out the bios for Jaxon, the Falcons infamous quarterback, that I just typed up. He grins as he reads through it and I'm glad he finds it amusing. That's what I was going for.

"What do you think?" Geez, fishing for compliments much? Speaking of fishing. My mind drifts back to when Braden fished me from the lake when someone tossed me in and later when he caressed my chest with vapor rub. A fine shiver goes through my body as it recalls the feel of those big palms coming so close to my nipples that night. And honestly, I never thought he was 'fishing' for compliments when I told him he was hot. Braden is hot. If a girl can't see that, she must be blind, but he's so much more than his hotness. He's the nicest guy I know.

"You've got mad skills, Cass." He makes a fist and lightly nudges my jaw. "You make Jaxon sound like a superstar. Maybe you should do this for the rowing team."

Excitement goes through me. Maybe I'm finally good at something. "I could probably—"

"I'm kidding." He laughs off my enthusiasm. "My family already gave a big donation. No need to waste your time."

Waste my time? Does he think this is a waste of my time?

I like helping out the team, and for the first time ever, I felt like I might be good at something. But maybe I'm not. Maybe this is all just stupid. I glance back at my screen. "I expect Jaxon to bring in a ton of money," I say, my voice lacking the enthusiasm from earlier.

Stefan pulls a chair up beside me and his scent fills my nostrils. I glance at his damp hair. He must have showered just before he came here. He grins at me and goes almost statue-like as I stare—like he's gifting me with a look. I suppose he's used to a lot of female attention. Returning my focus to the job at hand, I hit print on my keyboard and the printer spits out Jaxon's bio.

"These are the players I have left," I tell him and slide my notebook over so he can see the list.

He quickly scans it. "You haven't done Braden yet?"

"Saving the best for last," I say, playing into our ruse. He nods, and it's easy to tell he has something to say. "What?"

Blue eyes leave the list and meet mine. "How long have you two been together?"

I wave my hand. "I've known Braden my whole life."

"Yeah, but how long have you guys been together, you know as a couple?" he pushes at my non-answer.

"It's fairly new," I tell him. I point to the list. "So what I've been doing is reading their bios on the Falcons website and pulling up some stats to list in the bio. It's actually kind of fun." He looks at me like I might be insane. "What?" I ask again.

He laughs. "If you want to take my donation and forget about all this, we can get out of here and I'll show you what real fun is."

My stomach sinks a bit. He thinks what I'm doing is stupid. "No, I want to do this for the team, and for...me."

He shakes his head. "Okay, let's get this done then."

A moment later, he produces his laptop and sets it on the table. He brings up the Falcons website and starts reading about the players.

Curiosity gets to me. "What...what do you do for fun?"

"Lots of things." His leg brushes mine beneath the table, and it's odd. The touch fails to arouse anything in me.

"Such as?"

He stretches his long legs out. "I like movies, parties, rowing. Things like that."

A couple of girls come into the building. Their eyes go big as they glance at Stefan and me. Whispered words follow as they take a seat at one of the tables and open their laptops.

I lower my voice and ask, "Do you like it here at Kingston?"

"Yeah, my brother loved it. He highly recommended it, and I have no regrets. Here I don't have paparazzi documenting my every move."

I never thought about that before. Maybe his life isn't so perfect after all. "That must be hard."

He tugs on one of my curls, which I spent far too long getting just right. No ponytail for tonight. "I'm just glad you and I can hang out without starting rumors."

"Rumors?"

"You know, like we're secretly seeing each other behind Braden's back. Speaking of rumors..." He leans into me. "Are they true about Braden?"

"Are what true?"

"That he doesn't have sex during the football season."

"Yeah, that's true," I say, but I don't really want to talk about that with Stefan. It feels invasive, despite the fact that the entire campus must know. Still, I would never do anything to break Braden's trust.

He shifts closer and puts his arm on the back of my chair. "I don't know how he does it. If you were my girl, I'd be all over you." His gaze drops to my mouth, and I suck in my bottom lip.

"Well, uh...it's important to him, and he has a strong will." What am I even saying?

"Yeah, well if you were mine, I'd put you and your needs first and foremost."

"Braden is a good guy," I blurt out. I don't like that he thinks Braden is selfish, and doesn't think about me. If he only knew exactly what the guy was doing for me...although I can't very well tell him.

"Yeah, I'm sure he is."

Needing to change the subject, I say, "So, your brother. I didn't really know him when he went here, but he's married now, right?"

He grins. "Yeah, he and Bianca are super happy. She's pregnant."

My jaw drops with that announcement. "Really?"

He nods. "Why are you so surprised?"

"I don't know. I guess it just seems so fast to me."

He leans toward me, his shoulder brushing mine as he takes another peek at my notebook, running his finger along the list of guys. "Not really. An heir is expected in the first year of marriage in my family."

God, I can't even imagine bringing a kid into the world this young. Bianca just graduated. I didn't know her well, but she didn't seem like the type of girl to settle so quickly.

"Does she...what does she do in Sweden? She was in Kingston's PR program. Has she put it to good use?"

"She doesn't need to work, Cass. She has everything she needs. But yes, she's putting her degree to good use by having the best parties for her husband."

My mother's words bounce around inside my brain as Stefan starts typing into a document on his laptop. I'm not sure I'd consider hosting parties for her husband putting her degree to good use. I think I might want to do something more meaningful, like raising funds for the football team, or even the women's shelter. As that idea jumps into my brain, a bubble of excitement wells up inside me. What a great way for me to give back.

"Do you want kids?" I ask.

"Of course, how about you?"

"Yeah, sure. I guess." Wow, way to sound enthusiastic. Stefan arches a brow and I inject excitement into my voice when I add, "Well, of course I want kids."

Someday…well into the future.

"My parents will want my wife to have kids, sooner rather than later."

"Do you always do what is expected of you?"

"When it comes to family and obligations, yes, of course."

He's so deadpan, for a second I think he's kidding me and I wait for the punchline. When none comes, I say, "My mother would love you." I never did what was expected of me. I'm not sure I have that in me.

"Speaking of mothers, mine will be here in a couple of weeks and I'll be flying back home with her for the weekend."

"Oh, that's so nice, Stefan. It will be nice to do some sight-seeing with her in So Cal."

"She's actually here to rent the country club…"

"Oh, that's when you…"

"Choose a princess? Yes."

God, I really do feel like a contestant on the Bachelor.

"Mother has to meet and approve of her, naturally."

"Why?"

He laughs like that's a silly question. "Our brides have many duties and obligations. She wants to make sure I pick appropriately. Our lifestyle isn't for everyone."

If Kate and I are in the running, I don't stand a chance…She's a girl who knows how to talk the talk and walk the walk. I'm a girl who wears jeans and T-shirts and my idea of a dinner party is a pizza and beer.

"Stefan, why the rose ceremony?" I ask, genuinely curious.

He chuckles. "My brother has a flair for the dramatic and watches too many American television shows. He loves everything about the culture and wanted an American bride."

"Oh, I see. Why are you doing the same, though?"

"Why not? He had fun and he said I would have fun too."

"Are you?"

He winks at me. "Getting to know you is fun."

"I have a boyfriend," I state, and it comes out rather sharp.

He eyes me. "I'm well aware of that."

"Your brother gave a rose to a girl who had a boyfriend."

"If Bianca and her ex-boyfriend were meant to be together, she wouldn't be married to Jonas, now would she?"

"Is that sort of like saying fate had a hand in it?"

"Something like that." He stares at his laptop and taps the desk with his thumb. "How does this sound?" He turns his laptop my way. "Probably lame compared to yours."

"I'm sure it will be fine. Kate said you were a great writer." Why the hell am I bringing up Kate?

"Speaking of Kate," he says without lifting his head. He focuses on his screen as he nonchalantly adds, "I ran into her on the way over here."

My back instantly stiffens. "Oh yeah."

"She was on her way to the field for practice. We talked about the auction. I think she's bidding on Braden."

My heart lurches. "What?"

"She said something about wanting to help out and since you couldn't bid on him, she would." His lips twist, like what he's about to say next might sour his stomach—or mine. "I think she might be into your guy, Cass."

My brain spins. Okay, wait this is good, right? This keeps her away from Stefan, and gives me more time with him. But Kate and Braden? I can't even imagine. Maybe she's going after him because she thinks he's mine. God, does she have to win everything over me? The competitiveness in me rises to new heights and I don't miss the way Stefan is staring at me, waiting for a response.

"That's nice of her to help out like that," I say casually, not wanting to come off as a crazy jealous bitch, which I might very well be.

"You're not jealous."

I'm disgustingly jealous. But I have no right to be. Braden can be with whoever he wants. What's between us is fake.

"I trust Braden."

"Yeah, but do you trust Kate?"

No!

With my stomach in knots, I nod and say, "Kate and I go way back." He arches a brow at my non-answer, the second time in minutes—and I turn back to my computer, but all my concentration is gone. I can't write creatively when my thoughts are on Braden and Kate, and how he could be giving her a piggyback ride to the locker rooms right this very minute.

"Want to get out of here?" Stefan asks.

I take a deep breath. I should get this done, but I'm suddenly too worked up and if I'm going to get to know Stefan and impress him, I should probably get out of the student union building, and show him my fun side.

"Yeah, okay." I close my laptop, and Stefan jumps up. I shove my laptop into my bag and he does the same. "Where are we going?"

"It's a surprise." I eye him and he laughs. "Come on, you'll like it. I promise."

We head outside and the night air is cooler. I cross my arms and rub them, wishing I was in jeans and a T-shirt, not some stupid dress fit for a princess. He walks close to me down the path that leads to the lake, and takes a key from his pocket when we reach what looks like a storage building that I've never been in.

He slides his key into the lock and swings open the doors to reveal the rowing team's boats. I peak in. "Are we allowed in here?"

He smirks. "Worried about getting into trouble?"

"Yeah."

"Such a good girl. I like that, but don't worry, Cass. You're with me."

"Aren't we breaking the rules, though?"

He steps into the building and flicks on the light. I stand still, hesitant to follow him. "Most rules don't apply to me, and when you're with me, they don't apply to you either."

Nervousness curls through me. "I don't want to do anything that will jeopardize my education—or yours."

"Trust me, this is fine. There's nothing I can't get out of if I throw a little money at it."

He tugs one of the big boats outside and I'm not really sure if I want to do this. "I'm not really dressed for this."

"You're dressed perfectly fine." I cautiously follow him to the water, and he holds his hand out to me. "Let me help."

"I've never been in one of these before. What if I tip it?"

"All you have to do is sit and look good, Cass. I'll do the rest."

Once again, feeling like I'm a contestant on the Bachelor, I give him my hand and he holds me steady as I climb in and sit, adjusting my dress around my body so I don't flash him under the moonlight.

"I'm not a very good swimmer if we tip."

"Relax. I'm a great swimmer and we're not going to tip. I know what I'm doing." He sits facing me, and puts the oars over the sides of the boat, taking us deeper into the lake. I glance up at the night sky and take in all the stars.

"Gorgeous," I murmur as I try to relax.

"Very," he says, and I glance at him to find him looking at me.

"So this is what you do for fun?"

"Among other things."

I nod and struggle for interesting conversation. What can I talk about? It's not like we have anything in common. "Are you enjoying your courses?" God, I'm not even sure what he's studying, or why.

"Business management," he says, like he can read the question on my face. "Pretty boring."

"What do you want to do with your degree?" Braden is taking accounting so he can fall back on it if he doesn't make it into the NFL.

"After college, I'll return home and take up my duties to my family."

"That sounds interesting." I want to ask what those duties are, but don't want to come off as stupid.

"I'll be working as a charitable entrepreneur."

I perk up. "Oh, that is interesting. I volunteer at the women's shelter here in town."

He nods. "Very impressive. Great to pad your resume."

Honestly, while that's true, there are other reasons to volunteer. I'm well aware that I grew up with privilege, and with privilege comes advantages. I want to give back. Nothing makes me happier than putting a smile on Lacey's face.

"I really like it. There's this little girl Lacey who I adore. I brought her and her little friends a bunch of dresses, and a tiara, from my pageantry days," I say. "They were so excited." I snort out a laugh and catch myself. "The other day she asked if I was going to marry a prince. They obviously heard talk that there was a prince at Kingston. They would die if they met you." *Okay, stop rambling, Cassidy.* "Just a few seconds ago I decided I'd do a fundraiser for the place. Maybe a silent auction. Contact a few stores for donations..."

Oh my God, shut up already?

He arches a brow. "And your answer."

"My answer?"

"She asked you if you were going to marry a prince. What did you say?"

"Oh, well, I had to say yes, she looked so hopeful, and I didn't want to say anything to upset her. I think all little girls grow up dreaming about marrying their very own Prince Charming."

He leans into me, his blue eyes glistening beneath the moonlight. Being the sole focus of his attention should thrill me, not send fight, or flight sensations rocketing through my body.

"Did you?"

20

BRADEN

The Growler is packed tight and alive with excitement. Why wouldn't it be? Cass is on stage, getting ready to auction us off, and tonight's fundraiser is supposed to be well...fun. I think I might be the only downer in the crowd, not just because I hate everything about this, but because Cass has been acting strange and distant all week, and I fucking miss her.

What have you gotten yourself into, Braden?

The truth is, I've barely seen her since she's gotten together with Stefan to do up the bio cards last week—not long after I put my fingers in her and she left her sweet scent all over my bed. I thought I was going to see her later that night, and I waited, only to receive a text telling me it was too late to come over—James would have been suspicious—and she wasn't wrong.

Throughout the week, she came to the house to make dinner, keeping up her end of the deal. Once completed, she'd disappear and not even stay to enjoy the meal with us. Maybe

Stefan is giving her all the attention she wants and maybe she doesn't need me anymore. Or maybe I'm being a complete asshole baby, and she's been busy with school, the fundraiser and her volunteering.

A glass is thrust into my hand and I turn to find James. "Thanks," I say and take a big drink, swallowing nearly half the contents in one gulp.

James takes a swig of his own beer. "You looked like you could use it."

"Yeah."

He goes quiet, thoughtful, and I shift, not wanting him to read my thoughts. When Jaxon suggested we all remain celibate, I had a feeling James knew more than he was saying. But Cass and I have been careful. There's no way he can know what we've been doing behind closed doors, right?

He angles his head and I brace myself. "You okay, Braden?"

"Fine," I say and gesture to Cass on stage. "Let's just get this over with."

He nudges me with his shoulder, as I spot Kate moving through the crowd toward us. "Come on. It won't be so bad, will it?" he asks.

Just then Chloe comes running up to me and jumps on my back. I curse as I spill my drink all over my button-up dress shirt. Yes, Cassidy wanted us in our best clothes tonight and since I'd do anything for her, I even ironed my shirt.

"Oops, sorry," Chloe says and giggles in my ear. I arch my brow at James, everything in my look suggesting, yes, it will be bad. "I'll grab some napkins." I'm about to tell her it's fine, but she dashes off and comes back with a handful of napkins to dry me. She pats them against my shirt, and when she gets close to my dick, the hairs on my neck tingle. I lift my head to find Cass watching us closely. She frowns and looks a little lost, or dazed, or...something I can't quite put my finger on. Stefan jumps on the stage and puts his hand on the small of her back as he leans in to speak to her. Anger and jealousy flare through me and it's all I can do not to go up there and lay claim to my girl.

She's not your girl, dude.

A big smile lights her face as Stefan stays close, whispering in her ear, and my fingers fist, nearly breaking the cup in my hand.

Fuck me.

"What did that cup ever do to you?" James asks.

I shake my head. "Just thinking about last night's game."

"You killed it out there, Braden. Is that really what's got you so worked up?"

"Yeah." I put my hand over Chloe's to stop her from running the napkin all over me. "I'm good," I tell her.

"Yeah, you are and I'm going to bid on you, Braden," Chloe tells me.

"Hey," Kate says her nose crinkled as she steps up to me. "Chloe, I think Miranda was looking for you."

"Oh, don't go anywhere Braden, I'll be right back."

I'm about to tell her that I have a girlfriend, but what's the point? I can't stop her from bidding on me. I turn to Kate. "Help me."

"I just did. Miranda wasn't looking for her."

I laugh, despite everything. I think Kate is one of the good ones. Too bad Cass is always in fierce competition with her.

She puts her hand on my shoulder. "Don't worry, Braden. I'll outbid her and I'll use the spa passes myself if you don't want to go."

I put my hand over hers and squeeze. "Thank you." I lift my head, once again feeling Cassidy's eye on me, but when I find her on the stage, she's deep in conversation with Stefan. Guess I was wrong. I take a minute to admire her confidence as she gets ready for the auction. She's definitely in her element tonight and it looks good on her. So does the sweater dress that hugs her at mid-thigh, and boots that come over her knees. She's stunning, outshining every other woman in the room. Then again, she could be in a potato sack and I'd still think she looks amazing.

"What do you think?" James asks me.

I tear my gaze away from his sister and hope he hadn't caught me ogling her. "About?"

"Stefan and Cassidy. They make quite the couple, don't they?"

I hold back what I really want to say. Maybe James has taken one too many hits to the head on the field. How can he think they make a good couple, or that his sister should be with a douche bag like Stefan? I'm beginning to believe I don't know James at all anymore...that I don't even know his sister. Why is everyone changing before my eyes? I don't like it. Not one little bit.

I drink what's left in my cup and set it on the bar. Cassidy taps the microphone, and I drop down onto a stool as she brings Derek, her first victim—or rather, baller—up on stage.

Stefan hands her a card from the pile in his hand, and as she begins to read his bio, the girls in the crowd go wild.

Joker that Derek is, he begins to pose, and even I begin to laugh. James leans against the bar beside me as the bids get higher and higher. I glance around, and for a second I think I see Jonny (Red) in the crowd. The guy's got some fucking nerve showing up here. I push off my stool and go in search of him, ready to toss him out of the bar. The crowd is packed so tight it's hard to move. Thank God I'm taller than most here. I glance over their heads and spot Jonny in the hall. He's talking to someone with a blue Kingston ballcap on their head, but I can't tell who it is. All I know is I have a bad feeling mushrooming in my stomach.

I squeeze past a group of screaming women. By the time I reach the hall, it's completely overcrowded, and Jonny is nowhere to be found. I don't see anyone in a blue Kingston ballcap, either. I turn and Chloe is right there. She jumps onto me and wraps her legs around my body. My hands instantly go to her ass before she falls.

"Chloe, what are you doing?"

"You're up. Cassidy has been calling your name. Didn't you hear her?"

"No."

"What are you doing in the hallway?"

"Nothing." Maybe Jonny wasn't here. If he had half a brain cell, he'd be hiding out in his house. She slides off my body, grabs my hand and drags me through the crowd. Cassidy gives me a smile as her eyes meet mine, and it feels like she's miles away from me—emotionally. What went on that night with her and Stefan?

She crooks her finger and calls me onto the stage and the crowd goes crazy. I fucking hate this. Every muscle in my body tightens, and she frowns. "You don't have to—"

"It's fine."

She hesitates for a second before turning to Stefan. He hands her a card, and she looks a little torn as she silently reads it over.

"Cass," I begin.

"Yeah."

"You're doing great. Everyone here is having a good time, and you're really good at this. Now, make me sound as good as you made Derek sound. I want to bring in the most money tonight."

A big smile lights up her face. "Competitive much?"

"You're one to talk." I'm actually kind of worried that two things are driving her actions where Stefan is concerned. One, her mother, and two, her need to win something over Kate, and that's just messed up.

"True." She shakes her head, a new kind of sadness moving across her face. "One of these days I'm going to come out on top, B."

"Maybe all those other times weren't meant to be," I say, assuming she's talking about her pageant days, and not making the cheerleading team. "You're a winner, and in this game Stefan is playing, you're the prize, Cass, don't ever forget that." She cocks her head. "What?"

"You're not the first one to tell me that."

"Then you'd better believe it." She's about to bring the mic to her mouth, and I put my hand on her arm to stop her. I don't miss the way my body reacts to touching her, nor do I miss the little hiss of breath she exhaled. "Nice guys don't always finish last, Cass."

"Are you saying I'm nice?"

"The nicest, and don't ever change...for anyone."

She snorts a little and it's so adorable, I press my lips to hers for a kiss without thinking about it first.

Her fingers go to her lips and her eyes go wide. She casts a fast glance at Stefan, and it's a reminder of what we're really doing here. "What was that for?"

"Can't a guy kiss his girlfriend before she auctions him off and sends him on a date with another girl?" Her gaze sinks to the floor, and once again she has that strange, almost lost look on her face. I touch her chin and lift it until her eyes are on mine.

"Let's kick ass."

I grin at her and it brings her smile back. With the mic to her mouth, she introduces me and Chloe starts jumping up and down. I seek Kate out with pleading eyes and she nods at me. Cass reads off my very impressive bio, and I nearly choke on my tongue when she brings up the Halloween that I went out with her and her brother as ketchup. Everyone gets a kick out of it, and I give her a look that suggests she's going to pay for that later. She laughs, hard, and it lightens my mood. I love seeing Cass happy and in her element. Her future is definitely in public relations, not in being a party planning socialite princess. But that's just my opinion and it clearly holds no weight.

A few of the girls begin the bidding, and Chloe jumps up on one of the tables and waves her arms in the air as she ups the bid. The bouncer steps up to her and hauls her off and she kicks up a stink, but Cass continues. Kate bids on me, and I don't miss the way Cass stiffens beside me, but she recovers quickly and continues to incite the crowd, getting them all excited.

She waves an envelope in the air. "Come on, we can do better than that, can't we. A spa date with this guy," she says and holds her arms out and waves them up and down the length of me.

Someone bids and once again Kate outbids them and I'm eternally grateful. Beside her, James is talking to Becca and I can't see them well, or hear what they're saying, but it seems to be a very important conversation. I don't know what's going on with my buddy. One second I think he likes Kate, then the next he's all hush hush with Becca—who has a boyfriend. He's not the kind of guy to steal another guy's girl, though... right? He's not Stefan. Maybe I should have a word with him anyway.

"Looks like Kate is the winner," Cass says into the microphone, and it pulls my thoughts back.

"Thank God," I say under my breath and scrub my chin as I smile at Kate. She gives me two thumbs up and I give her two back.

Cass puts the microphone back in the cradle. "It seems like you knew she was going to bid on you," she says, her voice so low I have to strain to hear.

"Yeah, she's helping me out."

Her mouth twists. "I bet she is," she shoots back.

"What's that supposed to mean?"

"Nothing."

I narrow my eyes, dip my head, and take in her body language. "Cass, you sound like you're jealous."

"Of course I'm not jealous," she hisses and stands closer to me, her words for my ears only. "You can go out with anyone you want." She waves a dismissive hand, and I'm pretty sure we're having our first couples quarrel—in front of everyone. Well, we would be if we were a real couple, and Jesus, I'm on this stage for her. I want to tell her why Kate bid on me, how she's saving me from Chloe and the other girls, but Cass presses the tickets into my stomach, turns her back to me and calls up her brother.

What the actual fuck?

I exit the stage and when I turn back, she's staring at me. Okay, one of two things are going on here. She's staging a fight for all to see, so she can break up with me so she's free for Stefan, or she's actually jealous. Jealousy would mean she's into me every bit as much as I'm into her.

Is the latter wishful thinking on my part, or could it be true?

Maybe it's time I found out.

21

CASSIDY

I wake after a restless sleep and stretch as I glance at the clock. My thoughts instantly go to Braden, as they usually do, and my stomach tightens as a groan crawls out of my throat. I haven't been avoiding him...much. Okay, I have been. It's totally true. But what choice did I have? After my night out on the boat with Stefan, it occurred to me that I'm having real feelings for my brother's best friend, and he's only in this to help me out. He's a nice guy and would do anything for James and me. Now...now I think he's falling for Kate, and I don't know how I feel about that. Okay, I do know, and I freaking hate it.

Pull yourself together, girl.

I pound the bed, and hate the way I treated him last night. God, I shoved the tickets into his stomach and basically told him to leave and leave he did—with my frenemy. How did this get so messed up? I don't know, but I figured avoidance was my best course of action, and today, his sister is coming for a visit and staying with me, so there is no way I can keep running the other way. I'm sure he must be totally confused by my erratic behavior. He probably has whiplash from my mood swings.

I kick the covers off, my mood dark and confused as I pull myself up to a sitting position and glance around. While I'd like to sit here and mope and feel sorry for myself, I have to pick up Lauren at the bus stop in a half an hour, and then I have a full day of events planned, followed by a football game and a girls' night in to watch some chick flicks. My phone pings, and I pick it up to see a message from Braden.

Braden: Heard from Lauren, and her bus should be here around eleven.

Me: Yup, I'm on it. Going to shower, eat and walk to the bus stop to meet her.

Braden: Okay, I'll be there shortly to walk with you.

Me: It's okay. I can get her. You probably have a lot to do today.

Braden: Do you not want me to come Cass?

Leave it to Braden to come right out and ask. His honesty is one of the things I love most about him—until today.

Me: No, it's not that. I just thought you were busy. Sure, come on by and we'll go together.

Braden:

His little happy face makes me smile and I just shake my head as I make my way to the shower, where I'm not going to spend one second thinking about the time Braden joined me, washed me and then gave me a ridiculously intense orgasm.

Nope, not one second at all...because it will be more like one minute or two. Groaning, I shower, dry and tug on my shorts and a T-shirt. I'm about to make some coffee when a knock comes on my door.

I open it to find Braden standing there, and my knees give a little at the mere sight of him. God, he's so rough and rugged on the field, and so soft and tender with my body. As I stare, he holds a paper cup out to me, and I can't help but think I want him again—all of him.

"You brought me coffee."

"Americano."

I breathe in the delicious aroma. "You are the most awesome guy in the world."

"Most awesome boyfriend, you mean."

I smile. "Yeah, that's what I mean."

Before I can open the tab and take a sip, Braden kicks the doors shut behind him and presses his lips to mine. At first I'm surprised, but he tastes so good, I sink into his kisses, and a little moan catches in my throat. His tongue finds mine, and he takes the cup from my hand and sets my coffee as well as his on the table, and spins me around until I'm pressed up against the door, his arms pinning my hands above my head.

Okay, this is new, and I like it.

He presses against me, his hard cock indenting my stomach and an awful, horrible thought hits. Did he get all worked up from being with Kate, and come to work out his sexual frustrations on me? I freeze a bit, and he inches back. He lightly brushes my face with his knuckles.

"Everything okay, Cass?"

"Yeah, everything is okay." Liar, liar, pants on fire.

He presses his head against mine. "I have to tell you something."

Oh, God. I brace myself, and prepare for bad news. "What is it?"

"My practices are going great. I've been playing better than I've ever played before."

"Really? That's great news."

His warm breath falls over my face as he exhales. "I think...I think it's the sex we've been having."

I can't help but grin. "So, contrary to what you believe, sex is making you a better player this season."

"Everyone is noticing the difference, the coach, the QB...your brother. They're all talking about going celibate. Jesus, can you imagine?"

"No, not really," I say with a chuckle. "I don't think any of them have the ability to do that. I like that you do, though."

"Well, I haven't really been celibate, now have I?"

"We've not gone all the way. So in my book, you're still holding your convictions close."

"That's logic at it's worst, Cass."

We both laugh at that and while I like this intimate conversation we're having, like the way he's standing close, I say, "We need to get to the bus stop. I don't want your sister lost on campus."

"You're right." He keeps me pinned to the door a little longer. "I want to finish this tonight."

"You have a game tonight."

"After the game."

"But Lauren will be here."

"She has to sleep sometime." Why am I making excuses? I want this. I want to finish what he's started here. If I do, though, I'm afraid it's going to pull me in deeper. "Do you want me again, Cass?"

"Yes," I admit. "Especially if it's going to help your game." I give a stupid unlady like snort. "And of course, I still need lessons. It's a win/win, hey?"

He frowns, and inches back and I immediately miss his warmth. "Yeah," is all he says as he shoves his hands into his pant pockets.

My stomach sinks. What, did I expect him to say he wanted me for other reasons? That he's not falling for Kate, but is falling for his best friend's kid sister?

Grow the hell up, Cass.

He clears his throat. "When does Stefan give out the roses?"

"The what?" I blink, and lightly shake my head, hoping to get it on right so I can understand what it is Braden is trying to say to me.

"The roses...his princess."

"Right, um, soon. His mother will be arriving in a couple of weeks, and they rent out the country club and all the girls are invited. Apparently, she has to approve. It's all a bit strange. Why do you ask?"

"Just curious. We'd better get going."

He reaches for our coffees and hands mine to me. I pull the tab back and take a drink. It was really thoughtful of him to pick me up my favorite morning drink. Outside, we walk to the bus stop, and we're both quiet. It's nice, though. The quiet doesn't feel strained, and I don't feel the need to engage in conversation. We can both just be silent in the presence of one another.

"I thought Lauren might want to go to the women's shelter with me tomorrow. Her bus doesn't leave until the afternoon and I thought she might like to see the little girls and learn about giving back to the community."

"That's a great idea. I think she'll love that."

"Last night's auction went so well, I was thinking about doing something for the shelter. The nights are getting colder and the holidays will soon be upon us. I could raise money for warm clothing and toys."

A smile touches his mouth, and I don't miss the appreciation in his eyes. "You want to do an auction for them?"

I take a sip of coffee and nod. "Maybe a silent auction."

"I think it's great. I can help. Whatever you need. I can even hit up the local stores for donations if you want."

My heart squeezes. I love that he's so willing to jump in both feet instead of throwing money at my idea. "You don't think that's stupid, do you? Like...a waste of time."

"Stupid? Why the hell would I think that's stupid? And how is helping others a waste of time? Who put that idea into your head? You never used to think like that."

"I don't know. I've never really been great at anything, and maybe my ideas—"

"Your ideas are brilliant, Cass. Don't ever think they aren't or let anyone tell you otherwise. The way you pulled that auction together and made it fun. Not a lot of people could pull that off in such a short period of time. When you graduate here, every public relations firm from here to Hawaii is going to want to hire you. Just follow your heart, like you always did when you were young."

I go up on my toes and kiss him just as the bus pulls up, and I push off quickly, not wanting his sister to think we're an item. No sense in confusing her.

The bus doors open, and a few people exit before Lauren. She steps to the ground and Braden picks her up and spins her around. My heart swells. She's lucky to have such a loving big brother. Heck, I'm lucky too and I know it. Guilt niggles me. While there is nothing wrong with Braden and me having fun in the bedroom together, my brother wouldn't see it that way. When he asked about Becca and I thought he might be interested, it tested my gag reflexes too. I'm still not sure why he asked. Maybe he was just messing with me. I have noticed them talking a lot more lately, though.

"Cassidy," Lauren yells and throws her arms around me. "I'm so excited about being here. How did the benefit auction go last night?"

I give her a hug and Braden tosses her bag over his shoulder. "It went great," I tell her.

"Don't be modest," Braden says with a grin. "She commanded the room, Lauren, and everyone had fun."

"Not everyone," I say and whack his stomach. Although maybe he did have fun—afterward with Kate. My stupid stomach sours, and Lauren talks a mile a minute. She'd clearly done her research on the college and wants to see everything.

We walk toward my sorority, and she stops outside the building. "I love everything about this sorority," she says. "This is where I want to live."

"It's a great place. After the game tonight, we can come back and have a girls' night. Becca is going to join us."

She claps her hands. "Yay, I love Becca. I'm so excited." She steals a glance around at the lush campus grounds. "My friends are all so jealous that I might get to meet Stefan."

"You'll get to meet him. I promise."

"Really?"

"For sure." I take a fast glance at Braden. He's gone quiet, and I'm guessing he doesn't like the idea of his sister meeting Stefan. At least he doesn't think Stefan was responsible for roofie-ing me anymore. But I'm smart enough to know he's still doesn't like him.

Do you like him, Cassidy?

"If you want, you can do a girls' night at my place. We have the big screen, and a fully stocked fridge."

Lauren looks at me, waiting for an answer. "Hey, whatever you want to do. This weekend is all about you."

"I'd love to see the sorority, but a big screen and stocked fridge sounds great."

"That's what we'll do then."

Braden kisses his sister on the forehead. "You two have fun, and we'll catch up after the game, okay?"

He walks away, and I turn to Lauren. "How about I give you a tour of the house? Afterward, we'll drop your things off at

Braden's place, and I can show you around campus. All the places you want to see."

Instead of answering, she stands there, her eyes wide, her body shaking and I'm almost certain she's having a seizure.

"Lauren," I say quickly and put my hands on her shoulder to check out her pupils, not that I have any idea what I'm looking for. I think I need to get her to the clinic.

"Is that...him?"

I turn my neck so hard, I kink it. The second I set eyes on Stefan strolling our way, Kate beside him, I realize Lauren's not having a seizure, she's star struck.

I lift my hand and wave. "Ohmigod, he's coming this way. What do I do? What do I say?"

I chuckle at her enthusiasm. "Just be yourself, Lauren." It's great advice, and I wonder why I'm pretending to be something I'm not. "He's just a guy like any other guy."

"No, he's not, he's a prince."

Stefan's smile is big and brilliant as he steps up to us.

"Lauren, it's so good to see you," Kate says, and what I hate most about all this is how good Kate looks with Stefan.

I do the introductions and I'm pretty sure Lauren's stopped breathing. Stefan takes her hand and kisses the back.

"I didn't know Braden had such a beautiful sister."

She swoons as he runs his lips over her palm. God, is that what I looked like those first few times I met Stefan?

"She's interested in the PR program, so I thought I'd show her around this weekend, and take her to the game tonight."

"Sounds like fun. I'll see you at the game, then."

"O...kay," she murmurs, her body vibrating.

"I'll see you too, Cassidy," he says, and Kate gives a little finger wave goodbye as they walk away.

"Do you think he's going to pick Kate?" Lauren asks.

"I don't know."

I'm not sure what she heard in my voice that made her jaw suddenly fall open, but as she stares up at me, my phone pings.

"You...you like him, don't you? Oh my God, Cassidy. I think he likes you too. Did you see the look on his face when he said, see you too? He's into you, Cassidy!"

I pull my phone from my pocket and slide my finger across the screen without checking who's calling.

"Cassidy, darling. How are things going?"

"Oh, hi Mom." I cover the phone and tell Lauren it's my mother, and she walks away, and begins taking selfies as she gives me privacy. "Things are good. Braden's sister Lauren is visiting with me this weekend. I'm showing her around."

She goes quiet for a second. "That's lovely, dear, but do you think you have time for that?"

"It's a slow weekend. Mid-terms aren't until next month."

"That's not what I mean."

Yeah, I know...but sometimes I just like to piss her off.

"You should be spending time getting to know Stefan."

I realize my life has been a good one. My parents have always been generous and giving and they think they know what is best for me, but I'm not so sure they're right about this. "What...what if that's not what I want?"

"Of course it's what you want. Who wouldn't want that?"

I'm about to tell her not me, but she continues with, "I talked to Kate's mother yesterday. She said Kate and Stefan have been spending a lot of time together."

"And..."

"Cassidy, you're not going to let her beat you again, are you?"

My throat squeezes so tight I can't seem to breathe. The world goes a little fuzzy as I glance around at all the towering stone buildings—some similar to a castle that a princess would live in.

Maybe I should just keep trying with Stefan. It's not like Braden wants a future with me—sex sure, to help his game— and maybe I will be happy once I marry Prince Charming, and become his childbearing, party-throwing princess.

FML.

22

BRADEN

After playing a kick-ass game of football, knowing my girl and my sister are in the stands watching me, I steal a glance toward them as Chloe jumps on my back for her after game ride into the locker rooms. Okay, technically Cassidy isn't my girl, but damned if I'm not hoping for that outcome. Yes, I will have to deal with her brother, and that's a conversation I'm not looking forward to. I just pray to fuck he doesn't hate me. But I'm getting ahead of myself. As of right now, she's still trying to get a rose from the douche bag prince.

I catch sight of them in the stands, and my pulse pounds when I see Stefan standing there talking to them. With any luck, the more time she spends with him, the more she'll realize he's not the guy for her. I am.

"Hey bro, great game," James says and slaps me on the shoulder. "Maybe you're on to something with your superstitions."

"Yeah, maybe."

Chloe slides off my back when we get inside and runs to meet up with the other cheerleaders.

"So this ruse between you and my sister is definitely working. Stefan can't seem to stay away. He's up in the stands with her now."

"Yeah." I tug my helmet off.

"How do you guys plan to stage the breakup?"

"I don't know. Do you think we have to? Stefan's brother Jonas gave Bianca the rose when she was still dating Carlos. How fucked up and entitled is that?"

"You're not wrong."

I shake my head, confused by James's behavior. "Yet you seem okay with Cassidy marrying a guy like that."

"She's a big girl, like I said. She can make her own decisions in life."

Once again, I wonder what happened to my best friend. This is so not like him. Everyone is acting out of character, and it baffles me.

He chuckles and tugs off his helmet. "You know Cass. If you tell her to do one thing, she'll want to do the other." I stare at him, not really sure what he's getting at. I open my mouth about to ask him if he has a brain tumor or something, and he says, "Let's hit up the Growler."

"Sounds like a plan." We shower, and dress and head out into the night. The atmosphere is lively after a win, and tons of people drive by in cars and honk their horns. My mind is occupied, however, my thoughts on Cassidy as we make our way to the Growler, with everyone congratulating us and giving fist bumps.

Kate catches up to us, and she and James start talking. I hang back a bit, and look around for a quick escape. Would anyone even know if I don't show up? I'd like to turn and head back to my place, but I do want to give the girls time for their girls' night and I'm expected to show up at the Growler, so that's what I'm going to do.

The doors open and I step inside the crowded pub, and a drink is thrust into my hand. The crowd begins to chant my name, and honestly, it's a little embarrassing. I don't love being thrust into the spotlight.

"Enjoy it, bro," James says.

"You know I'm not into this shit."

James laughs and throws his arm around me. We head to the bar, and chat with a few people. Kate comes back, and I excuse myself, fibbing that I'm headed to the little boys' room. With James and everyone else partying, I step out into the night and breathe in the fresh night air. I slowly make my way back to my place, giving the girls time to hang out.

I reach my house and open the door to laughter. I poke my head into the living room and find Cass, Becca and Lauren eating ice cream and watching something on TV.

Cass turns my way, as if she can feel my presence, and a smile lights up her face. My insides warm at the sweet, welcoming greeting.

"What are you doing here?" she asks.

I casually roll my shoulder. "My sister is in town. I thought I'd hang out with you guys."

"And miss the after party?" Becca says, incredulous. "You must really love your sister."

"Yeah," I say and keep to myself that I might love one other girl in the room, too. "What are you watching?"

"Die Hard," Cass says.

"Really?"

"No," she blurts out and Lauren and Becca laugh as Cass throws a cushion at me.

"How naïve are you, brother?" Lauren asks.

Okay yeah, that was a dumbass response. I hope I'm not naïve in believing Cass and I could have an amazing future. What if I am, though? What if I'm in my head too much, making more of this than it really is?

"Anyone need anything in the kitchen?"

"Can you make some popcorn?" Lauren asks, before shoving another spoonful of ice cream into her mouth. I grin. She looks like she's having the time of her life and I really appreciate Cassidy arranging this for her.

I head to the kitchen and opt for a soda instead of a beer. I don't want my judgment clouded in any way tonight. I toss a bag of popcorn into the microwave and when it's done, I dump it into a bowl. As I walk back into the living room I ask, "Okay, what are we really watching?"

"The Princess Diaries."

I roll my eyes so hard I nearly give myself a headache. "Of course you are." I hand the bowl of popcorn to my sister and take a seat beside her at the end of the sofa. I reach into the bowl, grab a fistful of popcorn and shove it into my mouth as I sit back and prepare to be tortured for the next couple hours.

Hours later, after the movie lived up to my torturous expectation, my sister yawns. She was up early getting the bus and she must be exhausted.

"Why don't you take my bed?" I tell her. She was planning on crashing with Cass in her bed, but this way they'll both be more comfortable.

"Where will you sleep?"

"I can crash with James, or take the sofa. Either is fine."

She stands and stretches. "Thanks for today, Cassidy. It was so much fun." Cassidy pushes to her feet and hugs her.

"I had a great time too."

"I wish you were my sister." Her eyes go wide. "If you married Braden, you'd be my sister-in-law and that's like being a sister." Cass's gaze lifts and flickers over my face. I can't tell what she's thinking, which is odd. I can usually read her. "Oh, but you like Stefan and he likes you, and no offense, brother, but no girl in their right mind would choose a baller over a prince."

"Jeez, why don't you tell me what you really think?"

She puts her hand on her hip. "I said no offense."

"Oh, none taken. I'm pretty sure there was a compliment in there somewhere, and it's called trading up, Lauren." I put her in a headlock and lightly run my knuckles over her hair. "Now get to bed. Tomorrow is a busy day for you again."

I let her go and find Cassidy smiling at me. "I should get going too."

I nod my head toward the front door. "I'll walk you guys back."

"No, you should stay here. I don't think you should leave Lauren alone in the house. James knows she's here and won't bring anyone back, but that doesn't mean some random cheerleader won't come banging on the door...for him...or you."

Banging. Yeah, that's what I'd like to be doing right now, with Cass.

"You guys both go. I'll stay here and guard the house and Lauren until James gets back, so no need to hurry home, Braden."

Why do I get the feeling that she's waiting for James? I'm so confused. I have no idea who he wants to be with and who wants to be with him. I do know Becca has a boyfriend, and James would never hone in on another guy's girl—that's Stefan's department.

"Okay, Becs. Talk to you in the morning," Cassidy says.

Becca has her phone in her hand, busy texting someone, with only half her attention on us she says, "K, bye."

We head outside, and we can still hear people partying late into the night. It's always like this after a winning game.

"You did really good tonight," Cass tells me. "Your sister was very proud of you."

"Were you?" Shit, way to sound like a needy asshole.

She purposely bumps me as I walk. "Of course, I was."

"I saw Stefan talking to you guys in the stands." She opens her mouth like she wants to say something but closes it again, clearly changing her mind. "Have you given any thought on how you want to stage a breakup?" I take a breath, hoping like hell she wants to tell me she doesn't want to break up, that she wants this for real.

"No, I'm glad you brought it up. I haven't had much time to think about it, but I'll definitely get on it."

Christ, I really am a dumbass.

"Although I'm not sure it matters," I tell her.

She wraps her hands around herself and I pull her into me, offering her my warmth. My skin has been burning hot since the game, and even hotter after finding Cass on my sofa, spooning ice cream into her mouth. My damn cock has been aching to replace the spoon ever since.

We reach her building, and I head inside with her. Our steps are hurried as we go upstairs and down the long hall leading to the room she shares with Becca. With Becca at my house, however, we have the whole place to ourselves. Damned if I don't want to worship her body again and show her what she means to me—that she's the prize.

We step inside and I close the door and lean against it. She blinks up at me, a new kind of urgency about her as I pull her to me and put her between my spread legs. She quivers, and I lightly brush my thumb over her pouty bottom lip. I dip my head, dying to kiss her, but she speaks and it stops me.

"B?"

"Yeah." Jesus, is she thinking of the breakup? Does she want to do it now?

"What was that you said this morning, about wanting to finish what we started." She moves against me, and I can barely think straight.

My dick instantly hardens and deciding to show her with actions instead of words exactly what I mean, I scoop her up and carry her to her bedroom. I set her on the bed and drop to my knees, positioning myself between her legs.

"Cass," I murmur, and pull her head to mine for a deep, mind-numbing kiss. She kisses me back. It's slow and soft at first, but changes when I put my hands on her sides and slide upward, stretching my thumbs out to caress her hard nipples.

"Braden," she whimpers and breaks the kiss, her head falling back slightly as she takes pleasure in the way I'm touching her. I grip the hem of her shirt and peel it over her head. With a quick flick, I remove her bra and toss her clothes away.

"These," I say and run my hands under her breasts. "Are perfect." Her fingers rake through my hair and she tugs on my head, bringing my mouth to her nipple. God, I love a girl who knows what she wants. I take her bud into my mouth and her moan vibrates through me. "Fucking perfect," I groan around a mouthful of breast.

I suck on her, and her body rocks, clearly needing my atten-tion. I treat her other breast to a lick, before I sit back on my heels and give her an easy push. She falls back on her bed, her hair framing her face, and I instantly go to work on her jeans. I push open the button and she squirms as I tug her jeans to her feet and toss them away. I gaze at her near nakedness and I swear to God, I could sob with joy. How did I get so fucking lucky to have a girl like her in my bed...my life?

"B...please," she cries, and I widen her legs, and push the flimsy fabric covering her hot pussy to the side. I lightly brush her clit.

"Is this what you want, Cass?"

"Yes, God yes."

I play with her wet pussy, sliding the rough pad of my thumb all over her swollen clit until she's writhing like a hot mess. I inch a finger into her, and she tightens around me. She's so close already. Hell, so am I. I've missed her. Missed touching her, kissing her...missed simply being with her.

My finger is so slick, I easily glide in and out. As I continue to finger fuck her, I take her clit into my mouth and suck hard. Catching me by surprise, she comes all over my fingers and her hot juices run down my hand.

"Braden..." she whispers, her voice low and breathless. "More...I want more. I want you to fuck me." I steal a glance up at her, and all coherent thought leaves my brain and drains to my cock. She can't be asking what I think she's asking, right?

Her lids fly open and there's a deep need in her eyes, when she says, "Please..."

And just like that—and let's blame it on the fact that I have no blood in my brain to think—I stand, and tear open my button and zipper. I kick off my pants and shorts in record time and stare at the woman squirming, aching, begging me for me. How can I say no to that? I take my thick cock into my hand and stroke from base to crown, and she cries as she positions herself in the bed.

She widens her legs for me, and I groan as something niggles in the back of my mind. Think, Braden, think. "You're too far away," she murmurs, and I tear off my shirt and climb over her gorgeous naked body. I kiss her, and sink into her warmth as her legs go around my back and squeeze tight. "I want you inside me, Braden."

I take my cock into my hand and brush it over her sex, and she's so hot and ready, I could explode without ever entering her, but she wants me inside, and Cass always gets what she wants—from me.

Her hand slides between our bodies and she touches my cock, pressing it into her sex. "You want me?" I ask, needing desperately to hear that she does.

"Yes, please, B..."

I inch in, and again something niggles at me but it's too far out of reach for me to grasp onto. Pleasure swarms my brain, nothing else matters except this woman and how she wants me inside her. She moves, and her legs tighten around my back, forcing me in deeper. I power forward and she gasps, as I break through her barrier, and that's when I remember she's a virgin. What the fuck am I doing?

I'm about to pull out, yet can't bring myself to do it. Not when she feels so damn good, her body so needy for more. "Cass..."

"Fuck me, Braden," she says, and cups my face, bringing my lips to hers. She rocks her body, and I rotate my hips. Her eyes close and she whimpers into my mouth. Her hips lift, and I pull almost all the way out, and power back in again, going so gloriously deep, I hit her cervix. She moans, and grows wetter. I begin to move with her, our two bodies as one, as we both give and take.

Her hands go to my back and she runs her nails lightly over my skin. I press hot, hungry open-mouthed kisses to her neck as we rock together. My pelvis caresses her clit every time I push deep and she moans and grinds against me. I'm close, so damn close, I don't know if I can hang on. I want this, I want her, but I want this to last forever.

I change the pace and rhythm, hitting the bundle of nerves inside her until she's completely soaked and easily taking my cock. Her breathing changes, becomes rapid and her nails scratch harder on my back. I close my eyes, waiting for her to come around my cock, knowing nothing in life could ever compare to the pleasure it's going to bring me.

"B..." she moans, and I cup her face, stare into her glossy eyes as her body lets go, her liquid heat scorching my dick. She whimpers and claws at me as a powerful quake goes through her body, bringing my orgasm to life. My chest expands, filling with everything I feel for Cass.

"Fuck yes." I grunt, and hold her gaze as I come and come and come some more. Her muscles tighten around me, hold me deep inside her until I'm completely depleted. I pant, and groan, and collapse on top of her, my damp body sated and spent. She hugs me to her, and we stay like that until I grow soft. I inch back, and gaze at the beautiful woman beneath me. I love her. I fucking love her with my entire being.

"Cass," I murmur, and shift to the side. I'm about to pull the blankets up and snuggle in, but stop when I see a bit of blood. Jesus fucking Christ. I just took her virginity. That thought sends shards of guilt through my heart, and my lungs seize as reality slowly creeps back in. "Cass, did I hurt you?"

"No." She cups my cheek, and I take in the dampness in her sleepy eyes. Is she crying? "Cass, I'm..." God, how can saying I'm sorry, ever right this wrong? I should have been stronger, should have left the second after I gave her an orgasm. This was a mistake. A huge fucking mistake that neither of us can ever come back from.

"Let me clean you up."

I can barely walk, or think straight as I stumble to the bathroom and grab some tissues and warm a cloth. That's when another thought hits. I didn't use a condom.

Motherfucker.

I go back to Cassidy, and she's on her side, waiting for me. "Cass," I croak out. "I didn't use a condom."

"It's okay," she says quietly, a hitch in her voice, like it's difficult to speak. Jesus, is she regretting this as much as I am? "I'm on the pill to regulate my periods."

I breathe a sigh of relief. "I'm clean, Cass. I always use a condom. I don't know why..." I shake my head. How did I forget to use a condom? I've never lost it like that before. Keeping my head down, I'm not sure I can look her in the eyes, I wipe away the blood and press the warm cloth to her pussy to soothe her.

"Thank you," she says quietly.

Once I have her clean, I lay beside her, and while there's only an inch of space between us, it might as well be a chasm as she emotionally pulls back. I turn to face her, but she looks the other way, her body stiff, not at all relaxed as it should be after sex, and I get it, she's as upset by this as I am. We both got carried away in the heat of the moment, and I took something that wasn't mine to take. I take all the blame for that. Cass was saving herself for the right guy, and I'm not sure I'm the one. If I was, she wouldn't be so upset at the moment, right?

Could I have fucked things up anymore?

23

CASSIDY

I pinch my eyes shut and try to slow my breathing before I hyperventilate and pass out. I'm not having much luck. Okay, I'm having zero luck. Is it any wonder? I just begged Braden for sex. Begged! Sure, he told me sex was helping with his game. This, though, what we just did, shouldn't have happened. I took things too far and I damn well know it.

Braden might fool around during football season, but he doesn't go all the way. No wonder he'd gone deadly quiet once reality sank back in. God, he can't even look me in the eye. He must hate me. I would if I were him. I certainly hate myself. In my heart, I know he'll always give me what I want, and I asked—pleaded—for the one thing I never should have asked for.

You really fucked things up, Cassidy.

I swallow uneasily, and coward that I am, I roll over and pretend to be asleep. I don't know what else to do. God, I never expected my first time to be so horrible. Correction.

The sex wasn't horrible. Sure, it stung, but it was also intimate, and sweet and loving and my body is still tingling in delicious ways. Everything from the way he touched me told me I was in good hands, and the way he gazed at my body with such appreciation made me feel cherished. He's the guy I wanted to give my virginity to. I'm not trying to justify my actions here. While it was everything I ever dreamed it could be, that doesn't make what I did right.

He moves beside me, shifting to face me, judging by thc heat of his breath on my neck. I get the sense he wants to say something. I'm a hot emotional mess after giving myself to the guy I'm falling for, and I'm not sure I want to hear the disappointment in his words, or see it on his handsome face. Pain slicks through me, flaying my insides open, and it's all I can do not to give in to the tears. If I do, it's going to be a big blowout ugly cry session.

Neither of us move for a long time. I begin to wonder if he's asleep. His breathing hasn't slowed, so I'm guessing he's not. The bed bounces as he puts his hand on my arm, just resting it there. He breaks the quiet, and whispers, "Night, Cass."

The bed dips on his side, and I roll a bit. My throat squeezes so tight it hurts as he shakes out his jeans and climbs into them. Rustling sounds reach my ears, followed by light footsteps, and he sneaks out of my room. As my door closes tight, my heart splinters into a million tiny pieces because I sense he's not just closing the door to my room, he's closing the door on us. Everything in my gut tells me that. Tears I can no longer hold back spill down my face, and I fist my sheets and tug them over my head.

I cry and cry and cry some more, until I have no more tears left to shed. I stay in my bed, his scent all over my sheets, and by the time Becca gets home, well past midnight, I finally fall into a fitful sleep full of bad dreams.

Morning brings rain, and it's a fitting match for my mood. I roll over, wanting more sleep, but it won't come. Maybe I'll go drown myself in a hot shower. I kick the blankets off and tears threaten again at the sight of blood. I put my hand between my legs, recalling the tender way Braden wiped me clean last night. How am I going to make it through the day with his sister visiting? One look at me, and she'll know something went down last night. Something beautiful and horrible at the same time.

I walk quietly to the bathroom and take in the dark smudges under my eyes. Not even a bucket of makeup is going to help with those dark circles. I brush my teeth and shower, hoping to wash the sadness from my skin. Jeez, I didn't even know skin could be sad until today.

After washing with my favorite grapefruit wash that only reminds me of Braden and his hands on my body, I hurry back to my room, check the time, and pull on some comfy clothes. In two hours, we'll be heading to the shelter, and it's going to be damn hard to put a smile on my face. I plunk down on my bed and instantly hate myself. After last night, I already hated myself, but this time it's for a different reason. My heart might be broken, and I forced Braden to do something he didn't want to, but those women and kids at the shelter have it way worse than I do. How selfish can I be?

I stare at my phone. Should I text him? Call him? What is the protocol after having sex with the guy you've fallen for when he's trying to remain celibate and doesn't love you back? Yeah, I'm pretty sure there's no protocol for that.

My phone pings and I jump two feet in the air. I scramble across my bed and grab my cell from my nightstand and my heart jumps into my throat when I see the text is from Braden. I quickly slide my shaky finger across the screen.

Braden: Just wanted to see how you're feeling this morning.

God, he is the sweetest guy on the face of the earth, and I'm a horrible, horrible human being. If he knew what was good for him, he'd run as far away from me as possible. Wait, he already has. Last night he left in more ways than one. I'll never forget how the air had chilled tremendously after we had the best sex of my life, and he walked out and shut the door on me...on us. Yes, I know, it was the only sex I've ever had. I'm still positive everything else will pale in comparison. I run my fingers over the screen.

Me: I'm good. How are you?

I stare at the screen. Is that lame? Should I be apologizing? I start texting and stop as three dots appear. Breathing deep, the world closes in on me as I wait for his words. They finally come and my heart stops.

Braden: Sorry about last night.

Oh, God, he's sorry. Sorry that I begged him and made him do something he didn't want to do. Tears pool in my eyes and one falls, splashing on my screen and blurring out his words. I swipe it away, and struggle to find the right response.

Me: I made a mistake. I'm sorry.

There. Honest, clean and simple. I hold the phone so tight, I'm sure I'm going to snap it in half. I sit silently waiting, hoping he'll forgive me for my mistake. Three dots finally appear, and I hold my breath.

Braden: Lauren wants to know what time she should be at your place.

Is that it? It's over and done with and we're going to forget it ever happened and simply move on. I guess there is a protocol after all. I take in a huge breath, fill my lungs, and message him back.

Me: Anytime. She can come hang out if she wants. We leave for the shelter at one.

Braden: It's raining. I'll drive.

I'm about to say no until I glance out my window. It rarely rains here, but when it rains, it pours. Sort of like my life right now.

Me: That's nice of you. Thanks.

Braden: I ran into Kate last night, and she offered to introduce Lauren to some cheerleaders and show her around the gym and practice room this morning. Is that okay with you?

Me: Yes, of course. Whatever Lauren wants. She's interested in cheerleading, so that's awesome.

Awesome, my ass. I swipe at a stupid tear. I never know if Kate is being nice, or just trying to one up me on everything.

Braden: Okay, I'll let her know. We'll see you at one.

I drop my phone, and cover my face with my hands. I don't want Becca to hear me crying and come running in here. She's convinced I should marry a prince and it would shock the hell out of her if she knew I'd fallen for Braden, and how I did a bad thing last night, even though everything about it felt right. I'm really not in the mood for an inquisition, which she's sure to give. I realize she only has my best interests at heart, and part of her must think I want to marry Stefan or she wouldn't be trying so hard.

I spend the next half hour layering on makeup, trying to make myself look somewhat presentable. I stare at myself in the mirror, and I don't recognize this version of myself. Braden once told me I didn't need makeup. He likes me just the way I am. But who the hell am I anymore? I'd never do anything to hurt Braden, and yet I've become some selfish bitch, and I'm not sure I like that girl very much. Braden certainly wouldn't like her, hence his reason for leaving last night.

I tip toe to the kitchen, not wanting to wake Becca, but I hear her door open. I throw a pod into the coffeemaker and get it brewing. Maybe caffeine will help me hate myself less. Doubtful, but I'll try anything.

Becca pokes her head into the kitchen and her smile falters when she sees me. "What's wrong?" she instantly asks.

I give her a bright smile. "Nothing. Just getting ready to take Lauren to the shelter. Coffee?"

"Yes, of course I want coffee. Did something happen between you and Braden last night?" she asks, stepping into the room to grab a mug.

"What do you mean?"

She eyes me. "You have a ton of makeup on today, so I'm guessing you didn't sleep well last night, and he was in a shit mood when he got home last night. James asked him what was wrong, but he stormed off to the bathroom and jumped in the shower."

No doubt to wash my deceit off his body.

"Why were you still there if James came home?"

She frowns, and glances down like she's trying to think of an answer. Does she and my brother have a thing? Recovering quickly, she waves her hand and answers, "Oh, he'd just gotten home. I was just saying goodbye when Braden stormed in. I figure you two had a fight or something?"

I don't miss the way she turned the conversation back to me. "No, we didn't have a fight."

"Oh, are you staging the breakup, then?"

"Something like that."

"It was so nice of him to do this for you. He's one of the good ones, isn't he?"

"Yeah." Wait, is she interested in Braden? "Braden is going to drive us to the shelter this morning. It's pouring."

"Okay." I take her mug and put it under the machine and fill it with coffee. She goes quiet, contemplative and starts texting someone. "Thanks," she says her attention elsewhere as she takes the coffee and disappears. A few minutes later, I hear the shower turn on.

I try to study, concentrate on my homework, but can't keep my focus. By the time Braden and Lauren arrive at one, I'm a hot mess. How will I face him? Will he even meet my eyes? I glance out the window and into the parking lot, and Lauren waves to me from the front seat.

"They're here," I call out to Becca and she comes running from her room. I grab an umbrella and we both tuck under it as we head to the car and jump into the back seat. I catch his reflection in the rear-view mirror and find him looking at me, his brow furrowed. He's probably wondering why I'm caked in makeup to go to the shelter. He quickly averts his gaze and my heart sinks.

"Lauren, did you have fun with Kate today?"

"She showed me around the locker room and said I could Facetime her to get pointers for tryouts next year."

I nod, and note the way Becca is staring at me. "That's nice of her."

Lauren talks non-stop about her adventures with Kate and I'm glad I don't have to make conversation. The rain has lightened as we pull up to the shelter, and Braden gets out of the car with us.

"What are you doing?" I ask.

He angles his head, his gaze moving over my made-up face. "Do you not want me to come in?"

"It's not that."

"What is it then?"

"Becca, Cassidy," Lacey screams from the doorway, a little more excited to see us than usual. I glance over my shoulder, and spot Lacey with her arms open for a hug. What is going on with her?

"That must be Lacey," Braden says.

His body brushes mine, as I turn back to him and it sends shockwaves through my veins. "How do you know that?"

"Because you talk about her."

I nod. "Come on, you can meet her."

As we get closer and closer to the door, a strange sense of dread overcomes me, and I glance around, trying to figure out what's wrong.

"Hurry, hurry," Lacey says, waving us in.

Becca glances at me. "What's going on?"

"I have no idea."

We step into the big shelter, and my knees nearly go out from underneath me when I spot Stefan sitting in the living room, all the kids and mothers gathered around him.

"Stefan…" is all I manage to get out. I turn to Braden, and take in the strain on his face. What, does he think I knew Stefan would be here, and is assuming that's why I'm all made up? I'm about to tell him I knew nothing about this, but don't get the chance when Lacey's mother Patricia comes up to me.

"He wrote a big check to the shelter," she explains. "We'll be able to get supplies and toys for the kids. It's so very kind of him."

"Very kind," I say and note that her look is more cautious than elated. She frowns, and leans into me, her words for my ears only. "Remember you're the prize, Cassidy."

She goes back and sits and I try to wrap my brain around everything that is going on. Stefan stands and comes up to me.

"I…I was going to have a benefit auction," I tell him.

"Yes, but now you can free up your calendar and have time for other more important things."

"More important. What could be more—"

"This."

He presses something into my hand and my heart jumps into my throat at the sight of a rose and a small envelope. Cheers go around the room, so loud I can hardly keep my thoughts straight.

"Cassidy, you're going to be a princess," Lacey says, her voice rising above the others. I spin, to tell Braden I don't want this, that I want him, only to find him walking out the front door and taking my heart with him.

24

BRADEN

I can't even begin to describe the rage, anger, love, hate, and disappointment still raging through every fiber of my being. I haven't seen Cassidy since last Sunday when I dropped her at the shelter—where Douche Bag gave her a rose. Everyone was so happy for her and as I heard all the screams of joy, my sister's words echoed in my brain: *no girl in their right mind would choose a baller over a prince,* I knew we'd accomplished what she asked me to do, and it was time to make my exit. I left quickly, and only went back to get my sister to take her to the bus stop. Cass didn't accompany us. I guess she no longer needed anything from me.

If I hadn't taken something so precious from her, I might have stayed and fought for her. God, we were so good together and there was a part of me that thought she realized that too. I was wrong, though. I'm not the guy for her. I'm not the guy she needs in her life. If I was, I would have stopped things before we'd gone past the point of no return and reminded her she was saving herself for someone she loves.

Why the fuck does it have to be Stefan, though? I hate everything about him, and just the fact that he could hand a rose to a girl who has a boyfriend speaks so much of his integrity... his sense of entitlement. I'd hoped the more time they'd spent together, Cass could see past the shininess of his title and get a glimpse of his rotten soul. The old Cass, the one I grew up with, would have. Why is everyone changing on me?

Here it is, Saturday afternoon, and I'm sitting at the damn campus pub while Cassidy is off to some fancy country club with the hopes of becoming a princess. Honest to God, I'm still stunned by everything that's happened and sometimes I think I'm in the middle of a nightmare. No matter how many times I close my eyes and open them, no matter how many times I pinch myself, I still wake up to the same reality. Cassidy accepted the rose from Stefan and could soon very well be his princess.

Fucked. Up. Much.

I gesture for another beer and it's slid in front of me. Zach, the bartender, stands there a second longer. I lift my head and arch a brow. "Yeah?"

He tosses a rag over his shoulder. "You okay?"

I take a swig of beer and put it down. It hits the counter a little too hard. "Living the dream my friend."

"Yeah, you kind of are."

Fuck, he's right. I'm here at Kingston getting a great education, my game has been top notch and my chances of making it to the NFL is looking pretty good. Underneath all that, I did wrong by the woman I'm in love with, and her brother. Fuck, I'm lucky to still call James a friend. The door bangs open, and I turn. Speaking of James.

"Hey," he says and plunks down next to me. "What's the matter with you?"

I shrug. "Nothing."

"Then why are you at the pub, drinking alone? Not your style, Braden."

"I guess you don't know me anymore." Christ, I'm not sure I know him anymore. He's been acting strangely for the last couple of weeks, and I have no idea what's going on with him and Becca. They're always whispering, and when I got home after making love with Cassidy, I found them sitting close, deep in conversation. They broke apart quickly when I arrived, and I was in too much of a shit mood to investigate. James apparently doesn't want me to know anything, so I'm not asking.

"Have you seen Cassidy today?"

"No, why?" I take a big drink and try to wash away the lump the just jumped into my throat, the way it always does when he brings up his sister.

"She's gone to the country club. She looked amazing."

"Yeah." I toy with the bottle and begin to pick at the label, anything to occupy my hands. What I really want to do is punch Stefan in the face and throw Cass over my shoulder and carry her away caveman style, but I'm not the guy for her. Even James knows that.

"She was in this gown, similar to what she always wore to the pageants, and..." he pauses and I glance at him. He runs his hands in front of his face. "Tons of makeup."

"Sounds just like her," I snort out.

"You wouldn't even recognize her."

"Yeah, well, there's a lot I don't recognize lately."

"What's that supposed to mean?"

I pinch the bridge of my nose. "I don't know. Everyone is acting weird. Things are changing and I don't know what is going on."

"You're one to talk. You're acting weird too."

I angle my head to see James, not sure if I want to ask him what he's talking about. Does he know what Cass and I have been doing? Does he know I'm sitting here feeling awful for taking her virginity, yet wanting to claim her as mine?

The door opens again and in walks Becca. "Looks like your girlfriend is here."

He turns to see Becca and laughs. "She's not my girlfriend."

I take another sip, and finish what's in my bottle. I gesture for another. "Could have fooled me."

"Check it out," Becca says and produces her phone. I stare at the picture of Cassidy, looking like a princess in her dress, her hair up and her face shining. "Doesn't she look gorgeous? I think Stefan is going to pick her."

I snort and look away. Fuck this. Fuck everything. I'm about to leave, go somewhere, anywhere, where the conversation isn't centered around the girl I love. I push from my stool and catch the strange way James and Becca are looking at each other.

"What?" I ask.

"If you love her, why don't you go fight for her?"

James' words take me by surprise and I sink back onto my stool. "Fuck."

"You said Becca was my girlfriend. I said she wasn't. You said, could have fooled me." He slaps my shoulder. "Well, guess what, we have been fooling you, Braden."

My brain spins as my heart thumps hard, making it difficult to know if I heard him correctly. "You've been fooling me? I have no idea what you're talking about."

"Remember I told you that you're the only guy I ever trusted with my sister?"

Guilt hits like a linebacker, and a groan crawls out of my throat. Everything I feel for James, for his sister rushes to the surface and I can't do it anymore. I can't lie to my friend. "James, I'm sorry. I'm not the guy you thought I was."

His palm tightens on my shoulder. "Yeah, you are. Which is why I sort of pushed you into helping Cassidy when she needed a fake boyfriend." My gaze goes to Becca, and I note the worried look on her face.

"That's why I sort of pushed you into giving her sex lessons," she admits.

My gaze jerks back to James and I expect to see anger and shock in his eyes, but I don't. Instead, I see worry and love.

"James, I slept with Cassidy," I blurt out, unable to hold the secret for another second.

"I know."

I sit there and try to center in on my friend as the room spins. "You know?"

"Um, yeah. I know you love her."

"I'm sorry." How do I make this right? "I didn't mean for it to happen."

"No, but we did," James says and throws his arm around Becca's shoulder.

I blink a few times, trying to put the pieces together. Wait, did he say he knows I love her and he meant for the two of us to happen? I must be hearing things. "Are you saying that you and Becca were working together to set us up?"

"There it is!" James says and grins at Becca. "I told you he wasn't that dense."

She holds her hand out palm up. "I never used the word dense. More like clueless."

"They pretty much mean the same thing," James says.

"I don't know. If you looked them up in a dictionary—"

"Guys," I yell. "What the hell?"

They both turn to me, and James begins, "You love her, which means you'd better get over to the country club. Honestly, Braden, you had us worried for a bit."

"She doesn't love me, guys. She straight up told me sleeping together was a mistake."

He mouths the word *dense* to Becca, and she nods her head.

"I'm right here. I can see you."

"She loves you, Braden," Becca says. "I'm not sure why she said that. You'll have to ask her. I just know you two should be together and should be banging like bunnies."

"That's my sister you're talking about," James says and puts her in a headlock. As they both laugh, I sit there and stare at them, completely dumbfounded.

"You guys wanted us together?" I say, still trying to wrap my brain around all this.

"You're the best guy she knows. She told me that," Becca explains. She jerks her thumb toward James. "And you're the only guy James trusts. James and I knew with a little time together, you'd both see that you were right for each other."

"You guys have been fucking with our lives," I say quietly. I guess that's why they've been secretly whispering for weeks now. I shake my head as everything begins to make sense. "James, I couldn't understand why you would go along with this farce or why you seemed okay that your sister might marry a douche bag. You weren't okay with Stefan at all."

"Nope, and you'd better get your ass over there and make it right before all our hard work is for nothing."

"Where is she?" I ask and jump up, a new kind of urgency ripping through me.

"Cypress Country Club. You'd better get a move on," Becca says.

"Say hi to Kate for me," James says.

I briefly pause. "Kate got a rose."

"Had you taken your head out of your ass this week, you would have known that."

Wait, if he and Becca were conspiring, and he was spending as much time with Kate... "Was Kate in on this with you too?"

James shakes his head. "No, we're kind of a thing. I really like her."

I stare at him as a million questions race around in my brain. He's into his sister's frenemy? Fuck, Cass won't like that.

"Why is she at the country club if you two are kind of a thing?"

He shrugs like it's nothing. "She wanted to go check it out, see what the foolishness was all about. She doesn't want a rose from Stefan, she never did, and I liked the idea of her being there to keep an eye on my sister, and why are you still here, Braden?"

"Right." I run outside and run all the way to my house. I jump in my car, and I'm glad I didn't drink too much, and quickly back out of the driveway. I plug the directions into my phone and go as fast as I can without getting a ticket to the country club. I park, and jump from the car. Guys I recognize from school are all standing around talking and I guess they must have been invited to witness the narcissistic prince choose his princess.

My stomach turns at the thought. I glance around in search of Cassidy. She must be out back. I shove my keys into my pocket and circle my car, only to find Jonny throwing his guts up on the ground.

"Fuck," I say.

His head lifts and he wobbles and smirks when he sees me. "Well, if it isn't Braden Murphy."

I want to punch him in the face, but he's down and out and my only concern right now is getting to Cassidy and telling her how I feel about her.

"You're too late, bud."

"I'm not your bud." I'm about to leave. "Wait, what am I too late for?" My throat clenches. Jesus, did Stefan pick Cassidy?

"He doesn't have to drug her to fuck her now," he says and starts vomiting again. I jump back to avoid the spray.

"What are you talking about?"

"He likes to win, man. You never stood a chance. One way or another, he was going to get what he wanted from Cassidy."

"Are you fucking telling me that Stefan was responsible for roofie-ing Cass?"

"Shit, fuck. I don't know what I'm saying." He uses the back of his sleeve to wipe his mouth.

I step up to him, grab his shirt and practically lift him clear off the ground. "You'd better fucking tell me."

"Look, he paid me. He said he was just fucking with you." His eyes roll. "Shit, man, don't tell him I told you." I toss him away and he falls to the ground. "Don't tell him, man."

I see red as I run toward the building, and my heart is pounding so hard, I'm lightheaded when I spot Kate stepping from the building.

She goes still, and her mouth drops. "Braden, what's going on?"

"Where's Cass?" I take a fast breath as she jerks her thumb toward the back gardens.

"Come on, I'll take you." She captures my hand, and I let her blindly lead me, my anger flaring so red hot I'm not even able to see straight. We reach the back, and she continues to hold my hand as she points. "She's right there."

The next thing I know, Cass is marching straight for us, a glass of wine in her hand. Her gaze is venomous, as she stops inches from Kate, and splashes her red wine all over Kate's white gown.

What the actual fuck?

25

CASSIDY

I have no idea what came over me. Okay, maybe I do. Five minutes ago, I got a text from Mom pushing and demanding to know what was going on and asking if Stefan was going to choose me. That simply added to the stress and anxiety building inside me for the last week, and the second I saw Kate walk in holding hands with Braden, the thin string holding the shit show known as Cassidy Collins together snapped, and ruled by emotions, jealousy, fear and loss, I crossed the garden and threw my wine on her pretty white dress.

"I...I..." I begin, as Kate gasps and Braden stands there and stares at me like he has no idea who I am or why I would have done such a thing. He's right to look at me like that, because I have no idea who I am anymore either. I don't want to be here at this country club. I never wanted to be here, yet I spent the last few weeks doing everything in my power to get a damn rose, including using Braden, the sweet boy who would do anything in the world for me, and has...including having sex with me during football season. Honestly, I couldn't hate myself any more than I do. The look on Braden's face, though. Yeah, he hates me more than I hate myself.

"Cassidy," Braden says, his eyes full of shock and disappointment.

"I'm…I'm sorry."

A waiter walks by with a tray, and Braden grabs a few cocktail napkins and presses them to Kate's dress. "Thank you," she mumbles quietly, and pats her dress, which is completely ruined thanks to me.

"Why would you do that?" Braden asks and rubs the back of his neck, completely agitated, which I think might be about something other than Kate's dress.

"I'm sorry."

He shakes his head, his dark eyes arctic cold as he looks me over, taking in my hair, and gown. His throat works as he swallows and I get the sense he's searching for the right words. When he finally opens his mouth, he says, "Who are you?"

Tears pool in my eyes. "I'm me, Cassidy."

"You're not the Cassidy I know. Not anymore."

"Underneath this dress, I am…" I say and I'm not sure if I'm trying to convince him or myself, because the old Cass never would have done that to Kate. Braden has every right to be with her. I only asked him to pretend to be my guy. I have no claims on him.

He captures Kate's hand and they take a distancing step back, like he's not sure what I might do next. "Underneath the dress is a girl who cares only about the competition. That's what's become of you. Do you even know what you want anymore, or who you really are?"

"B, please..." I take a step toward them and they take another step back, a huge chasm between us—physically and emotionally.

"You're certainly not the Cassidy I love...the Cassidy I've always loved."

"Love? You're here with Kate," I say, my broken heart shattering just a bit more.

He shakes his head. "I'm here for you, Cass. You. I was never with Kate."

"You were glad she bid on you."

He shakes his head. "I tried to tell you that night she was doing it to save me from Chloe. She told me she would and that I didn't even have to go to the spa. She was helping me, and your cause, out."

Oh God. "I didn't know."

"There's a lot you...didn't know." His voice hitches and he adds, "There's a lot I don't know. Like who you are anymore."

"I'm me..."

"No, Cass. You're someone else now. Someone I don't know, and someone I..." He pauses to glance at the ugly stain on Kate's dress. "...someone I don't like."

Stefan steps up beside me and Braden stiffens, his gaze going dark and angry as he fists his hands at his side.

"If this is the guy you want to be with, then you need to know he's the one who drugged you that night. It wasn't Jonny."

Stefan smirks. "I don't know where you got your information. I was saving her that night, taking her to safety because you were off doing something else."

Braden looks like he's going to pounce and knock Stefan to the floor. Kate puts her hand on his arm. "Don't, Braden. He's not worth getting kicked off the team."

"No, but he hurt Cass, and even though I don't know this version of her anymore, that doesn't mean I won't protect her."

Kate nods and lets go of his arm as Stefan summons two big ass security guards.

"Will you please escort these two out of here."

The guards stand beside Kate and Braden and he holds his hand up. "Please just ask him, Cassidy."

I turn to Stefan, my insides tight as the hairs on the back of my neck tingle in warning. "Did you?"

"Of course not." He smirks at me. "He's only here because he's upset that you want me now, and not him."

"No, I don't want her. I don't even know her anymore."

A cry catches in my throat, and I suspect he's not just talking about the wine, or me being at this horrendous event I despise, or in a dress I hate. He's also talking about the night we spent together. I made a mistake, and dammit, I keep making them.

Stefan releases the button on his suit, like he's preparing for a fight, but I'm pretty sure he doesn't fight his own battles. "You wouldn't be here if you didn't want her." I take in his grin. He's clearly completely pleased with himself. He likes that Braden came here looking for me.

"You need every girl to want you, don't you, Stefan?" Braden says. "When they don't, you'll do whatever it takes to get them. It's all about the chase and challenge for you. You want what you can't have. You became interested in Cass the second you knew she was with me." Braden continues with, "When she was with me, and didn't want you, you were going to drug her to have her." As volatile energy pours off him in waves, he runs his hands through his mess of hair and paces like a restless animal. "What kind of a guy are you and what kind of sick game do you think you're playing here? Do you have any idea how fucked up this is, how fucked up you are?" His jaw ripples as he clamps down. "If you don't know, let me tell you. You're a fucking douche bag, with zero respect for women."

"Don't be jealous that she wants me and not you, dude."

Braden stares at me. "He thought you were with me and still gave you a rose." Sadness and incredulity cross his strained face. "Hell, I thought you were with me for a bit there too, but you were never with me, Cass." Stefan gestures to the guards, and one grabs Braden's arm while the other grabs Kate's. "Is that the guy you want to be with, Cassidy?"

Tears spill down my eyes, and blur my vision. I swipe at them to see the disappointment in Braden's eyes when he says, "Then again, this has been all about the chase and challenge for you too, Cass. No matter the costs or the consequences, you'd do anything, to win over Kate." His disgusted gaze goes from me to Stefan back to me again. "I guess you two are more alike than I realized."

"Braden," I call out as the guards lead them out.

"Bye, Cass."

"Braden please, I'm sorry."

He doesn't turn back, doesn't want to hear what I have to say, and I can't blame him. He hates me as much as I hate myself, and there is absolutely no coming back from any of this. My future isn't clear, but one thing is for sure. It won't be with Braden.

"Well, that was fun," Stefan says with a smile.

"You think that was fun?" I practically screech.

"You didn't?" he questions and it's all I can do not to smack that pretentious, gloating smirk off his stupid face.

As my fingers curl, I consider everything Braden just said to me. One thing I know for sure is, he isn't a liar. If he said Stefan drugged me, he must have drugged me. Know what else Braden isn't lying about…that he no longer wants me. I can't blame him. The competition got to me and I spilled wine on Kate's dress on purpose. That's not who I am.

"Come on, let's get some champagne and celebrate," Stefan says, clearly proud of himself, that he won some battle. I pull my arm away.

"Don't touch me."

"You can't be serious, Cass. That guy is a loser."

"A loser? He has more integrity in his pinky finger than you have in your whole body."

"Fine, go after him. If you want to give up a life full of fame and glamour, then there's the door."

Cripes, I never wanted that life. My mother did, and I'm sick and tired of her running my life. I hike up the skirt on my big stupid dress, and storm outside in time to see Braden and Kate drive off. I glance around, completely alone and lost in the big parking lot. I should walk home. I don't deserve a nice comfortable cab ride.

My phone buzzes and I pull it from my small bag. I slide my finger across the screen.

"I screwed up, Becca. I screwed up big time."

"Yeah, I know. James is talking to Braden right now. Are you still at the country club?"

I sniff, and nod, even though she can't see me. My throat is too damn tight and sore to get words past it. "I'm coming to get you," she says.

I cry silently and she ends the call. I plunk down on a bench in front of the majestic country club's main lodge and spot a red headed guy vomiting between vehicles. Lovely.

Thirty minutes later, Becca pulls up in her small car. I open the passenger side and climb in, my dress puffing up around my face. I beat it down and pull on my seat belt. She gives me a small, pained smile, and starts out of the driveway. I cry beside her, even though I'm doing my best to pull myself together, and neither of us say a word as she takes me back to our sorority.

She helps me inside, and out of my dress when we get to our room, and I crawl between the sheets. She says only one word, 'rest,' and puts a glass of water on my nightstand before closing my door. The place goes silent, and I lay there until I cry myself to sleep.

My room is dark as I stir awake, and as I sit up and glance around, memories flood my brain, and I take my pillow, put it over my mouth and scream into it. I drop the pillow at the sound of my door creaking open.

"Hey," Becca says.

"Hey, thanks for picking me up."

She crosses the room and the bed dips as she sits beside me and wipes my hair from my face. I can only imagine I look like a raccoon, my makeup running down my cheeks. Braden never would have cared about that. Tears start again as I think about him.

"I screwed up." Ashamed of myself, I lift my eyes to Becca's. "I spilled red wine all over Kate's dress." I press the palms of my hands to my eyes.

"I know."

My hands fall. "How do you know?"

"I know everything, Cass." She almost looks ashamed of herself.

"Oh right, you said James was talking to Braden."

"It's more than that." She takes a deep breath, lets it out slowly and tells me how she and my brother were working together to get Braden and me together. As I sit there listening, there is only one word to describe what I'm feeling. Shock.

"You guys wanted to see us together?"

"Yeah, we both knew you were right for each other."

"When James asked if you were available, that's because he was…"

"I don't know what that was. I think it's just a big brother's job to mess with his sister. He might have been trying to find out where I was, though."

I shake my head. "Yeah, well he sure did mess with me this time, only for me to mess up big time."

She tucks a strand of hair behind my ear. "I have one question."

"Yeah?"

"Do you love Braden?"

I nod, my vision growing blurry again. "Yes."

"Okay then, not all is lost."

"You weren't there, Becca. You didn't hear the things he said to me, the finality in his voice. He hates me."

"He might hate what you did, and hate the person you were pretending to be..." She puts her hand over my heart. "But he loves the girl with the big heart. You just have to show him that girl still exists and is really who you are."

"How..." I give a big hiccupping sob. "How do I do that, and even if I do, will he ever forgive me?"

"You can do one of two things, Cass. Figure out how to show him you're still that sweet girl he fell for, or forever ask...what if?"

26

BRADEN

I glance out my bedroom window and take in the quiet streets. It's Sunday afternoon, a sleepy day for most students here at Kingston. Not for me, though. I have practice in twenty minutes and would much rather stay home and remove my toenails with pliers than chase a ball up and down a field. Drastic I know, it's just that I didn't sleep much last night, and currently feel like a hot bag of shit. Christ, after what went down at the country club, and seeing the changes in Cass, I'm not sure I'll ever sleep again. They say time heals a broken heart, and while I'm not sure who *they* are, I really hope it's the truth.

At least I found out the truth about who really drugged Cass. It's hard to believe Stefan planned to take her to his room and do God knows what with her, simply because he was determined to 'have' her one way or another. I told Cass the truth, and she knows I don't lie, so what she does with that now is up to her. I just hope she comes to her senses and walks away from the douche bag and lives the life she wants to live—not the one anyone else is pushing on her. She might not love me the way I love her, and I'm still sorry for taking her virginity, but I really want what is best for her. That will always be a given, no matter how much she's changed.

I toss my bag over my shoulder and stifle a yawn. I've been playing great ball these past few weeks, and now... Well, now I'm afraid that spell might be broken. I don't even feel like going to practice, and that's not like me at all. I live for the game. I used to, anyway. I need to get that motivation back if I want to continue my winning streak and make it into the NFL.

In the hall, I find James coming from his room. He has much more energy than I do, and I'm glad that one of us seems to be fired up for practice. He puts his hand on my shoulder. "You look like shit."

I shrug, and it takes pretty much all of my energy. "Why don't you tell me what you really think?"

He frowns and gives my shoulder a squeeze. "I'm sorry, Braden."

"Have you talked to her?" I ask and wish I hadn't. I can't help but wonder if she's okay. I really hope she realizes what kind of guy Stefan is and comes to her senses.

"Yeah, last night." His brow furrows as he stares at me, and my stomach clenches. Why do I have the feeling he's going to deliver bad news? "She's okay, Braden," he says but I know him well enough to know that there's something he's not telling me. "After you called me on your way home from the country club, I filled Becca in, and she went to pick her up."

I let out a long, slow breath, and while I'm sure he's holding something back from me, I'm glad she walked away from Stefan and is home safe. "Thank fuck."

"I guess you knew all along something was off with Jonny's story."

"Yeah, but now I want to kick Stefan's ass but good."

He nods, and I know he's itching to get a few good punches in too. Stefan better keep those security guards close by, although between James and me, I'm sure we could go through them to get to Stefan.

"You really love her, huh?"

I swallow against a tight throat, his question cutting into my frayed heart. "I do. No matter what, I only want what is best for her. I just didn't recognize the Cass she's become. The way she acted. All she cared about was the competition and beating Kate. She was so...different."

His arm falls from my shoulder. "Maybe she's not so different after all."

"What's that supposed to mean?"

He shrugs, like he might have said too much, tosses his bag over his shoulder, and nods to the stairs, putting the conversation to rest. "I don't know what I'm saying. Let's get to practice before Coach hands us our asses and makes us run laps."

"Yeah," I say for lack of anything else, my emotions on a rollercoaster ride as we take the stairs two at a time and grab a quick bite before we walk outside. I take a deep breath of morning air. I have to say, I'm fucking elated that Cass came to her senses, yet so fucking sad that we have no future. We head down the road, opting to walk, and every now and then, James casts glances my way. "I'm fine," I say.

"Yeah, sure," he responds, his voice full of disbelief, worry, and something else. What is going on with him? He's still acting odd. Surely, he and Becca have quit conspiring.

"Okay then, once I work off my stress on the field, I'll be fine." It's a lie. I'm not sure what it's going to take for me to be fine.

We reach the field and head inside the locker room to get changed, and as the guys all chat about last night and their conquests, I go through the robotic motions of smiling, piping in when I'm asked a question, and changing into my gear. I'm slower than the rest, and they all file out of the locker room, leaving me behind. I notice the way James is stalling. He doesn't have to wait for me. I guess that's what best friends do, though. He's worried about my mental state, and I love him for that. I still can't quite wrap my brain around the fact that he and Becca were trying to get Cass and me together. Here I thought James would hate me if he ever found out what was going on with me and his sister, only to find out I'm the guy he wanted her with all along. I guess he knows that no matter what, I'll always put her best interests first.

"Ready?" he asks, and I nod and follow him onto the field. I walk onto the grass, and my steps slow as I gaze down the field and spot Cass standing beside Coach Meyers, a megaphone in her hand.

My gaze jerks to James, and a small, tentative smile curls his lips. He obviously knows what's going on, otherwise he wouldn't be smiling. "What the fuck..."

James puts his hand on my shoulder as I begin to back away. He clamps down, to keep me rooted. "Just hear her out, okay?"

"James, come on. Why didn't you tell me about this?" I look around and spot Becca and Kate standing in the bleachers. They both wave. I don't wave back. I'm not at all happy about making a spectacle of myself—again.

"You love her." There's a pleading look in my best friend's eyes as he adds, "You just told me that, so you need to hear her out, okay?"

"James…" I complain, even though I owe him that much.

Cass lifts the megaphone to her mouth. "Hear her out, Braden. If you want to walk after that, you can walk. Hell, I'll walk with you."

I search his face for answers, and nod. "Fine."

"Braden, can I have a word with you?" Cass asks and all the guys on the team begin to holler and wave me over.

"Fuck, I hate being the center of attention like this," I grumble. I slowly walk toward her, and James takes my helmet out of my hand. As I get closer, I notice Cass has her hair in pigtails, like she used to wear when she was a kid. It drove her mother crazy. I, however, always thought it was adorable. Sometimes I think she did it just to piss her mother off and show a bit of her stubbornness. I guess she lost that stubbornness over the years. Apparently, that can happen if you're battered enough. I'm sure her mother is going to be livid that things hadn't worked out between Cass and Stefan.

I move close, and I take a minute to register that her face is freshly washed and make-up free. My gaze travels lower to take in her T-shirt and jeans. Everything about her is a complete contrast to last night. She looks more like the Cass I know and love. On the outside, anyway. I can't be sure about the inside.

"What's going on, Cass?"

"I know you hate me, and probably don't ever want to talk or see me again, so I figured this was the only way I could get your attention. James said he and the entire defense line up would block you if you didn't listen to what I had to say."

Did she really think this was the only way I'd hear her out? I guess after some of the cruel things I said yesterday, I can see why. "I don't hate you, Cass," I tell her as my heart squeezes so tight, I can hardly breathe. She smiles and I close the distance between us, the sight of her standing there reminding me of the night of the auction when she took center stage to sell us off to the highest bidder. "I don't hate you, but I do wonder what you're selling here."

She drops the megaphone and her arms fall to her sides, and she looks so sad and lost, it's all I can do to stop myself from pulling her into my arms and telling her everything will be okay.

"Okay, let's give them some privacy," Coach Meyers says and I'm grateful when he leads the team to the other end of the field, giving us the space we need.

Once everyone is out of earshot, I repeat, "What are you selling?"

"I'm not selling anything, Braden." I eye her, and her chest rises and falls quickly as she continues with, "I wanted you to look at me, and see that this is who I am." She waves her hand up and down her body. "I'm the same girl you always knew."

I shake my head and close my eyes as the vision of her splashing wine all over Kate's dress plays in my mind's eye.

"What you did to Kate was wrong. She's a nice girl, but you couldn't see past the competition."

"You're right. I know, and I'm sorry." She glances at the bleachers. "I apologized to her. I'm not sure she'll ever want to be friends, and I can't blame her, but I did tell her how sorry I was for...the wine and everything else over the years."

"Good." I scrub my face as a breeze carries her warm scent to my nostrils. I fill my lungs, and memories of her beneath me, me inside her, weaken my knees. I love her so fucking much it hurts to breathe. "Is that it? That's what you wanted me to hear?"

"No, I wanted to show you that I'm still me. Inside and out. Actually, I'm a better version of the girl you always knew." She puts her hand over her heart. "In here."

"I loved who you were in there. You were always a good person...until this stupid fucking competition. It changed you."

"I have changed, Braden. It's true. I don't deny that. In fact, I'm a new and improved version of me, and I'm hoping you'll love this version, because I am who I am right now thanks to you. You make me a better person. Everything about you is good and kind, and even though you were disappointed in me, you still wanted what was best for me."

"I love you, Cass," I state matter-of-factly. "That's why I want what's best for you. That's all I ever wanted and it's not going to change."

"I've adored you my whole life and always knew you were one of the good guys. Okay, sometimes you were annoying, chasing away all my boyfriends, but when you pretended to be my boyfriend, it awakened something in me. Maybe it was always there, and I never explored it before because you were my brother's best friend. All I know is after our first kiss, I started to imagine what it would be like if you were my real boyfriend, and the more I imagined, the more my feelings grew. I fell in love with you, Braden."

As her words ping around inside my brain, the field closes in on me and I grow a little lightheaded. I take a couple of deep breaths, but it only makes it worse.

She loves me...

She looks down, shame and sorrow spreading across her face. "I lost myself for a bit there, letting the competition get the better of me, but more importantly, I lost you. I don't ever want to make that mistake again."

Mistake.

That word hits like a slap and my mind races back to the morning after we had sex. "You said...you said sleeping with me was a mistake." I swallow hard and glance around the field before zeroing back in on her. "I know I never should have taken your virginity...you were saving it..."

Her eyes go wide, and her mouth drops open. She stares at me for a second, incredulously, and I have no idea what's going through her head. "It *was* a mistake, Braden. It was a mistake because you don't have sex during football season. Giving my virginity to you was never a mistake to me. I only ever wanted it to be with the right guy, a guy I cared about, and hands down, that guy was you."

"Christ, Cass." I rub the knot at the back of my skull as I try to sort through everything. "I thought you were mad that I took something I shouldn't have taken. I've been so angry with myself, thinking I should have been stronger and stopped it."

She grips my jersey with both of her hands and tugs. "I was angry with myself because I was the one who begged you for it. I was worried you hated me because I made you do something you didn't want to do."

I shake my head as the tumblers all fall into place. "So we were both angry with ourselves for all the wrong reasons."

"You're not sorry..." A little grin tugs at her lips as she lets go of my shirt to do air quotes and continues with, "...that you *gave it up to me* during football season?"

"Not sorry." I capture her arm and pull her until she's pressed against me. My heart fills with love as my chest expands. This is where she belongs, right here in my arms, her body meshed with mine. "I'd do it again." My cock twitches as it presses against her softness. "In fact, I'd like to do it again."

Tears fill her eyes. "I want to be with you, Braden."

I brush her hair from her face. I gaze into her big eyes, take in the love shining there. "Are you done looking for your prince charming?"

"Yes, I'm trading up."

I cock my head, remembering my sister saying no girl would choose a baller over a prince. How is wanting to be with me trading up? "I don't understand, babe."

"You were always the prize, Braden. Not *him*." The word *him* spills from her mouth like she'd just tasted something nasty, and I'm glad she didn't use his given name. I don't ever want to hear it on her lips again.

"You think I'm the prize?" I question, a grin on my face as she presses against me, her heart beating hard against my chest.

"Yes, you're Prince Charming."

"I'm no one's Prince Charming, Cass."

"Wrong, you're mine."

I hug her tightly. "You're the prize, Cass. You've always been the prize."

She goes up on her toes and presses her lips to mine. "Now I'm your prize."

"Damn right you are."

I scoop her up and the guys behind us start cheering. I plant a hard kiss on her mouth, and say, "After practice, we're going to finish what we started here."

She grins and says, "I can't wait."

———

EPILOGUE

Cassidy

I walk into my office, and every time I do, I want to pinch myself. I graduated a few months ago, and landed a job at Blazed, Santa Monica's top public relations firm. I'd been shadowing for months, and was just given my first project to create brand awareness for a new organic kombucha drink. I couldn't be happier, and I can't wait to dive in. Becca also landed a position here and she's working on a different project. We get to spend our lunch hours together and it couldn't have worked out better.

I honestly don't know what I did to deserve this life, or this future. One thing for certain is that I'll never take it for granted, and I'll never be that jealous person who would do anything to win.

After Braden and James graduated, they both went on to play for the Panthers, and I entered my senior year at Kingston. While long distance relationships are hard, we're making the best of it. I smile, because after the fiasco known as Stefan, in the end I landed Prince Braden. My mother was shocked at first, needless to say, but she came to terms with it, and hey,

Braden is a professional football player and that's pretty damn impressive."

All this time later, I still feel guilty and embarrassed for pouring wine on Kate. We never saw much of each other after that, and she went on to become assistant manager for the Panthers. I'm happy for her, really. I just wish I could have made things better between us or have done something to show her that I'd like to be closer. I was afraid of rejection, and she had every right not to trust me.

I'm about to circle my desk, maybe pinch myself and get straight to work on my first big project, until I hear footsteps behind me. I spin and spot Patricia and Lacey. Shortly after landing a position here, I found out they were looking for a copywriter, and Patricia had experience in the field, so I encouraged her to apply. She did and landed the job, and every time I see her doing so well my heart fills up a little more. Little Lacey goes to daycare across the street and sometimes they join Becca and me for lunch.

"Hey Lacey, don't you look pretty today?" I say as she stands there with that old tiara on her head. I'm not sure she takes it off. "Are you going to marry a prince?" I tease. I pretty much ask her that whenever she's wearing it, and she always answers yes. I really hope one day she finds a prince as wonderful as mine.

"You're needed outside," Patricia says, a frown on her forehead. "There's some kind of emergency."

My gut tightens. "What's going on? Is someone hurt?"

"I'm not sure."

Lacey chuckles and her mom tugs her close to quiet her. Lacey clearly knows what's going on, and I suspect Patricia does too. She just doesn't want to tell me.

"Lead the way," I say, and everyone stands at their office doors, smiles on their faces, as I head down the long hall. If someone were hurt, they wouldn't be smiling and now I'm all that much more confused.

Patricia opens the front door and I follow her out onto the sidewalk. "Braden!" I screech when I see him. He was off at summer training camp and isn't supposed to be home this week. Behind him, people bustle about, and I assume it's all his fans. As Braden comes toward me, his arms outstretched, I shade the sun from my eyes. It's then I realize it's not his fans standing there, it's my friends and family. What is going on?

Braden wraps his arms around me and hugs me so tight it's almost impossible to breathe. "Braden, what's going on?" I ask. "Why is everyone here?" My gaze races over my smiling mother and father, Braden's smiling parents, sisters and even his grandmother.

Instead of answering, he sets me down and drops to one knee. Tears spring from my eyes and my hands cover my gaping mouth. "Braden," I murmur.

He opens a gorgeous velvet box. "Will you marry me, Cass?"

"Braden..." I murmur, barely able to get that one word out. From the corner of my eye, I spot Patricia and Lacey back away. "No," I blurt out.

Braden stiffens and gasps come from my family and friends. My God, everyone I've ever loved is here. So is Kate, and she's standing awfully close to James. Becca comes toward me, worry in her eyes. "Cass..." she says.

I shake my head. "No, I mean, no, Patricia and Lacey. Don't go."

Patricia turns. "I didn't mean to interrupt. You're here with family, and..."

"You are family," I say to her. "Besides, we're going to need a flower girl and I can't think of anyone more perfect than Lacey. Isn't that right, Braden?"

"That's right."

A big smile lights up Lacey's face, and Patricia gives me a warm, loving smile. My heart swells, and I fear it could burst with all the love inside me.

"Cass," Braden says.

"Yeah."

"Um, you didn't answer me."

I drop to my knees and hug him. "Yes, a million times over." He puts the gorgeous diamond on my finger, and I'm pretty sure he's fighting off tears. I love it so hard. He's a big, powerful football player, yet so soft on the inside. We kiss and everyone claps. After we break apart, Lacey comes close and puts the tiara on my head.

"I believe you're going to need this."

I laugh and hug her. "Thank you, Lacey. I'll give it back when you find your prince, okay?"

She nods and her mother tugs her against her legs to give us privacy. I stand, and smile at my family and friends. "I can't believe you guys are all here." I put my arm through Braden's. "Thank you. This is perfect. Actually, it's not quite perfect."

He frowns. "No?"

I shake my head and meet Kate's eyes. She smiles at me, and I walk up to her. Becca is obviously my maid of honor, but I want to do right by Kate. "Kate, would you do me the honor and be a bridesmaid?"

Kate shakes her head. "I'm sorry, I can't."

A hush goes over the crowd as my heart sinks into the pit of my stomach. "I understand," I say, and fight back embarrassed tears as Braden comes close, his hand on my back to offer support.

"I can't because of this." She holds her hand out and shows me a gorgeous engagement ring, and my jaw drops open as my gaze goes from her to my grinning brother who has his arm around her, back to Kate. "You...two..."

"We were thinking a double wedding," James says, and a big happy squeal rises in my throat.

"Are you serious?"

Kate gives me a brilliant smile. "I'd be your bridesmaid if I could, but..."

"No, this is way better." I throw my arms around Kate and as we both hug each other tight, I know we're going to be okay, and I plan to be the best sister-in-law ever.

I turn to Braden, and the mere sight of him sets my heart racing. I throw my arms around him, and say, "Now everything is perfect."

A popping sound reaches my ears and I turn to see Kate open a bottle of champagne as Becca hands out small plastic glasses. The champagne spurts from the bottle and spills all over my work clothes.

James laughs and Kate says, "Oops, sorry."

"Did you do that on purpose?" I ask her, not at all angry. I truly deserve it.

"Yes, but not for the reason you think." I stare at her dumbfounded, and she leans in and whispers, "It was Braden's idea."

"Braden?" I ask and turn to him

He grins. "Now you have no choice but to leave work, and go home and get out of these clothes."

I laugh. "You're right. I have no choice."

"And I have no choice but to help you."

"You don't have to sell it to me, Braden," I say, and everyone laughs as he scoops me up and plants a warm, loving kiss on my lips. I might not be Cinderella and he might not be Prince Charming, but together we've found our very own happily ever after!

***

Thank you so much for reading, **TRADING UP**, book 4 in my End Zone series. I hope you loved this story as much as I loved writing it. Please read on for an excerpt of **ALL IN**, coming April 2022.

ALL IN
Chapter One

Peyton

I spin on my cracked leather stool and take in the college football game playing on the gigantic TV behind the bar. "Ugh, I thought I'd never have to watch a Falcons game again after graduating from Kingston." I snarl a little. Ladylike, I know. But that's what watching Caleb Stewart get a touchdown does to me. "Why the hell are they playing re-runs from last year's game, anyway?"

"It's just the highlight reel," my friend and co-worker Lance says as he angles his head, like he's going into work mode, but I'm in no mood to be analyzed. As a social worker, I prefer to do the analyzing, but he's a social worker too, and it's in our nature to evaluate those around us. Still, I wish he couldn't read me so well. He arches a questioning brow. "It's not so bad, is it?"

Oh, it's bad. It's so incredibly bad, but I don't want to get into my past with him. It only depresses me. So does the fact that it's the holiday season once again, and come New Year's Eve, I'll have no one to kiss when the ball drops.

"Are you a football fan?" My gaze moves over Lance's fancy, square-framed glasses, to the perfect way the collared points of his dress shirt stay tucked into his sweater. He lifts his glass and I grin at the delicate frosty drink in his hands. I love the guy, I really do. He took me under his wing when I started work at the behavioural clinic right after graduation eight months ago. But he's so damn astute, and I prefer to leave my past in my past, yet he somehow always has a way of making me spill my thoughts and worries. Not this time, buddy. Not this time. I resist the urge to mimic the motion of zipping my lips and tossing the key away.

"I don't mind looking at their tight ends," he teases and takes a sip of his strawberry daiquiri, the highlights in his hair glistening beneath the Christmas lights strung across the ceiling.

I laugh at that. "Yeah, well, there's one tight end I never want to see again." I grumble and gulp my margarita, unable to take my eyes off one particular player's perfect backside. I hate the guy. Loathe him, actually.

Then why the hell are you staring so damn hard at the TV, Peyton?

"Look at him. He thinks he's God's gift to women," I mumble under my breath, and snarl a little more as I force my focus onto my friend. I'm sure even the plastic reindeer he has pinned to his ugly Christmas sweater can see right through me. Bah humbug! I really hope my mood improves before Beck and Eden's oceanside wedding tomorrow.

Lance's brows furrow as his gaze goes from me to the TV back to me again. "Who?"

I snort. "Caleb Stewart, of course." I wave a hand toward the screen. "Do you see anyone else on that field that thinks he's the cock of the walk?"

Dear God, why would I use Caleb and cock in the same sentence?

Do not think about Caleb's cock!

Do not think about it.

Dammit, too late. I'm thinking about it. Not that I have a visual buried in the depths of my memories, or anything like that. I've never seen it, nor do I want to. Okay, well, maybe back in college I thought about it a time or two, but that was eight long months ago.

Douchebag Caleb never gave me a lick of attention in college, yet he slept with every girl who looked his way. Every girl but me, that is. Bitter? Nah. Not much anyway. I mean I might have put on a bit of weight, living off campus food, but I wasn't a troll or anything. Still, he only gravitated toward model-thin cheerleaders, and honestly, I should be happy I never slept with him. Why would I ever want to be with a narcissistic asshole like that?

"So you like him, huh?"

I take in Lance's wry grin. "No, I don't like him." I sit up a little straighter and square my shoulders when he raises his brow. "Oh, please. He's a bastard. I hate everything about him."

"Doesn't seem that way to me."

"Your spidey senses are off this time, Lance."

"Spidey senses?" he says with a laugh.

"Can we please just talk about something else." I wave to the bartender, and he looks my way. "Would you mind turning the station?"

"Ooh, someone's got it bad," Lance says with a little finger wave.

I glare at him. "I hate him, end of discussion."

Wait, how did Lance get me talking about Caleb? I'm about to ask, when a deep voice beside me cuts me off.

"Why don't you tell me what you really think?"

I spin, and the second I come face to face with none other than the man who's been living rent free in my head for far too long, my blood drains to my toes. Lance makes a squealing noise behind me, and I reach behind me and try to whack him but only get air.

I swallow. Hard.

Speaking of hard. My gaze leaves Caleb's perfect, chiselled face, and travels down to take in the blue sweater that showcases broad shoulders, a tight chest and a perfect eight pack. Well, I can't really see the eight pack. That's just my stupid imagination at play.

"What...what are you doing here?" I ask him.

Silence hangs heavy for a moment, taking up space between us. "Nice to see you too, Peyton."

I snort. "I'm surprised you remember my name."

"Why wouldn't I remember?" He sidles closer and his warm scent curls around me. I nearly sob as it seeps into my skin and caresses every erogenous zone. I quiver from the top of my head to the tips of my toes. "You're far from forgettable."

As his gaze moves over my face, embarrassment jumps in to replace arousal, and I'm glad the bar is dimly lit. I'd hate for him to see the heat coloring my cheeks red as my mind goes back to the night I had a little too much to drink and seduced him. Seduced him? Okay, more like threw myself at him like I was one of his beloved footballs. Little did I know he was going to deflect, and I'd fall to my ass, mortified. Okay, I get it. I'm not your type. Move along.

"What exactly are you doing here, in this bar?" I ask again. Lance and I hit up the place every Friday because it's close to work and I don't believe in coincidences, and come on, this is kind of a big one, don't you think?

He shrugs and holds his beer up in salute. "Needed a drink."

Lance clears his throat, giving me a reprieve from Caleb's gorgeous blue eyes. "This is Lance, my friend and co-worker," I say, trying not to sound as breathless as I feel, but fail miserably. Lance extends his hand, a huge smile on his face as he and Caleb shake hands. I stare at his big, stupid hand, and no way on the face of this earth am I going to spend one second imagining what it would feel like caressing my body. Not right now, anyway. Not while I'm sitting at the bar.

Tonight, however...

Caleb turns his attention back to me. "I'm in town because it's Christmas. I'm home to visit with the family, and of course Beck's wedding tomorrow."

My mouth drops open. "You're going to Beck and Eden's wedding?"

"Wouldn't miss it for the world." His eyes leave mine, travel downward to take in my blouse and dress pants. What, does he like what he sees? Well, screw him. He didn't want me when I was chunky, which means he can't have me when I'm thin.

"I didn't know you kept in contact with Beck."

With his eye still lingering around my midriff, I'm about to tell him my face is up here, not on my breasts or between my legs when his head lifts, a sexy grin tugging at the corners of his kissable lips. "We go way back. Buds for life."

They played football together at Kingston, and I was friends with Beck's girl Eden, but I didn't realize the guys stayed in touch, especially after Caleb went off to play for Chicago.

"You'll be there too, right?"

Is that hope I see in his eyes?

"Yeah, I'll be there." A small grin touches his mouth, and I hate—HATE—that he's looking at me like I'm a sheep that wandered into the lion's den. "Lance is my plus one."

Lance makes a sound, and I reach behind my back and pinch him to shut him up. Caleb glances over my shoulder, the smile gone from his face.

"Oh, I didn't realize you two were..."

He lets his words fall off. "Yeah, we're a couple." I glance around and don't miss the way the women in the room are staring at Caleb. Heck, why wouldn't they be staring? I put my elbow on the bar and brace my chin on my hand, like I don't have a care in the world. "Who will you be bringing?"

"There was this one girl I was hoping to go with," he says, his blue eyes back on mine, eliciting shivers deep within my body. He picks up his beer, takes a long pull from the bottle and slams it back down. "But it appears she's already taken."

Dear God, is he talking about me?

"I guess I'll see you there," he says, and turns away.

I resist the urge to say not if I see you first, but I'm not twelve years old. Okay, that might not be the entire truth. I don't say it because my words catch in my throat as I take pleasure in his sexy swagger. Dear God, how am I going to make it through the wedding tomorrow knowing he's going to be there? My gaze drops to his sweet backside, and arousal races through me like a runaway freight train.

Dammit.

"Want to tell me what that was all about and why I'm getting dragged into this thing between you guys?" Lance asks.

"What thing?"

"This thing called hate." He snorts and holds one hand out as he looks at the ceiling. "I'm surprised it didn't set off the sprinklers."

"I hate him, Lance," I spit out with conviction, but from the smirk on his face, it's easy to tell he's not buying it.

"Yeah, he hates you too. If hating you means wanting to eat you alive."

That might be the case, but Lance has no idea how much Caleb embarrassed me back in college. But we're not in college anymore and he obviously likes what he sees—now. Maybe I could have a little fun with that. A little revenge for dissing the curvy girl. Maybe I'll show him exactly what he missed out on and leave him hanging like he left me. I grin. Oh, this is going to be so much fun.

To find out more check it out here!

The Wing Man

The Puck Charmer

The Troublemaker

The Rule Breaker

The Rookie

The Sweet Talker

The Heart Breaker

In the Line of Duty

His Obsession Next Door

His Strings to Pull

His Trouble in Talulah

His Taste of Temptation

His Moment to Steal

His Best Friend's Girl

His Reason to Stay

Confessions

Confessions of a Bad Boy Professor

Confessions of a Bad Boy Officer

Confessions of a Bad Boy Fighter

Confessions of a Bad Boy Doctor

Confessions of a Bad Boy Gamer

Confessions of a Bad Boy Millionaire

Confessions of a Bad Boy Santa

Confessions of a Bad Boy CEO

Hands On

Hands On

Body Contact

Full Exposure

Dossier

Private Reserve

House Rules

Under Pressure

Big Catch

Brazilian Fantasy

Improper Proposal

Boys of Beachville

Good at Being Bad

Igniting the Bad Boy

Bad Girl Therapy

Stone Cliff Series:

Crashing Down

Wasted Summer

Love Lessons

Wrapped Up

Eternal Pleasure Series

Instinctive

Impulsive

Indulgent

Sun Stroked Series

Seaside Seduction

Deep Desire

Private Pleasure

Captured and Claimed Series:

Yours to Take

Yours to Teach

Yours to Keep

Firefighter Heat Series

Fever

Siren

Flash Fire

Playing For Keeps Series

Slow Ride

Wild Ride

Sweet Ride

Breaking the Rules:

Hold Me Down Hard

Pin Me Up Proper

Tie Me Down Tight

Stand Alone Title:

Hands on with the CEO

Torn Between Two Brothers

Holiday Spirit

Unleashed

Knocking on Demon's Door

Web of Desire

ABOUT CATHRYN

New York Times and *USA today* Bestselling author, Cathryn is a wife, mom, sister, daughter, and friend. She loves dogs, sunny weather, anything chocolate (she never says no to a brownie) pizza and red wine. She has two teenagers who keep her busy with their never ending activities, and a husband who is convinced he can turn her into a mixed martial arts fan. Cathryn can never find balance in her life, is always trying to find time to go to the gym, can never keep up with emails, Facebook or Twitter and tries to write page-turning books that her readers will love.

Connect with Cathryn:
Newsletter https://app.mailerlite.com/webforms/landing/c1f8n1
Twitter: https://twitter.com/writercatfox
Facebook: https://www.facebook.com/AuthorCathrynFox?ref=hl
Blog: http://cathrynfox.com/blog/
Goodreads: https://www.goodreads.com/author/show/91799.Cathryn_Fox

Pinterest http://www.pinterest.com/catkalen/

www.ingramcontent.com/pod-product-compliance
Lightning Source LLC
Chambersburg PA
CBHW060518220726

48290CB00015B/1774